Praise for *Black Cloud Rising*

"Faladé's fast-paced narrative is filled with dramatic confrontations. But its military skirmishes are made even more tense and powerful by the personal clashes that set some soldiers against one another and illuminate the dangerous uncertainties that shadow both the hurriedly assembled Black forces of the Union Army and the local communities being wrested from the Confederacy."
—Alida Becker, *New York Times*

"There are no braided points of view here, no too-pretty words, no splintered syntax. No leaden diagnoses of the human predicament belch on the smoky skyline. The nature of the American experiment is implicitly questioned but not burned to the ground . . . This is a classic war story told simply and well, its meanings not forced but allowed to bubble up on their own."
—Dwight Garner, *New York Times*

"The story of the African Brigade, a unit of Black freedmen who fought for the Union during the Civil War, gets its due in this superior adult debut from Faladé . . . [Richard] Etheridge is made a fascinating figure, well suited to serve as the focal point for Faladé's exploration of the complexities of Etheridge and his comrades's rapid shift from powerlessness to armed military duty. Engrossing and complex, this will have readers riveted."
—*Publishers Weekly* (starred review)

"Wright Faladé's richly detailed, grippingly told story breathes life into a revolutionary moment when the US moved a vital step forward toward achieving the ideals we've always proclaimed."
—Charles Frazier, National Book Award-winning author of *Cold Mountain*

"David Wright Faladé's thrilling, revelatory *Black Cloud Rising* turns Civil War history upside down and makes America give up one of its darkest secrets—that our racial tension is literally a family feud."
—James Hannaham, Pen/Faulkner Award-winning author of *Delicious Foods* and *The Pilot Imposter*

"*Black Cloud Rising* is riveting and authentic—an intimate and brilliantly written portrayal of former slaves who risked everything to fight in the African Brigades during the Civil War. It's a compelling and deeply moving story of race, war and the eternal pursuit of freedom."
—David Zucchino, Pulitzer Prize-winning author of *Wilmington's Lie*

"The brilliant portrayal of crucially defining matters of racial history in America will rightly draw great acclaim to David Wright Faladé's *Black Cloud Rising*. But this novel's power is transcendent. Told in an exquisitely distinctive and nuanced voice, it reaches deep into the universal human condition and engages the core yearning of us all: our yearning for a self, for an identity, for a place in the universe."
—Robert Olen Butler, Pulitzer Prize-winning author of *A Good Scent from a Strange Mountain*

"*Black Cloud Rising* is the story of a minor engagement in the Civil War, a footnote in most history books, but it is the story of a major part of American history: the hard fought, still continuing battle of African Americans to rise from slavery to equality. From a single time and place, like a hologram it generates a three-dimensional picture of the difficulties, complexities, and nuances faced by Black people then and now. If you like history, if you want to better understand the struggle for equality, no matter your personal history or race, and if you want a good story, read this book. It's a triple threat."
—Karl Marlantes, *New York Times*-bestselling author of *Matterhorn*

BLACK
CLOUD
RISING

Also by David Wright Faladé

Fire on the Beach

Away Running

A Novel

BLACK CLOUD RISING

DAVID WRIGHT FALADÉ

Grove Press
New York

Printed in the United States of America

First Grove Atlantic hardcover edition: February 2022
First Grove Atlantic paperback edition: February 2023

This book was set in 12-point Adobe Caslon by Alpha Design & Composition of Pittsfield, NH

Library of Congress Cataloging-in-Publication data is available for this title.

ISBN 978-0-8021-6039-3
eISBN 978-0-8021-5920-5

Grove Press
an imprint of Grove Atlantic
154 West 14th Street
New York, NY 10011

Distributed by Publishers Group West

groveatlantic.com

23 24 25 26 27   10 9 8 7 6 5 4 3 2 1

For Mom, Myriam & Chantal

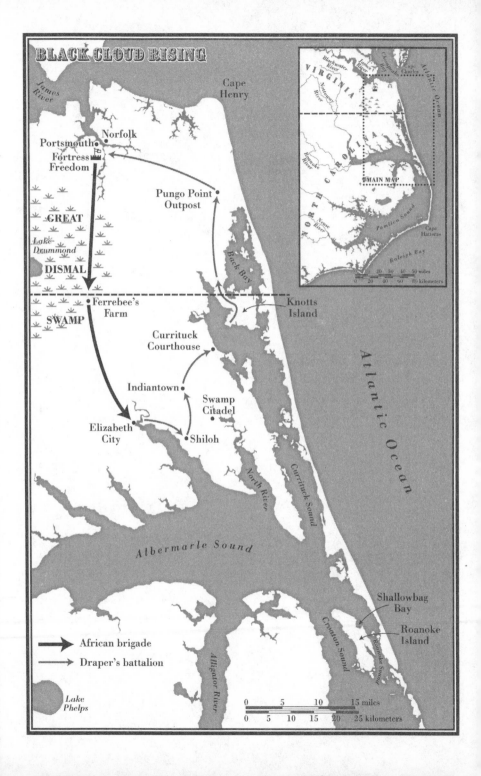

Nature has done almost nothing to prepare men and women to be either slaves or slaveholders. Nothing but rigid training, long persisted in, can perfect the character of the one or the other. . . . We were both victims to the same overshadowing evil. Nature had made us friends; slavery made us enemies.

Frederick Douglass, *My Bondage and My Freedom*

Don't you see de black clouds risin' ober yonder
Whar de Massa's ole plantation am?
Nebber you be frightened, dem is only darkeys
Come to jine an' fight for Uncle Sam.

Look out dar, now! We's a gwine to shoot!
Look out dar—don't you understand?
Babylon is fallen! Babylon is fallen!
And we's a gwine to occupy de land.

From the Civil War song "Babylon Is Fallen,"
by Henry C. Work

PART ONE

Mass Claps'n Come-Up

Wednesday, November 25, 1863

CHAPTER ONE

We are just boys, ten-, eleven-, and twelve-year-olds, five colored and one white. But for our smallclothes, each of us is most-all naked. We stand on the rickety reach of pier, its planks care-laid but well used, us colored boys' black glistening in the noontime bright, the white one not yet leathered like the sunbeat beefs that free-range the Island. Our britches and coveralls and burlap shirts lie pell-mell near the spot on the shore where Ebo Joe Meekins kneels, inspecting the line of the skiff he is refitting. The old Negro is either fifty or a thousand, the one age as imponderable to us as the other, and he pays us no more mind than we do him. On the water, cleat-hitched to the pier, rocks the dugout full of oysters that we are supposed to be ferrying over to Ashbee's Harbor. Up and down it rolls with each leap or dive, as we plunge into the water one at a time or in twos and sometimes all six at once.

I am young, square-shouldered but elseways long of limb, with knots for knees and elbows, and I climb from the Croatan Sound up onto the dugout. Straddling it, a foot on each gunwale, I begin walking its edge. The wood's rough grain digs into the pads of my feet with each shuffle-step forward. The other boys wade nearby, wondering at my balancing act.

"You look like one of Uncle John's barn cats," Patrick, the white one, shouts up, and he splashes water to challenge my progress.

I halt my walk so as to keep my balance and taunt back at him: "That the best you got? You can do better than that, Paddy-boy." Then I start rocking the dugout in place—down and up each gunwale, down and up—pushing out waves and making the others work to stay aloft.

"I'll fix your arse," says Patrick.

He swims forward, grabs a gunwale, and yanks down hard. But I spring overtop of him and stretch a splashless dive into the briny water beyond. The others swarm, wrestling to keep me below the surface, all but Patrick, who has pulled himself onto the pier.

"Youall hungry?" he calls.

He goes to his trousers, retrieves a penknife, and returns with one of the larger oysters from the floor of the dugout. He pries at it until it cracks open.

I climb up after him. "Smokes, Paddy, that's as nice a knife as I've seen."

The mother-of-pearl handle, the spey blade.

"Uncle John gave it to me." Patrick holds it out for the others to see. "Said I was becoming a man and deserved such a thing." He throws his head back and slurps down the oyster, then opens another and extends it toward me.

I just stand there looking down at it. "Mass John B. told us to plant those out past the second duck blind," I say, "not to eat them."

The other boys gather up behind me.

"Half the Sand Banks are laughing at his fool notion of plant-ing oyster beds," says Patrick, slurping down the one I've refused. "Hellfire, there will always be oysters."

Fields Midgett, protectful of me, tells Patrick, "Richard don't need none of that. Besides, Easterns taste like snot."

"Naw, they good," says Bill Charles, "but fried and on day-old bread."

The rest chime in then, proffering the ways and hows of oyster-eating—this, without any of us noting the somber white man who has emerged from the thicket of pitch pine.

John B. Etheridge walks up the shore, smoking a pipe. He wears bibbed dungarees over a white work shirt, closed at the collar by a string tie, his everyday duck-cloth coat over that. A slouch hat shades his face. John B. owns the dugout and the oysters, much of the Island, in fact, including me and two of the others. He stops a short distance from us.

"Patrick! Those oysters are for my oysterage!"

The others scramble to gather up their clothes, all but me. I remain aside Patrick. We both stand stock-still on the pier, heads hanging.

John B. storms up. "What are you thinking?"

"Me and Dick were just letting the boys have a break is all," says Patrick.

John B. glares at this boy whom he has taken in as a son upon a dear older brother's death. "How many times do I have to tell you? When I leave you in charge, you have to *take* charge." His voice evens, though the hard look in his eyes does not. "Not Dick, *you*."

He doesn't look at me at all.

"Yes sir, Uncle John," says Patrick.

John B. often punctuates a point by the length of tense silence that follows.

"You can't be pals with every nigger on the Island," he says. "Dick is no exception."

Though it is Patrick who's been scolded, I feel that it is I who have disappointed my father.

Turning, John B. says, "Make sure those beds are planted before I see any of you around the house. You two, with me." And, though he is already headed up the shore, each of us knows which order is for whom. Patrick and I scoop up our clothes and follow after, the others unhitching the dugout and pushing off.

John B. speaks briefly to Ebo Joe, who immediately stops what he is doing and removes his hat, then John B. continues on. Patrick carries his boots over a shoulder, tied together by the laces. In short pants and a burlap shirt, I have no shoes to carry. With John B.'s back now to us, Patrick apes his posture and gait, but I ignore him. I rush after John B. as he disappears into the trees.

We make the mile-long march across the Island in silence, Patrick aping, me ignoring. At Shallowbag Bay, where most Roanoke Islanders live, we join up with John B.'s younger brother, Tart, and our party of four takes the sloop *Margery & Sarah* and sails across the Sound to Nags Head. We land south of Jockey's Ridge and trek over the stark dunes, through patches of dwarf pine and thorny scrub, toward the sea. Topping the last rise, we see a wrecked schooner, pitched on her side near shore. A three-master, though only two remain. A party has already set upon the carcass, six or seven men rummaging through the hull and the debris scattered nearby for whatever might prove of value. They make piles high up on the beach, gulls wheeling overhead.

The wind rips steady and strong, whipping up sand, a stinging reminder of the recent storm that blew through, this wreck a vestige of it. William Creef, clearly in charge of the other party, starts up the dune as John B. leads us down it. "I was wondering when the Roanoke Island Etheridges would come inquiring."

"What do we have?" asks John B.

"Near sunup I seen her lurching in the surf, all torn apart and her sails blown to hell," Creef says. "There ain't much to prog for. A few salvageable barrels of salt is all, most of them shattered before coming ashore."

That is very likely prevarication, it seems to me. I look over toward Patrick and find mirrored in his face a like skepticism.

"And there is three dead," Creef adds, pointing up the dune.

Patrick and I stare in the direction his finger has indicated, at the bloated corpses of three mariners. It appears to be two men, each one the pale blue of death, and a woman, her skull crushed and half torn away. She is recognizable as female only by the tattered remains of a muslin dress that clings defiantly to her body. I know to drop my eyes.

John B. doesn't react to the news of the loss of life any more than he has to Creef's claims of a want of bounty. He and Creef move off down the beach, discussing the particular apportionments of this shared find. Tart joins the other Creefs, working the wreck. Patrick and I follow after. Two Creefs have stacked the larger pieces of planking into a single pile and begin to burn off the wood to salvage the iron. Giant fingers of smoke stretch skyward. Tart picks his way through the scattered timber. He lifts what remains of the arch board, the name MOLLY MCNEAL inscribed thereon, then tosses it aside. Patrick, walking along the wrack line of the beach, kneels and retrieves a pair of bent spectacles and puts them on.

Before I can join him, Creef's youngest, Colie, a year or so my junior, tosses a pick and shovel at my feet. "Go on up there and bury them dead," he says.

A punishing, arduous task—and grisly, even for me, a boy who has seen death before, for what Sand Banker has not? Our stretch of coast is called the Graveyard of the Atlantic and known the world over for just this reason: numberless ships and likewise many men have not survived it. But these ones here, these three dead? I find them hard to stomach.

Turning toward Patrick, I ask, "You coming, Paddy?" It is more plea than query.

And even now, all these years later, I ask myself still why I'd done this. Why had I lowered myself to begging? And what had I expected of Patrick? That my blood cousin, who sometimes

professed me "nigh on a brother," might assist in the dire undertaking? Or, better yet, that he might call on the advantage of our
shared name, and the rank that it implied, and remove me from
the grim chore altogether? The solidarity of family, that fool and
infantile notion?

Patrick stands only a few feet past Colie, the wire-rimmed
frames sitting skew-whiff across his face. "Hellfire, no! Why would
I?" His anger is sudden, his bravado clearly a show for the Creef
boy. He turns and saunters down the beach.

"Go on, Dick!" The boom of John B.'s voice startles me, his
towering figure staring over, face stern. "Do what you were told to."

So I have at it, dragging one sagging corpse at a time up to
firmer ground. Their wrists where I grab hold feel of pickled pork
knuckle, firm yet giving, but the bodies are deadweight so it is
impossible hard, even with the woman, whom I cannot bear to lay
eyes upon, particularly when what is left of her dress falls away. I
work out my anger with the spade, gash at my hurt with the pick,
digging a pit deep enough to guard against the sea's overwash and
to keep off gulls and gnawers—and likewise deep enough to topple
Patrick over into, had I the chance.

I catch sight of John B. staring at me when it is clear he
thinks me not looking. The set of his eyes betrays an aspect that
surprises. At moments like this, I recognize the father in the man
who owns me.

Later, the salvaging done, the two parties stare down the dune
as the last of the MOLLY MCNEAL burns, while nearby I continue
with the burials. The men speak among themselves as though I
possess no more hearing than does the spade that I wield. Tart and
the younger Creefs josh that one of the dead sailors looked to be
a Brazilian nigger, and they wonder lewdly at the role of the lone
woman in such a piebald crew. Patrick lingers among them.

Old man Creef presses John B: "I expect you could take all seventeen barrels and sell them up to Norfolk or thereabouts, if you had a mind to."

John B. goes into his pocket and brings forth paper tender and a few silver coins, then pushes them into Creef's outstretched palm. "You must be a religious man. Fortune just washes up at your door."

"The Lord giveth, and He taketh," says the other. "Who am I to question?"

As the Creefs gather to leave, John B. waves Tart and Patrick toward him. I overhear him instructing: "You see, that there is *his* place. *This* is yours."

I don't have the heart to look over. I know my father to be talking to my cousin about me.

"When he's done," I hear, "have Dick load those barrels into our boat. If it appears he'll not be able to finish alone, you may lend a hand."

"Yes, sir," I hear Patrick say, though the helping hand never does arrive.

My memories always spoke at me like this, in colorful pictures, telling tales. I expect their dream-story aspect was from all the book learning, the romances of knights and courtly love that John B.'s daughter, Sarah, taught me letters by—Maria Edgeworth, Sir Walter Scott—or the travel gazettes and magazines that she had me read at her. Or maybe it was John B.'s doorstop about the vengeful whale that by candlelight I made my way through. My memories, when they would come unloosed, were lively places I could feel and smell, full of people I knew, speaking at each other. Only their edges remained hazy, the what-fors and why-nots of these happenings that had already been but refused to leave me.

And on that morning, I needed them to. I needed a clear head. I was a full-grown man, with purpose, and had pressing matters at hand.

It was late November 1863, the Wednesday before the feast day recently proclaimed by President Lincoln for giving thanks for the blessings of fruitful fields and healthy skies. We were aboard the Union steamer *Express*, pushing down the North Landing River, headed for a farm in the neighborhood of the Princess Anne Courthouse. I figured our paddle-wheel's daybreak passage to be about as welcomed by the Virginians living along the shore as the oaths of loyalty that each of them had lately signed his name to. Such was the price of occupation.

And once the lot of us colored troops spilled out onto their docks? Why, I expected they'd find this boatload of musketed Negroes a mite disquieting. And bully for their distress.

"What you knowing?"

I'd not heard Fields Midgett's approach over the *spsh-spsh-spsh*ing of the wheel on the water.

"Is it wise, do you think," said my old friend, "for a Negro garbed in Yankee blue, with sleeves festooned with sergeant's stripes, to linger atop-deck a Yankee steamer as it steams through Secesh territory?"

He was right, of course. Adrift in memories of long-ago times, I'd allowed myself to drop my guard. This was nothing of the behavior of good sergeanting that I was being taught.

"Well, this is officially Union territory now," said I by meager way of excuse.

"Any Rebby-boy with a musket, be he regular, irregular, or mere passerby, would find a fine target of you."

"I expect so," I said. "But only after leveling his best aim at the general."

Fields turned to where I was indicating with my chin. A-forecastle, at the very tip of the steamer's advance, stood General Wild, stiff and tall, red-whiskered and red-haired beneath his slouch hat, the one arm left him after South Mountain crooked behind his back. A ship's prow has rarely worn a more striking figurehead.

"Ain't that something?" said Fields. He turned back to me. "I mean it seriously, Richard. Ain't that white man something, standing out there, a more prized target than even you?"

Sunrise had peeped early for late autumn, and with the brightening day, the wall of bog birch and oak began to emerge as more than merely shadows, revealing a spray of leaves going to russet with the turning weather. Fields and I settled in at the rail of the *Express* and surveyed the line of trees along the shore, as though aforehand spotting the muzzle flash of the shot meant to fell the general might somehow forestall the ball. Not a soul in sight.

"What you worrying on?" Fields said over the racket of the wheel. "Still troubling over our leaving to join up?"

Since we were boys, he had always seemed a right clairvoyant at divining my thoughts.

"Not the joining," said I. "That was right."

Just a few months into the war, Union bluecoats and Confederate butternuts from inland had faced off at Hatteras Inlet, then set to racing up from there, intent on capturing the Sand Banks. A string of long, thin islands wedged between the Atlantic and the broad Pamlico Sound, the Banks seemed as remote from the mainland South as it was from the far-off North, but it was prized by both, on account of our distinction as a linchpin of shipping. The Union boys won the contest and soon overran Roanoke, which Fields and I hailed as our home. We Island colored celebrated Jubilee that night. An army recruiting officer gave the call for Negroes a few months after, and Fields and I signed on together right then.

"No, not the joining up," I repeated. "The leaving part, though, is a hole that seems bent on filling itself in with chance memories."

The lowing of some beefs, just beyond the trees, turned our attention that way.

I said, "It reminds of home, doesn't it?"

"It ain't nothing like there!" said Fields. "The Sand Banks is all sand. This here is stretches of crops and peopled farms."

"I don't mean Kill Devil Hills and Nags Head and out there, but Roanoke Island. Home!"

Home—not just the place, but also those left behind. My ma'am, my girl Fanny.

"Them memories are what we're out here fighting to forget." He sighed, long, looking off into the trees. "Why not instead fill the hole with new, free-born thoughts?"

"Naw," said I. "I'm fighting for my right to prerogate claims to home."

"*Prerogate?*" Fields laughed in his easy, mouth-broad-open way. "That ain't even a word."

"Why ain't it?"

"Always boasting your book learning," said he, elbowing at me for effect. "Hincty!"

A few of our troopers wandered up from below deck and I righted myself, adopting the bearing prescribed by my rank.

"Sergeant, Corporal," Simon Gaylord greeted us.

"Men," said I. I kept my gaze out to shore.

Besides Gaylord, there were Miles Hews and Josh Land. They chatted idle with Fields, who, as a corporal, was meant to hold a closer place to them than I was.

Our commander, Colonel Alonzo Draper, appeared on the forecastle and made his way out toward the general. The colonel sported a gesture of dark beard, the aim seeming to be to trick the eye from lingering on his youthful countenance, not quite succeeding. He was the African Brigade's second-in-command, below Wild, and he and the general exchanged what seemed a solemn correspondence—at least, to read Draper's stern demeanor, it did. General Wild wore his habitual smirk.

"Hear tell we're out after one rank Secessionist today," said Josh Land to Fields. But it sounded more a question and he said it deliberate loud, loud enough for me to hear.

"Otherwise, why else would they have us out hereabouts on our own," Simon Gaylord added, "with guns and hardly a week's training in the use of them?"

Gaylord, who hailed Little Washington, North Carolina, as home, was broad in the beam but shy-eyed, the sort to always ask permission. How he had found his way into our lines was a mystery, and not only on account of his fearful disposition. For Gaylord had been a free man where most of us others in the Brigade had been slaves. He often crowed about his foregoing self-rule, much as he did about his erstwhile trade as a roving merchandiser; he thought this stamped him as special. Colonel Draper seemed to see it likewise, lauding the man's enterprising spirit, but I knew cannon fodder to be more to the mark. We sergeants took it upon ourselves to posit a peck of buck into the ones like Gaylord. He come in a puppy, but mister, he would leave a dog.

Fields told Gaylord, "We done paraded and hup-twoed and about-faced, and now the general has procured our company Spring-fields enough to take the field. We will put them rifles to use."

They were Harper's Ferry muskets, actually, not Springfields, manufactured at the arsenal where old John Brown had made his raid. I'd overheard the general telling Draper this. Though he'd been able to procure only enough rifles for one company, he'd made a point that it be this particular model, liking the intimation of it.

"It ain't that, Corporal—" Gaylord was saying, looking at his feet, when Hews jumped in.

"That ain't what we come up about. It's just all the hushedness behind this business."

I was a young-looking twenty-one, or so I was told, but Miles Hews made me seem a right grandpappy. He was seventeen, maybe, and everything about him was long, so much so that his pant cuffs only reached his ankles and the knobs of his wrists showed below the ends of his sleeves. He'd directed his words at me, their sergeant, rather than at Fields, my adjutant, and I could see that he was antsy like Gaylord. This was not Hews's natural bearing.

I dead-on faced him a pause before cutting into the three of them. "We will do what we're told and do it well, by God! The general elected Company F for this sortie because we've got bottom and we've got grit."

"Yes, sir!" snapped Hews.

"The Yankee buckra at Fortress Freedom just like those Copperheads in the North think all we're fit for is building up gun emplacements and hauling off their shit. Well, that ain't what you ran off from the farm to do. Today we show them different. Today we're soldiers. *We* wield the guns."

The *Express* rounded a bend just then and a wharf came into view. We all went quiet, for we'd arrived at the site of our mission.

Out on the prow, Wild and Draper scrutinized the landing spot. I pushed past my men and descended the narrow stairs to the hold and called into the splay-lit dark. "Ready up below! We land in ten minutes!"

Our company counted some sixty-odd men, grouped into three squads. Lieutenant Backuss, the only commissioned officer aside from the general and the colonel, commanded the first, so Revere—F's other sergeant—and I had charge of squads two and three. As the troopers assembled at the gangplank to disembark, I signaled

Revere to meet me outside the stateroom. It seemed prudent to review our roles.

"The Secesh will look on us as monkeys manning muskets," said I. "Let us show them otherwise."

I'd told him a thing that clearly didn't need telling, and he made me know it by ignoring the comment and staring off into the dark down the corridor, though he did not move to leave.

Like the rest of us, Revere had been conditioned in obedience, but the man was for certain not born to it. You could see it in his eyes—a sort of wildness—and hear it by his frequent silences, persisted in even as others were speaking at him. He and I shared a similar, lighter complexion, which I took to mean that we shared a similar history as concerned our paternal origins. But this was about all we shared. It took you aback how sturdy he was, solid and thickset, though tall. Me, I was of the Sand Banker type, wiry of build and an average height, more wax myrtle than broad-trunked oak.

Finally, he said, "I hail from this neighborhood, so the general will want my squad out front."

Of course Revere would assert this—as if he knew commander tactics or had the general's ear.

I countered, "Let's wait and see how Colonel Draper calls us out."

But it would bear up as Revere had predicted, with his squad in the lead. And as I had predicted, too, earlier. For from the moment we formed up on the wharf, white faces filled up windowpanes and half-dressed men spilled from doorways, glaring.

Upon quitting the *Express*, Colonel Draper gathered Backuss, Revere, and me, his squad leaders, and with the general looking on, apprised us of the mission. A runaway by the name of Cuffee

had offered up intelligence upon his arrival at Fortress Freedom—
what we colored troops called Fortress Monroe, our base and the
primary Union Army stronghold in the region. The farm Cuffee
had set off from was owned by Edgar Clapson, known to the Union
command to be a notorious Rebel bushwhacker, responsible for
many of the ambuscades and much of the sabotage from Princess
Anne to Great Bridge. With reliable knowledge of his location, we
aimed to arrest him.

Our column marched four abreast down the North Landing
road, with us squad commanders moving up and down the flanks,
keeping things smart. General Wild had no aim of surprising. He
wanted our presence announced.

"Hup, one, two! March, one, two!" I called to my squad, as
Colonel Draper had instructed during drills on the parade ground.
Sergeant Revere, ahead two lengths, left his men to march to my
cadence, offering inducement to individual troopers whose gait he
deemed below standard, paddling roughly at their backsides with the
flat of his sergeant's sword. Lieutenant Backuss, behind my squad,
added his own "Hep! Hep! Hep!" in time with my count.

Where Draper sat heavily upon his mount, I could see that
Wild was a natural horsebacker. Man and beast trotted casually
among the three squads. His was an easy sort of leading, that smirk
alit upon his face.

A general had no place and held little use in minor forays such
as this one. But neither had colored troopers made forays such as this
before today. Other Union commanders wouldn't abide it. General
Wild, though—he would abide nothing short of seeing our sortie
done. Since forming the African Brigade three months before, in
August, he had been searching for a way to get us into the field, wager-
ing that, afterward, many more such missions would be sanctioned.

Northerners were set in debate on the value of arming us colored, Abolitionist firebrands against Copperhead pols. Each one's

logic wasn't but different sides of the same coin, so far as I could make it. The Abolitionists hoped that bedecking slaves in Union blue and enlisting us in a fight for our own freedom would make men of us. The possibility inspired divineful awe, long-awaited witness that the monkey was ready to grind his own street organ. For Copperheads, the idea of us bearing up as fully men would damn near signal the apocalypse. Wouldn't be no returning from that.

But every blessed one of us colored knew it all to be bunkum for self-interested purpose. A Negro who has been owned knows he is a man from well before the first follicle florets his south forty. He knows accountability and responsibility and the fate that awaits any mistake and every misstep, for him as well as his.

General Wild knew like we did. For Wild, a bondman in a blue coat wasn't a spectacle, a benighted child being elevated to manhood. No, a nigger with a weapon was pure terror. Just that. The general recognized the blue coat as a dread costume on a freed slave's back. He knew that our weapons would be primed with the percussion cap of memory. And I cried huzzah for that man's discernment.

Before setting off from the *Express*, Colonel Draper had advised us squad leaders that, given Clapson's standing among the Rebels, contact with their Home Guard was possible. The dawn hour lessened the likelihood, he'd said, but be ready all the same.

Ready? I looked up toward Sergeant Revere, chiding his squad along; at my old friend Fields, towing tight his command.

We were ready, that and then some.

The general, too. That man was one of us.

It was an Indian summer morn. Yellowjacks like we had out in the Sand Banks rousened alongside the day's heat, petulant and unrelenting, lighting onto whatever skin lay exposed—your cheek, the nape of your neck. And like back home, they bit down to let you know that they'd stopped by, as though the buzzing at your ears hadn't already done that. Troopers swatted at the air despite Revere's scornful gaze. I strove not to, to maintain his same air of authority.

The distractions ceased as we parade-marched past the Princess Anne Courthouse. Old Glory whipped back and forth on her staff atop the white stone building, though it was clear that she was begrudgingly flown. I silenced my hup-twos, but each and every one of the men kept a steady beat all the same, even unsure Simon Gaylord. Our footfalls had the cadent boom of thunder. Whatever citizen, loyal or not, had not yet learned of our landing surely did so then.

We'd hardly gone two hundred paces past the courthouse when the Clapson farm appeared, across a stretch of unflowered and rustling stems where flax had not so long before been harvested. Cuffee, the runaway, finger-pointed it out. General Wild raised the one good arm and our column halted, the booming footfalls of a sudden still. Though nary a head turned, all eyes peeked as one over at the plantation house across the way that was our target. It was more façade than depth, boasting tall windows and a terrace out front but just dull planking on the sides, with little texture and no paint. A weatherboard barn stood to the left, a mess of chattel houses to the right.

The general had yet to speak word the first. He turned his mount and trotted back down our line, casual-like. Coming abreast of each row, he seemed to take in each man. As he neared me, I noticed that a yellowjack, furry and full, had lit upon his face, above his right eye. The man did not flinch as the deerfly did his due.

Wild met my gaze full-on. "No need fighting the inevitable," said he. "Let come what may. The pain cannot last." And he sauntered on.

Some minutes later, I heard him spur his mount, and man and rider dashed back to the head of the company. Colonel Draper, who waited there a-saddle, ordered us forward—Backuss's squad on one flank, Revere's on the other, where the chattel houses were, and mine down the center, straight through the crackling flax. The three lines fanned a half circle around the main dwelling house. Slaves stirred. Some emerged from the barn to take a look-see, even more from the chattel houses, which weren't but shacks with uneven joints and unglassed slits for ventilation.

Then, a man with disarranged hair and considerable whiskers appeared at the door of the main house. Clapson for sure, for he carried himself as though proprietorship was his established due. He wore breeches and a long-sleeved undershirt, nothing more, his suspenders not yet raised over his shoulders, and he stepped out onto the broad porch and stared down the general, who'd ridden a-front him and not dismounted.

Colonel Draper came up, the runaway Cuffee following after. Aught other moved.

My squad being nearest, I had a box-seat view when the general finally spoke. "Edgar Clapson?" he queried.

"You know damned well it is," said the other.

"I am Edward Augustus Wild, Brigadier General Volunteers, commanding." He half-turned in the saddle and added with a flourish: "The African Brigade!"

We all just stood there at attention.

"I see your nigger pogeys," said Clapson, "and I do not recognize your authority." He hitched up the suspenders, an angry gesture, as though they, too, had vexed his peaceful waking. "I command the Tidewater Twelfth Home Guard, the Pungo Raiders! And this here is my property."

Wild signaled with a nod and Revere, who was nearby, flew up onto the porch in two quick strides and seized Clapson meanly by the shirt and by the nape.

"Unhand me!" said Clapson.

Two troopers joined Revere, and they forced the man down the steps and wrestled him to his knees, beneath the general's gaze. "Pogeys, sir?" Wild said. "Did you say pogeys?"

Clapson would not respond, so General Wild continued: "These men are Armageddon's agents, both Gog and Magog. Your world is no more."

He turned toward us, the rest of the company. His voice boomed. "Guerrillas are cowards and murderers, without honor, no better than land pirates, and their fate is either quarantine or death. *This* land pirate's property is hereby confiscated. Seize all men, women, and tykes. Seize the grain and any implements and tools. Fill every hogshead, fill every buckboard. It is all contraband, and it returns with us!"

Fields broke the men into teams, and I sent this one toward the barn and that one toward the chattel houses where slaves were still falling out, and what had been puzzlement and gloom now turned to pure rejoicing. I could not know whether my own face showed it, but I was much overjoyed, too.

I was directing some men loading a handcart with farm tools—Miles Hews and Marsh Anderson and Lamb Rodgers—when I overheard the runaway Cuffee saying to the general, "All slavers buck they slaves." His head was bowed but his voice clear and strong. "But this one in the habit of stripping 'em head to heel, gals as likely as mens, whatever the age and for the least offense, and he lay it on sportly."

The general's expression did not change, but something was moving underneath.

"I know of at least one that ain't survived it," said Cuffee.

And I noted then what aforehand I had failed to see: a whipping post, well used, standing erect between the dwelling house and the barn. Or, what was more likely, my eyes had until then dodged seeing it. I had never suffered the lash, but what slave did not know it?

Revere without question did, for he held Clapson down on his knees, unassisted now and with what looked like pure relish. He forced the man's face to look upon that post. Clapson wasn't hardly fighting anymore. What must have been his wife and three young sons huddled on the porch.

General Wild, come abreast of Clapson, still disdainful of dismounting, leaned low from his saddle. "Even the women?" said he. "Even the women!"

Revere yanked Clapson to his feet, unbidden by the general but the order clear. The Secesh pulled like a colt then, knowing certain what was next. Revere, with a fistful of hair and a fistful of cloth, dragged him toward that upright timber. Shackles hung from its foretop point, and while two troopers wrestled the man's lurching and writhing, Revere hitched him on by the wrists.

The yard was dead still, us colored, slave as well as soldier, watching on. Mrs. Clapson's mouth lay wide open, lips aquiver, but no sound came forth. The three little boys, though—each one wailed.

The general marched his mount to the barn and into it, then returned with a bullwhip over the pommel of his saddle. He rode it over to Revere.

Clapson yanked at his wrists, crying to be released, all plea and no protest now.

"Pungo Raiders," said the general. "How quaint."

And with this, Revere, again obliging some unspoken command, lit the air with that long leather hide. Once. And again.

Fields was then aside me and I'd not heard him come up. "Damn, Richard," he said. "Damn!"

It was neither pity nor pleasure in his voice, just blunt astonishment. For who among us could have imagined this, the bottom rail on top, a nigger flogging a legal white man?

The general bid Revere to stop just four lashes along. Clapson's head slumped low, his lips whimpering curses. The general prepared to address us troopers gathered around—or so we initially thought. In fact, he was speaking at them others.

"Ladies," said he, his voice musical with sympathetic timbre. "I won't ask that you disclose this man's blasphemies against your virtue. Instead, I present the chance to settle old scores."

The yard stood still. Even Clapson's sons had ceased to wail.

From the crowd emerged an old mammy, head wrapped in a red rag, cheekbones like straight razors, a burlap dress hanging as long and plumb as her own long self. She crossed to the post, a deliberate stride that made the thirty-odd paces seem a damned sight more distant. When she got there, she unfastened a tie and the topmost burlap dropped to the waist. Dugs as flat as griddle cakes lay like sad folds of flesh against her chest.

It didn't seem she retained a tooth in her head. "This here the on'y virtue of being a Claps'n nigger," said she, her voice gravel and as purposive as her movements. She turned, and her back was a tangle of fleshy welts. "Ain't aught left here to blaspheme. But I expect I might take you up on that scoring bit. Mass Claps'n come-up is long due."

The general took the coiled cowhide from Revere and handed it to the old mammy. She let it out along the ground, reckoning the proper distance. Once she'd settled onto the right spot, the cowhide sang.

And then I heard the rest: the other slaves cheering, troopers too. "Oh, that I had the tongue to express my true feelings!" and "On the soil of Ol' Virginny! The mother state of slavery!" I heard Mrs. Clapson's rejoined wailing, her children's, and the Rebel Clapson, begging: "Mercy, Jenny! Oh, mercy!"

Revere stood so near Clapson that I thought the cowhide's lick might singe his cheek. His lips just off Clapson's right ear, he whispered at the man with each wallop—roughly, for sure, given Revere's dread aspect.

Vengeance can be justice, well earned and meted out fairly. And yet it be vengeance all the same.

The cowhide sang.

Fields and I turned toward the general, who anymore paid nil mind to the ministrations but spoke at Draper instead, the colonel stone-faced though not indifferent. "Dogum Goonoo!" I heard the general say—some such sounds as this.

"Sir?" asked Draper, as befuddled as Fields and I.

"Thirty-eight this day," the general said, as though this would clear things up.

The folded-over, empty sleeve flapped about with his mount's agitated jitters. "November twenty-fifth," he explained. "I'm thirty-eight today." He smiled a thin but generous smile. "'Dogum goonoo' is how the Turkmen say it."

Colonel Draper looked over at him, utterly perplexed.

The old mammy had lots more left than her spindly arm let on. She did not pause, and the general did not bid her to. "And it is a righteous good birthday at that," said he.

"The general . . ." Fields, gape-mouthed, looked unable to find the words. "That nigger wild!" he blurted finally.

"He sure enough be that," said Miles Hews, who'd come aside us without my noticing it. Rank and standing were right then of no import. Hews said, "I ain't yet met nobody the Lord had more aptly named."

Fields said, "That Rebel did not know we was men."

"He know it now," said Hews.

"And the general going to make sure they all know it, too," Fields said, "all them buckra."

"Naw," said I. "The general is letting *us* know that *he* knows it himself. Wild wants us to know that he will be with us to the end."

Clapson, his deadweight straining the iron shackles at his wrists, whimpered pleas that weren't hardly hearable anymore.

"Jenny . . . Jenny . . . Please . . ." And I imagined John B. as I'd last seen him, only transported here and slumped against that post. My ma'am—my mother, Rachel Dough—she too had scores to right. There stood I as proof. Justice, I supposed. Or maybe just vengeance.

"Good Lord, Richard!" said Fields, beaming like he was rare to do. "Lordlordlord."

CHAPTER TWO

It was a fitful dream that night, in the barracks back at Fortress Freedom—a thrashing between half-woke and full-on asleep. More a memory, really, the aftertaste of sleep that was either dusking or dawning but no longer fully dark. I was myself but back home on Roanoke Island. Walking up the lane that ran alongside Uppowoc Creek, past the barn and the windmill partly obscured by evening fog, toward the Etheridge House. Then standing in the vestibule, grayly lit by lantern light. Then afore the great doors to the dining room.

Had I knocked or just entered?

I watched myself, astraddle the threshold, dinner conversation of a sudden stopped. Mistuss Margery and Missie Sarah. Patrick. Mass John B. The silence of the room.

Ma'am Molly's Peter, the colored boy who served meals, was still now, too, his head bowed and eyes lowered, a platter outstretched toward Mistuss Margery but not close enough that she might successfully spear a fillet of the grilled bluefish.

"They are recruiting colored for soldiers up to the Contraband Camp," I heard myself saying, calling it what the Union boys called it and not the "Runaway Colony," like Sand Bankers derisively did. Nigh on as soon as the Northern Army had captured the Banks, slaves from inland, scores and scores, began to flee over the Croatan Sound to Roanoke, by whatever means—in pilfered canoes, dog-paddling on lengths of timber. The Northerners were collecting them together up by the Isaac Mann house.

"I will go there in the morning and enlist," I said.

I'd directed it at John B., but Patrick was the one who reacted. His face broke into a familiar, impish smile, as though I were taunting him with prankful play. Then it shifted, from amused to surprised and on to something other—darker—like I'd only on rare occasion seen.

"The hell you will."

None else moved, not even a flinch. Ma'am Molly's Peter stood stiff as statuary, the platter outstretched.

"The hell you will!" Patrick repeated, only stronger, as though it was him the master of the house and not John B.

Just then Mistuss Margery speared a fillet of bluefish—a sharp *clink!* of metal tine on metal platter. She refused to look at me. Ma'am Molly's Peter slipped out the side door, off to the kitchen, though aught other had been served.

"He can't do it, can he, Uncle John?"

I hadn't intended my announcement to waylay Paddy thusly. In fact, I had imagined the opposite. Even in this dream, I expected him to side with me.

John B. said, "The Yankees run the Island now. I suppose you will do as you wish from here on, Dick."

"Yes, sir," said I, wondering was the "sir" still mandatory or even appropriate.

I did not drop my eyes, though, as was custom and had always been my habit, and our gazes locked. Was it remorse I saw in his face, or was that merely what I hoped to see? I wished that the truth might expose itself. What did the man behold when he looked upon me? A son claiming his station, with the begrudging pride that this might inspire, or a slave of a sudden become ungovernable?

No such wish granted. Just his expressionless face and the sharp *clink* of tiny metal—Mistuss Margery hotly poking at pieces of fish, heedless that no one else had been served.

"But Uncle John! He can't," cried Patrick, less in protest than as a plea. He turned toward me. "It's their war, not ours. They will move on and things will . . . And who knows but that you might get . . ."

He seemed not to know at whom to aim his appeal, only that it was falling on deaf ears, as neither his uncle nor I would face him, each of us facing the other.

Then Patrick's voice changed. I heard something like contempt. "When you are killed and your nigger head is just some ornament hanging from the gum tree aside the square on Shallowbag Bay, we will leave it there for all to see what you have chosen."

He pushed off fiercely from the table and toward me, his chair toppling backward. Our statures mirrored one another's, as always, only now I felt taller, as though looking down upon his approaching form. My memory told me that our shoulders collided, perhaps deliberately, as he went past and out the door. But in this imagining of it, he spins back and takes my sleeve. "Dick," pleading. "Come on now, Dick. No . . ."

Was this truly said, any more than the part about the ornamented gum tree? I couldn't tell, the dream-memory breaking apart with the rustle of movement all around, with new sounds pulling me up through sleep. The metal-on-metal clinking of military gear, the bursting call of "reveille"—a din of fife and bugle in the distance. I forced open my eyes, saw my corporals moving between the rows of bunks, barking orders. I should have been up, too, rousening the men alongside them.

Instead, I lay there on my hard berth in the dawning November cold, remembering my mother's words, back at her cabin later the night of my announced leave-taking. "You couldn't just run off like other colored do?" Ma'am had said, her angled face unsparing. "You needed to beg for his approval?"

"Tell me," she'd added. "Did you get it?"

CHAPTER THREE

The foray to Clapson's farm turned out to be prelude to a grander pageant. In the days after, I overheard Cornelius Crowley and Henry Adkins, the first sergeants of Companies K and E, discussing an even larger-scale sortie devised by General Wild. It was confirmed when there arrived at our parade ground crate upon crate of Harper's Ferry muskets, this time sufficient for the entire Brigade. The troopers substituted these for the pretend rifles they had fashioned for training in the absence of proper weapons, and each company drilled all day and into the evening.

Thereon, General Wild summoned the great lot of us and apprised us of his intention for the immediate use of our new arms. "They fear you," he bellowed, standing atop a scaffold, a silhouette in the dusking light, straight and tall and rigid of posture. "They fear that, with weapons in hand, you will pillage and savage like the old preacher Turner did. Well, let them fear it!"

His one absent arm and the distressed other forestalled much possibility of gesticulation, but his voice—ho-ho! It was strong and cadenced, burning.

"It's their territory out there. General George Pickett in Raleigh has left the northeast of North Carolina to the Home Guard to defend, and it is where those guerrillas have taken root. But not for long. They think themselves safe in the forests and swamps, and from there they terrorize the loyal citizenry, they harass our outposts and expeditions. The African Brigade shall raise a voice that proclaims, 'No more!'"

His words carried us, each and every one, like camp-meeting Sunday. But none knew whether it was proper military decorum to shout back as we otherwise might have, and so no one did. Especially not with buckra troopers looking on. A spattering of white soldiers gathered along the wooden railing at the entrance to our parade ground, sharply silent, where they typically mocked our drilling and marching and whatnot.

"On four occasions previous," said the general, "Union forces have attempted forays such as this one, to bring the disloyal portion of the population to the side of allegiance. Ours will prevail, however, because unlike the predecessors, we will be terrible."

Just then, in the row afore me, Revere began waving his sergeant's sword back and forth above his head, the spirit in him.

"Sometimes, in order to be right, one must be infernal, and this we will be!"

Revere's platoon followed with huzzahs and foot-stomping, and I unsheathed my sword and took to waving it, too. Fields's back-and-forth brisked the company standard, and my men set in, stomping feet and whooping—Josh Land and Jerry Banks and Donald Newby, many more.

"Successful raids are characterized by surprise and speed," the general roared over our noise, "but this will *not* be a raid. We will march on their territory at our leisure and evacuate their hamlets that harbor the land pirates. Our bayonets, not stealth, will assure our safe return."

More huzzahs and stomps.

"For many of you, this will be a return home," said Wild, and the men of the Brigade fell still. "We shall not waste it. The Confiscation Act is our friend. It ordains us with the power to liberate the families you have left behind, to free your friends. This, too, will be our mission. We will endeavor to emancipate every bond-man in the region."

Those words struck the right chord, for even if some buckra volunteers like these onlookers at the wooden railing questioned what they were fighting for, nan one of us did, ever!

"Some label you 'contrabands of war,' mere property that the Secessionists have forfeited by their treasonous rebellion. I look at you, and I say, Bunk!"

Even old John Brown could not have spoken it more true. And all us colored were anew fevered then, stamping and hooting, clanging bayonet blades against canteens.

"Bunk, say I! You are men!"

As American as any and more man than most!

"This will be the largest military operation conducted exclusively by Negro troops," said the general. "You have shown to me that you are ready. Now, let us endeavor to show the doubting Thomases that you are, down where we're going, but up north, too."

We stomped and cheered in defiance of the doubting Thomases right there nearby us, on and on, for what felt like ten minutes or even more.

The white soldiers did not disperse as we broke ranks. They stared while we sergeants ushered our men past and back to the barracks. "Giving buck slaves guns?" I overheard one say to his friends, with voice deliberately raised, making it clear that he wanted it heard. "Why, that man is sure as hell a black Republican."

"The blackest they is," said another. "Blacker than old boy Abe hisself."

"That nigger Republican general is a lunatic," insisted the first.

"Lunatic and wild!" said one who had until then been silent.

A grizzled older soldier spoke up, making no pretense of talk-ing at his comrades, but rather, directing his poison words at me.

"I have come up agin them boys, them Partisan Rangers down in Carolina. They are awful to meet on the field, and devout. You monkeys will be shown your proper place."

I paid him back in kind, bad eye for bad eye.

Fields came over then, and we hup-twoed our troopers along with a barking style and a mite of dash, much as General Wild himself would have done. For we were the African Brigade! We were men!

December 5, 1863, ten days after Clapson's farm, just three weeks until Christmas. We counted a full regiment this time out, twelve companies, some one thousand men of the African Brigade, as we set off from Fortress Freedom at first light. Ours was the first column of two, led by the general himself. Colonel Draper had to stay behind to testify at Edgar Clapson's impending trial.

We sergeants were informed that our route south would follow the Great Dismal Swamp canal from Virginia into North Carolina. Orders came down that our column should look smart, at the ready, as we could not know when the Rebels would learn of our movements, if they had not already, and mount an opposition. And the men of Company F did. My troopers looked smart and snappy, marching to a silent cadence.

Maybe a touch too much so. More than a few looked downright jumpy, glancing about at the least sound. And why wouldn't they? This wasn't drills on the parade ground armed of carpenter's wood and suchlike planking, but marching off to war with muskets on their shoulders and bayonets on their belts, and none of the men had ever experienced it, not even us of F, who'd been on the Clapson mission. Not on this scale. Who knew what to expect or when to expect it, especially against bushwhackers? For it would likely be Home Guard like Clapson commanded that we encountered, the so-called Partisan Rangers. No stacked battle lines facing off across a broad field, as we'd trained for at Freedom, their formations mirroring our formations, tactics countering tactics—none of that. I imagined it would be ambuscades on our flanks and being sharpshot at from afar-off tree lines.

Marching through coastal pine toward a yet unannounced enemy, my men looked to be imagining it much as I was, as though some unrevealed specter was out there, for certain coming. So, I deemed it wise to forestall such inner workings and divert their attention elseways.

"Get it on step!" I shouted. "Hup, one, two! March, one, two!"

Fields recognized my intention. "Sing it out, Paps!" cried he.

Not missing a beat, Paps Prentiss, one of my privates, launched in: "Sitting by the roadside of a summer's day . . ."

My squad called back: "Sitting by the roadside of a summer's day!"

Paps sang: "Chatting with my mess-mates, passing time away . . ."

"Chatting with my mess-mates, passing time away!"

"Lying in the shadows underneath the trees . . ."

"Lying in the shadows underneath the trees!"

"Lawdy, how delicious, eating goober peas . . ."

"Lawdy, how delicious, eating goober peas!"

The chant became general up and down the column. And thusly the African Brigade made its way south, advancing through Virginia.

"**Allow me a few lines** to remark upon the bearing and style of General Wild," the newspaperman Tewksbury read aloud from his notepad by the light of a bonfire, our first night out. "His manner of dress is quite undistinguished from that of any other officer of the front line—a double-breasted blue frock of the old infantry style, with simple epaulets displaying his brevet rank and cinched at the waist by a leather belt holding his field officer's sword. But for the eyes! His ardent gaze unveils his chivalric creed. He is the ideal of gallant soldiery, no less so for his empty left sleeve."

The African Brigade was camped at Deep Creek, just outside the Great Dismal. We'd made only eight, maybe nine miles over the sloughy road. Pup tents were pitched according to company and rank, and most men not on sentry duty had turned in, as those first miles had been arduous and long in a drizzling rain. I was one of a few—officers, mostly—who had gathered around the *New York Times* paperman whom the general had recruited to accompany the expedition.

Tewksbury read on. "Much has been written of Colonel Shaw and his regiment of free Northern Negroes, particularly after their failure at Fort Wagner this summer past. However, General Wild has embarked on an altogether more demanding test—making men of slaves!"

"Will they fight?" he declaimed, thrusting a finger into the air. "Or, as so many believe, turn tail and run?"

I found myself cleaning at my fingernails with the tip of my eating knife, ceasing to listen. Tewksbury had a way with words and a certain style, and I'd sidled up hoping to hear luxuriant particulars on New York or on the North, and maybe for the chance to talk with him, a proper author. But he was a mite tough to tolerate for more than a few minutes going, what with his tragedian's manner and joyous self-regard and tittering at his own sad jokes.

I quit the gathering and made my way through the rows of pup tents back toward my own. We had not tents enough for all, and so some troopers slept under wagons with boards set up at one end to shield against the wind. Many just closed tight their greatcoats and rolled themselves up in gum blankets on the damp ground. Passing from pup to pup, from one bundled-up man to the next, I recognized myself not yet ready for sleep—for the nightly nostalgia about home, for the nightly pining for my girl there.

My mind was on the African Brigade and on our mission. *Will they fight?* Tewksbury dared to query, and in this moment of pause, I, too, found myself wondering, would we? . . .

Mister, we would! It was my duty as sergeant to ensure that General Wild's words of the previous evening were readily recalled and promptly executed by each man of my company, on each day of our sortie. And this, by God, I would do.

A campfire near the edge of the field drew me. As I neared, I saw that it was commandeered by other non-comms such as me, chatterboxing back and forth.

"Did you know that man a doctor?" said Moses Cornick, a corporal from Company K.

"A doctor of what?" asked his sergeant, Orange Redmon, a jolly, rolly man who'd run off from somewhere nearby the Secesh capital.

"Of healing!" said the first. "He gave it up for fighting."

"Guess his Abolition impulse was stronger than the curing one," someone said, to which Jake Whitfield replied, "Oh, he be curing, all right. The Rebby-boys just won't like the taste of his medicine."

We all laughed.

Rumors about the general were common currency throughout the Brigade, had been since I'd mustered in under his standard three months before. It was nice to get to share in them among men of my own rank, as I could enjoy the tall tales without having to rebuff troopers for talking out of turn about their commanding officer. Pushing in nearer to the fire, I loosened the buttons of my greatcoat, let the crisp heat cook at my shell jacket and pants.

"He took the Minié ball that took his arm at Antietam," Moses Cornick said, though I knew it to have occured at South Mountain. "We licked old Bobby Lee good up there at Antietam."

"I heard he amputated the arm hisself," was said by some voice at my back.

This was met by a chorus of *naws* and *ain't no ways*.

"Not the actual cutting," insisted the same voice, which I could not locate in the shadows afar-side the fire. "But they say he oversaw the doctor that was charged with it."

This seemed plausible to me, given the general's fire and grit.

"Our man is *wild*," someone said, echoing what, since Clapson's farm, had become a typical refrain throughout the Brigade. "That nigger be just plain wild!"

And the word *nigger* was not common parlance among us. Non-comms, in particular, were loath to use it, even when disciplining green troopers who needed to be taken down a peg. Yet it carried special meaning when used to refer to the general.

A sergeant from Company A, whose face I knew but name I did not, piped up. "I heard he has a record of arrest and has been court-martialed."

More *naws* and suchlike.

I saw Fields across the fire, standing between two corporals of Company G. I worked my way through the men to join him, as a skeptical Moses Cornick said, "How he come to be a general, then, if he has got jailed up?"

"Look who he a general of!" the sergeant from A shot back.

I squeezed in aside Fields, and he whispered the answer to the man's rhetorical query: "Of colored troops, of course." His face contorted into a look I'd known since boyhood, the one your ma'am shoots at your misbehaving antics or that colored folk sneak in disapproval of some foolish direction from their master—resignation born from enduring patience.

"Old Whitey think commanding us is a punishment," said the sergeant from A. "Their loss be our gain."

This was met by affirming grunts and *Yes sirs*. For Wild was our man, former convict or not, crippled or whole.

The campfire zizzed and popped. Abe Armstead of H, standing right alongside it, said, "This here war is not Wild's first. I once heard him telling the colonel how he had fought in an overseas place for a man name of Garibaldi."

"Baldhead Gary who?" someone said, and we all laughed.

"No lie," said Armstead, "Garibaldi. Some Italian that has fought wars like this war, but over in Italia, across the seas."

"A war agin slavery?"

"Naw," said Armstead, "one for union."

I knew Garibaldi to be a hero to folk over there. I'd read on him.

Moses Cornick said, "I heard the general telling this, too. He likes to tell such things to Colonel Draper." A smile inched up one side of his face. "Wild told him he had offered the voyage to his new bride—as a wedding gift. This was they honeymoon!"

We all harharred anew.

"Some gift."

"And what breed of bride did the man choose who would accept one such as this!"

"And youall think it ain't so?" was said sharply, and this calmed our raucous laughter.

It was Revere. How someone of his formidable bearing moved about unseen was a wonder, as I had not, before hearing his words, noted him among our group.

He said, "You fools think that man does what he does from some contrarian whim or for spiteful reprisal, on account of his wounds. I'm telling you otherwise. He is a zealot."

Since Clapson's farm, who could doubt this assessment of the general for its raw truth? Yet it seemed to forebode some other, darker implication coming from Revere's bone box.

To a man, we just stared over at him, and he stared right back at whatever of us would dare to hold his eyes. They burned brighter than the light of the bonfire.

"You, Etheridge," said he. "Is your heart in this?"

I hadn't expected to find my grit challenged and so, taken off guard, I just stood there mute—though I did not much care for the public chiding.

"And you, Cornick," he continued, "or you, Whitfield, with your doltish tales and joking comments?"

"Calm yourself, man!" said Henry Adkins, the first sergeant of E, aiming to forestall this before hotter heads prevailed and true confrontation resulted.

Revere went on as though Adkins had not even spoken, saying, but in a reciteful way, "For through the night I ride, and so through the night goes my cry of alarm . . ." And just then I realized he was indeed reciting at us, a poem or some such:

"A cry of defiance, to every village and farm,
A voice in the darkness, a knock at the door,
And a word that shall echo
Evermore!"

It wasn't the worst poem I'd heard, but if it was him who'd penned it, I knew myself to have a thing or two to learn him on metered lines and better rhyming.

"General Wild said that we were to be Gog and Magog," continued Revere. "Split-tail or hung, Secesh is Secesh. We should see them all dead, for they would thus see us."

With this, he spun on his heel and, pushing men aside, cut a path into the night—a final flourish to his theatrical apparition and just as sudden leave-taking.

A sight too stagy to my mind, but it had had its effect. A heavy silence reigned now, and more than one man stared into the fire or down at his brogans.

"Who that nigger calling Gog-Magog?" said Cornick to guf-faws and bellowing. Even Adkins, who didn't abide the use of the word, turned his face so we would not see his smile.

As the chuckles gave way to quiet, Hilliard Johnson said, "They say his come hard-earned." He indicated with his chin the darkness into which Revere had passed.

"Whose ain't?" was a general reply.

"Naw, Revere had a special cruel Mass," Johnson insisted. "Meaner than most."

"He sneaked himself letters is what I heard," said a sergeant I did not know.

"I heard the same," said Adkins. "Took stripes regular for pil-fering his master's books but kept on at it, yet and still."

Yet and still. It was amusing to hear when Adkins took to talking like the others of us did. He'd been born free in New York, a gardener by training, and his usual speech was more proper than ours. The African Brigade didn't yet have a regimental sergeant major, the chief non-comm above all others, but Adkins seemed a top contender for the position.

"*Revere?*" Livian Adams said. "Tst! I knowed that fool since he was foaled. His Mass's name was Peters, a hemp and hog farmer up by Isle of Wight. Called the boy Obediah, and he answered to it."

Obediah Peters, thought I. Ain't that something?

Livian Adams's revelation had seemed aimed for comical effect, but none of us laughed. The camp beyond had stilled and the night cold fiercened, and our meet-up was thus done.

Fields and I headed back toward our company. He said, "If that man weren't wearing blue, I might fear him."

He meant Revere.

"Maybe even in blue," said I, searching the dark into which Revere had disappeared, "a dose of precaution is warranted."

CHAPTER FOUR

The next morning, with the column formed up and marching on, the Great Dismal itself proved to be a more immediate foe than whatever bushwhackers might be about. The swamp was as inhospitable a patch as I had known. The road that ran adjacent to the canal—a towpath, really—was in disrepair, more packed dirt than graded stone, and was bordered on both sides by dikes fouled with black water. December spared us the raids of mosquitoes, but yellowjackets seemed untroubled by the winter chill. We swatted and marched, swatted and marched, it became a rhythm. Below the canopy of cypress and gum trees, full-on day could, of a sudden, with a passing cloud, become inky night, and we were often walled in by briar and head-high thorned bushes filled of frogs and insects so bold they did not let up their spectral calling even as marching soldiers stomped past. Moccasins and swimming rattlersnakes infested the area. More than one trooper was heard to call out for some other to mind his step, and Private Robert Hunter got bit just above his left brogan.

We made eighteen miles, just clear of the swamp, much to my great relief, as the idea of camping therein wasn't a welcome one. The column stopped at the trading station at Ferrebee's farm well past dusk.

Even at that late hour, the place was a-bustle with activity, including an unsavory lot idling about the porch. I organized my men on a corner of open field far enough from the store to disinvite temptation, on the off chance that an eighteen-mile slog through mire had not sufficiently done it. I likewise ordered Fields and my other corporals to be extra vigilant through the night, just in case.

Lieutenant Backuss, who, in the absence of an actual captain, captained us in Company F, joined the rest of the officer corps congregating around the general and the farm's owner beneath a kerosene lamp hanging from the eaves near the entrance to the store. Wild was coordinating with the old man about the expected arrival of two canal steamers sent down from Fortress Freedom, carrying rations to re-provision the Brigade. Ferrebee wore a straw hat and overalls over a white cotton shirt, and had a smile that too readily signaled consent and did not match up with his eyes.

As I watched, leaning against a falling-down stone wall, there sauntered over a youthful variant of Ferrebee—what I took to be a son, as he was similarly narrow of shoulder and false of smile. He was eleven, maybe twelve.

"Them there is Scratch Hall folk," the boy explained, pointing at the laze-abouts on the porch, lounging opposite where Wild and old man Ferrebee spoke, though I had not inquired after them.

They were a peculiar lot, yet and still. Each appeared a curious mix of poor white and colored, and nan one of them looked of the sort to inhabit any place meriting designation as a "Hall." They stared at the general and our officers, suspicious more than interested.

"How come is they so named?" said Fields, of a sudden standing aside us.

"Why, after their cousin Old Scratch, of course!" said the boy, bursting up with laughter, but mocking, not mirthful. "Swamp people," he explained. "They live in the pocosin and stay mostly to themselves, but come by the store for whatever they cannot make or catch on their own. Inbred mixbloods—Occaneechi, what's left of 'em, and Meherrin and run-off colored, to boot." He spat into the dirt. "Goddamn mongrels."

I turned from the porch toward this coarse and overly familiar boy then back, thinking: As though this ain't true of all, white and black, Indian and otherwise! It appeared to be so of the boy, in fact, whose tawny tinting looked to result from more than merely exposure to the sun. It was for certain so back home.

There weren't plantations out on the Sand Banks. There wasn't sufficient farmland for it, only small plots here and about on the scant arable bits, mostly on Roanoke. Fishing and oystering, lightering cargo and piloting the inlets were the primary means of money-making, and most Bankers did not make or have much. Few could afford slaves, and those few rarely kept more than one or maybe two. John B., who was a grandee by Banker standards, didn't own but nine of us. This, I learned at Fortress Freedom, was a paltry score for a Southern man of means.

Among an isolated people, increasing your slave stock was as difficult as finding new blood for brides. Mulattoes were the result, open secrets. I stood as a model illustration, a "scion" of the Etheridge House and broadly known as such, though a branch inscribed with my name would nowhere be found on the family tree.

Some Sand Bankers—though few—were not so guarded about publicly acknowledging the kinships. Millie Evans (white) and Abiah Owens (colored), out at Tommy's Hummock, and Vicy Bowser (colored) and Ben Dough (white), down to Kinnakeet, were openly coupled, with children and all, though in neither case were they legally married, as the laws of the state disallowed it. I would see Ben Dough on Roanoke with his tawny sons, Matthew, Mark, and Luke, regular if not often; he and John B. would barter fresh catch for whatever naval stores Dough might need from John B.'s supplies. White Bankers made no more fuss of the Doughs' presence than they might of wild Corolla ponies found pasturing in their yard of a morning.

Likewise for colored Bankers. We knew what we knew and so, among us, mixed blood was drylongso, just ordinary. Not for my ma'am, though. She'd been born a Dough slave, was bought in her teen years from Ben's brother Warren, and there was no love lost for anybody of that family, any more than there was for the Etheridges. She forbade me to interact with Matthew, Mark, and Luke. One time, I asked why.

"Vicy think having some tiny-small say in things with Ben be worth the price it cost to get it," she replied.

Ma'am was a lean woman, angled and taut. She could spark tinder with a shuddersome look and wasn't one to explain herself. But given that she'd started in, I asked more—the thing a mixblood slave boy knows yet still doubts the full truth of.

"With John B., was the price he offered too high?"

"Offered!" was all she said.

Her silences spoke louder than her words, and the one that followed merely reprised what I already knew without providing any connecting bits to help me make a song of the scattered verses. The worst of what I knew could wake me from sleep and seemed like an accusation against me, of what a man should do or had not done.

I quit the Ferrebee boy before he could recommence his gibbering. Fields followed. "Whatever that child says, he says with relish and might not nary a bit of it be true."

"Much like the father," said I.

I glanced back over at the older version, up on the porch, smiling oily at General Wild. A Southern man who had a broad patch of land, a store and goods for sale, and a barn and barn fowl and several beefs, yet not one slave? If the bushwhackers did not already have intelligence as to the Brigade's composition and hardware, they

would once we'd decamped from this location—that was certain—
either by Ferrebee or by the Scratch Hall folk.

Walking back toward F's place on the grounds, Fields
announced, "George Bowser is in camp."

"Bill Charles's brother?"

"He was paddle-wheeled in among the recruits that arrived
around the time we was out at Clapson's. They put him in Company
H." We stopped briefly to warm our hands over a campfire. "It's
said he's been looking for us."

This was gladsome news. Though three or four years younger,
he'd been part of our pack coming up. "Well, let's go find him, then."

H had pitched camp on the pasture abutting the west-facing
woods. Bowser's pup was easy enough to locate, after only a few
queries. When he saw us, he ran up all a-smile.

"Fields, Richard! I am pleased to see you!"

"It's *Sergeant* and *Corporal*, Private!" said I, sharp but not too
much so, so as he would recognize it for playful. "I'm likewise pleased
to see you, George, and glad you decided to sign up. Could you not
convince Bill Charles to do the same?"

"You know he ain't much for joining. He slipped off one night
and holes up down to Pea Island, with our people out there."

Fields asked, "And the rest of it—how are things back on
Roanoke? Much as to be expected?"

Bowser moseyed toward the nearest campfire, us following
along. He said, "It is why I asked after you, once I'd arrived to
Fortress Freedom."

His tone was foreboding. He full-on faced Fields.

"Don't tell me the Zouaves have changed their minds?" Fields
joshed, looking to lighten the sudden turn. "Do they not enforce
President Lincoln's call for deliverance? Are Roanoke colored no
longer free?"

Though said jokefully, such a thing was possible. Where numberless folk held the Northern Zouave regiments in high esteem for
their flashy attire and sense of dash, not so back home. They'd played
a live role in the battle for the Island but were a frightful occupier
afterward. Loud and braggadocious in their puffed-up pantaloons
and blood-red sashes and fezzes, disrespecting property and people,
and not caring one damn about colored. They treated us worse than
our owners had, calling us out as poltroonish buffoons, too stupid
to effect our own emancipation—this, even as streams of us were
coursing toward recruiting officers and enlistment.

"Well, more or less," answered Bowser, sheepish yet. "Refugees
keep flooding in, and the Union Army puts them to work in return
for offers of school learning and suchlike. But for us homegrown
Banker colored, if our Mass and Mistuss have pledged loyal, it is
not so clear."

Bowser stared at Fields, as though the implication of his words
was so obvious that he didn't need to say it aloud.

"Go on with it, man," said Fields. "Speak your piece!"

"Llewelyn Midgett"—Fields's former owner—"took his
remaining colored and sailed off from Shallowbag Bay, among them,
Riley and Lawrence."

These were Fields's brothers. "Naw, no way. They was to follow
me as soon as possible, to join me at Freedom."

Me, I could imagine it, though. The Midgetts were a rowdy
lot. Even after Roanoke fell and siding with the Union seemed
inevitable, many of them slipped off in a skiff or a lighter or whatever
craft remained after Zouave seizures, in order to resist it. Llewelyn,
being a Midgett and feeling bullied, might do just about anything.

And as though my thinking on it had made manifest the worst
thing possible, Bowser added: "Before shoving off, Midgett had
Riley flogged right there at Shallowbag Bay, for sassing."

"Sassing?" Fields protested, in vain, as Bowser was but the messenger. "That boy ain't sassed in his life. He hardly even speaks!"

It was an extreme of punishment, regardless the offense. Lashings were rare in the Sand Banks, and I'd never seen colored equipped of bits like horses nor the other manner of discipline that soldiers of the Brigade described as common fare where they'd come from. Yet Riley had been flogged, and out on the public square, to boot.

"That cannot be!" Fields's face was a churn of anger and confusion and pain. "It just cannot be."

Bowser dropped his eyes, which was all the corroboration that was needed.

"I'm sorry to be the one to tell you," he said finally. "But I wanted you should know."

I needed news of Ma'am. I'd left the Island with her emancipated, settled in at the Freedman's Colony. Now I wondered if this remained so, and under what conditions. I remembered Jenny at Clapson's farm. My ma'am bore the scars of memory like that old mammy wore the mess of gnarls that defaced her back, and for that reason she rarely held her tongue or masqueraded her true feelings. So long as tasks were done, Sand Bankers accepted it as her nature and let her be. But "sassing" could rightly describe her manner of talk, too.

I figured that if Bowser had something to disclose on it, he would have, but I asked all the same. "And my ma'am, George? Do you have any news?"

"Nothing out of the usual, so far as I know," said he, his eyes at once apologetic yet endeavoring also to add a dose of reassurance to his indeterminate report.

"And Fanny?" I asked.

My girl. She'd been safe when I quit the Island. I wouldn't have left otherwise.

But so too had been Riley.

"Fanny Aydlett?" queried Bowser.

"Yes," said I. "Any news about her?"

"Nothing out of the usual."

This "news" was hardly news, though much better than what Fields had learned. I reached a hand onto his shoulder, and he and I quit Bowser. We wended our way back to F's place on the grounds, both of us quiet, which felt appropriate. For what words could lighten a weight such as this one?

Outside his pup tent, Fields plopped onto the ground and sat at the entrance. "Man, we could sail from Roanoke of a morning, hire a hack for the rest of the journey, and reach this place by nightfall, that's how close it be. And here we is, in a patch of country I ain't ever even known of before, much less actually seen. So thick of white pine and juniper you wouldn't believe we was spitting distance to the Banks and the sea."

I could not follow his train of thought, but I sensed his eyes searching for mine in the dark.

"As a boy, I thought that freedom would be getting to rove about as I saw fit," he continued, "to decide my own choices." He faced down into his lap. "God is getting me, Richard, for shameful ignorance and prideful self-regard. It is wet and we are sleeping outdoors and I cannot go and do the things I need to do."

I wanted Fields heartened. "Come on, now, it'll be all right. We can . . ."

I could not finish the thought, much less my effort at consoling. If it was Ma'am and not Riley—or if it was Fanny!—I would be suffering it as he was, wrenched by my helplessness to do aught for her and restless for the chance to try something, anything, to make it right.

Troopers moved about around us. It was as though I'd only then noticed.

Fields said, "I run off despite offers of wage work and a share of the yield. Facing further threat of the loss of us, who knows what Mass Llewelyn might do?"

I'd not heard him call his former master "master" since we'd quit the Island.

"Listen," I said. "Packet boats are regular between Elizabeth City and Roanoke. I'll send a letter once we get there."

"Who to? Mass Llewelyn?"

"To the superintendent of the Freedman's Colony," said I, "or to the Northern missionary society there, or to both. But we will get the most current information and figure out how to act accordingly."

He seemed not overmuch convinced, despite the conviction with which I'd made my pronouncement. Nor was I, frankly. Even with news of their whereabouts, what could we do?

Our Old North State homecoming was not bringing the joy that the general's speech had heralded. Fields and I seemed farther from home and from our kin than had we been fighting over in Italia, like Wild had done. It left you feeling disillusioned, maybe even a little disloyal. After all, whom should we rightly be fighting for if not loved ones and family—for Ma'am, for my girl?

CHAPTER FIVE

Sentries were posted and company musicians commanded to play "Call to Quarters," though our quarters weren't but gum blankets, ponchos, and pup tents. The eighteen hard miles and recent sad news had tuckered me thoroughly, yet I could not get my mind to quell. Little Charley Brown was drumming "Lights Out" as I went to the campfire and lit the small candle I carried in my haversack and returned, cupping my hand over its topmost to keep the flame from extinguishing. One of the privileges of rank.

I set out to write Sarah Etheridge, John B.'s daughter. I'd all along imagined her as the recipient of my queries about Riley; I hadn't named her, though, as Fields didn't know that she and I corresponded. Etheridges and Midgetts were cousins, so Sarah was well-placed to have information on the latter, and given her contrary bent and fractious tendencies, she would be likely to gossip it, if prodded by clever enough inducement.

But before doing this, Fanny. I wanted to address my trepidations on her account.

I removed Sarah's letters from my haversack. There were only two—well, three with the postcard received the day before we'd quit Fortress Freedom. I went to the second, dated November 13. It was so fingerworn as to have become just about translucent.

Dearest Dick,

I very much appreciated your letter of October 28—the flourishes of plume, your earthy voice. You will be a great Negro author one day, and I shall always be glad—and proud!—to read you. Papa does not break laws on a whim, and that he sat idly by as I did so makes me all the more proud.

(Her roundabout claiming of credit for my "plume" always irked. She deserved some, for sure, for pressing that I be taught—just me and not nan other slave, man or boy. This I readily acknowledged. But I found myself a mite resentful of the insistence on gratitude from folks who'd taken much with relative little by way of return.)

All is much the same here on the Island. Yankees everywhere!—but this aside, much the same. Papa seems adjusted to the idea of their presence and our new circumstances. He has kept his ventures and enterprises humming right along—maybe even better than before, for the new business opportunities these Yanks present.

Very few have sided with the Secessionists and fewer still slipped off to fight with them, but not all are half so sanguine as Papa about our new way of life. I. C. Aydlett and family were over to dinner Tuesday last and Mr. Aydlett's vitriolic disposition on the Union occupation about ruined supper. Though neither his Caesar nor Troy nor Hercules have joined up like you did, they have made off to the Runaway Colony that the Yanks have established on the north end of the Island and refuse to return home! Mr. Aydlett was beside himself, and it was all I could do to not needle him with news of your successes in the Yankee ranks.

Mrs. Aydlett had her handmaid Frances along. The Aydlett girl could not hide her beaming when mention of the Good Soldier Dick came up—though given her master's disposition,

she tried mightily. Frances has yet to quit the family for the
Runaway Colony; Mrs. Aydlett supposes that she stays on to
care for old Uncle Pompeii.

The girl made a point to sidle up to me as we moved from
the table to the verandah and offered a message from your
mammy for me to pass along—that all you boys send news
to your people here, to Auntie Colleen and Mammy Betty
and Mammy Beulah . . . The list of names went on and on
and, if you will allow, I will abbreviate to merely, Your Negro
Adherents Hereabouts. Evidently, they are many on the Island.

But it is clear that one in particular wished for news of you
especially—and I do not mean your mother but her messenger!
(A lady recognizes these things, Dick. I am a little offended
that you did not think I would.)

So, do please, Dick, send word of your continued well-being.
Put that "buck larnin'" that I gave you to use and write. I will
see that Frances and Mammy Rachel get your news.

And Patrick, too. He assumes our correspondence to be
more frequent than it actually is and asks for particulars that
I do not know.

Perhaps one day when this is all over and done and you have
returned home, we shall have a great miscegenat banquet, all
of us together, at which black and white shall sit at equality
and give toasts and sings songs to Abraham Lincoln and to
freedom. Huzzah!

I write this only mildly in jest. I would enjoy such a festive
gathering, truth be told.

Yours affectionately,
Sarah

Seeing Fanny's name in script—"Frances," as the white folks
called her—brought on memories of her face, a face to shame the

angels! She'd had my eye since I was old enough to tell apart boys from girls and care about the difference. For some time now, though, we'd called each other more. It wasn't a proper courtship, of course. We were slaves. Some things were better kept secret.

If Sarah had deduced our affection, I was sure that it was because Fanny led her to it. Colored could mask for whites and all the while reveal to ourselves a world all our own. Fanny was a master of this. Beneath Sarah's report of the dinner were hints of Fanny's true meaning. It was a message of abiding love and longing like what I felt, and a promise to remain true until I should return to Roanoke to bring her away to freedom alongside me.

Given Riley, I also searched this time for indications of Fanny's continued safety in the Aydlett house. The old man's "vitriol," so easily toyed with by Sarah yet with no hint that Mrs. Aydlett and "her girl" were in any way uneased, reassured me.

Likewise rereading the mention of my ma'am. This, alongside Bowser's report of nothing being new, comforted. I surmised her to yet be residing with her sisters, Betty and Beulah, and her nearest friend, Colleen, in the hastily built cabin where I'd installed them in the Freedman's Colony. As this remained so, it was likely she was safe.

I folded the pages gently along their wearing creases and returned the letter to its envelope, then removed and unfolded the first one I'd received. It had arrived in mid-October and wasn't gratuitously sent. I'd beforehand penned Sarah a long and florid letter, detailing my safe arrival and immediate preferment to rank on account of the book skills I'd learned at her hand, and describing the conditions at the fort and suchlike—all of which, I will confess, had been intended to invite a reply. Other colored would have surely found corresponding with their former owner to be a shameful thing, but I needed a lifeline to home, a way to pass along news to Fanny and Ma'am back there. I knew that Sarah would be a game, albeit unknowing, courier.

But there was more to it, too—a sort of taboo satisfaction that I felt from my correspondence with her, if I was honest. I remembered our Sunday afternoons, Sarah and me in the downstairs library. With a spirited girl as unlikely captain and me, a slave boy, as even less probable first mate, John B.'s books made possible an elsewhere, fantastical and new. I read and reread her letters, not so much for missing Sarah but the time and place that her words recalled, a place that I found myself loath to see disappear—and one I'd enlisted to help destroy. It was a paradox, and uneasy in me.

The line between master and familiar is sometimes a gummy thing, and Sarah and I, as Patrick and I, had been friends. You grow up as babes together, suckling at the same breast. You make child's play in the yard, even after you alone come by chores and errands and they do not and this then rations the time that you have for it. One day they become white and you, their property. But you know what you know, even as they have forgotten this time not so long past.

And for me with the Etheridges, of course, it was more complicated than this.

"*Greetings, Dick,*" Sarah's first letter opened, coolly. (Not so much the "Dick" part—this was what the Etheridges called me—but the "Greetings." It sounded distant, as though we had not known each other.)

It has taken a little time for me to reconcile with your unexpected and abrupt departure—to forgive you, if you will; but I also felt it important to respond to your letter, to remain in contact. It is the Christian thing to do.

Papa always called me his "Abolitionist spawn" for insisting on teaching you to read, write, and cipher. But you know what? It was clear that he never meant it as an insult, only as teasing, as I always heard pride in his voice when he said it. Pride in you as well as me, I believe. Me, for doing as my conscience dictated, despite the legislature's injunctions otherwise and the broadly held ideas about a girl's proper place; and you, for being interested in learning.

I should have understood our "schoolhouse play" to be preface and not conclusion. And Papa should have, too. For does not the mere fact of you disprove the vile things that the Dixie Illuminati (such as it is!) would have us believe about the capacity of the Negro? Mammy Rachel turning up one day with child may have been an indiscretion on Papa's part, but your manner of upbringing was certainly not. Unlike the other servants, Papa reared you an Etheridge; he, just as much as I, should have predicted your departure from us with the Yankee arrival on the Island. We were both equally naïve not to.

You have wounded us all so, Dick, don't you know? Even me, though you might not realize it.

At dinner one night, Mama, who, as you well recall, can be quite prickly in matters dealing with servants, asked Papa how we should come by news of you. It was not mere curiosity. I heard worry in her voice and saw solicitude in her eyes.

And Patrick! He has been beside himself since you left. All the Island knows him to be prone to rashness, but it is always now either angry barbs or wild pronouncements against the "filthy Yankees" that "stole you off." I scarcely recognize him.

Perhaps it was not your intention to wound. Perhaps it was just your idea to be true to yourself, to attempt to be your own master.

There! I have said it! Such notions remain apostasy out here, but I knew you as a boy, raised in our house as one of the family. Where others will not admit it, I see it as my duty—as a girl become woman and, God willing, one day a proper lady—to acknowledge the sin committed by Papa and, in so doing, to thereby also recognize in you the qualities that your birthright, by blood, fittingly make yours, even if race and the Systema Naturae circumscribe your station.

I hope you will forgive me this candor. I have always felt us to be close, you and me. And I hope you will reply to this missive, as your military duties permit, and keep me—keep us all—apprised of your well-being.

Best regards,

Sarah Etheridge

I lowered the letter away from the candlelight and lay back against the hard ground. A bobcat wailed in the distance, the cry sharp, my stomach seizing up even as the sound was a good ways away.

I'd known my words in that first letter would find their way to John B.'s ear, and I'd wanted them to. I wanted him to know of my accomplishments. But my departure having been intended to wound? To wound him?

Patrick, sure. I'd figured he'd be hurt. We'd grown up "nigh on brothers," as he would often say, meant as a term of feeling (though not stating the obvious fact: that, given John B.'s regard for him as a son, we were, though merely cousins, nearly brothers as a matter of kin). But John B.?

I remembered the night I'd announced my leave-taking to them. Sarah's narrative so little comported with my recall of John B.'s indifference.

It was becoming a habit to not revisit the third correspondence, the recently received postcard. I always wanted to linger on my vision of Fanny after rereading the second letter, and the card's despondent tone broke the spell. The cover drawing was beautiful if glum, the backside message, mysterious and dark. But on account of Fields— on account of Riley—on this night, it was different.

I approached the card to the flickering light. The drawing was clearly by Patrick's hand: an ink sketch on a square of fancy paperboard, of a crumbling fisherman's shanty on a desolate stretch of beach engulfed of sea oats, the wind-planed trunk of a fallen oak twisting into the frame of the image from one side. It was finely wrought, with arcing lines that called to mind the somberness and solitude of the empty shack, and recalled to me Patrick's youthful enthusiasm for picture-making and art stuff.

In that time past, I'd more and more see him off in a corner of the library or out on the verandah with a pencil and pad, sketching, as I did chores about the house. I envied him this leisurely practice. We colored did most-all for them, so Patrick's inclination toward studied idleness did not surprise. Not me, anyway. For John B., the newfound interest was just one more thing that seemed to disappoint him about his nephew.

On the back of the postcard, Sarah had written:

Oh, Dearest Dick!
Patrick gave me this yesterday, with cryptic intimation. He said that, before, endeavors such as this pen-work were about all that he did better than you, but that soon this would no longer be the case. That was it, nothing more—cryptic, cryptic! He knows of our correspondence and it is clear he expects me to pass along his words. I wasn't sure I should, but here I have.
Yours truly,
Sarah

I still was not quite sure what it was he wanted me to know or suspected I would divine from those mystery words and the lonely image. With what I'd learned about Riley, though, I wondered if there was some connection. Had Patrick been attempting to inform me of the changed mood on the Island, of Llewelyn Midgett's turn? Or worse yet, did he have some hand in it? Though born an Etheridge, Patrick was more Midgett than not and had always been close with that branch of cousins.

Patrick, thought I, what did you do? . . .

I returned the card to its envelope and replaced all three in my haversack, then lay there in the brittle cold atop the hard ground. I hadn't penned the new letter to Sarah and admitted to myself that I would not get it done on that night. It wasn't only the bone-deep exhaustion, come by after eighteen hard miles, but just as much the rest—the dread about Riley and Patrick's crumbling shanty and the unknown that lay ahead.

I longed for sleep, bottomless and big. Easy sleep with my girl, Fanny, on my mind.

Good night, sweet angel. Good night.

CHAPTER SIX

Reveille was typically a paltry effort for colored troopers, as we'd been conditioned since boyhood to work from can't-see to can't-see. Such was not the case the next morning. Men milled about, breakfasting on hardtack and coffee long after what normally would have been the case. Me, I found a camp chair and used the early hours to write up my reports on Robert Hunter's snakebite and on Josh Land's turned ankle and on their subsequent removals to the Moses wagons, where the Brigade surgeons treated the sick and wounded. This work needed done before orders came down to prepare Company F to form up and move out, and I'd gotten behind on it.

Writing legible and reading true was a prerequisite of being ranked to sergeant, and this was the reason why: because of all the forms and whatnot that were constantly demanded of us—updated descriptive rolls, commissary requests, daily reports on the state of the sick and the wounded. Such was army life, a damned sight better than bondage but nothing of what I'd imagined of free-joined soldiering.

I heard, "Now is a good time to ensure that the official documentation is composed."

It was Lieutenant Backuss, come up behind me. A recently arrived Dutchman, he had little notable accent besides his English being a mite too correct. Like the other foreign-born I'd encountered at Freedom—Irishmen, mostly, and a few Norwegians—Backuss seemed especially discomfited among us colored, even more than did your typical Northern white, and he tended to overexplain things that didn't need explaining in the first place.

I lifted the forms from my lap for him to see, though they seemed clearly visible. "I will have these ready for you directly," said I.

"Sir" would have been appropriate, per military procedure, as well as rising from my seat. With him, it did not feel warranted.

He just stood there, awaiting further proof of my efforts or maybe something other—I did not know. I returned to my work.

Officers willing to lead colored troops had proved rare, so the Union offered commissions to non-comms from white outfits if they were willing to join a regiment of Negroes. Such was the case with Backuss. He'd been a corporal in the Ninety-Eighth New York, posted at Pungo Point, before mustering in with us. More often than not, those who transferred over were more of an opportunist bent than Abolitionist. When you made buckra privates and corporals into lieutenants and captains, they didn't of a sudden get more qualified to lead for the bars patched onto their collars.

Colonel Draper had cashiered out two of F's three officers in our first three months, a drunkard by the name of Ives who'd first captained us and, just a few weeks after, the lieutenant who'd replaced him, Joe Longley, for misappropriating company rations. Even more than the rummy, F had been glad to see Longley go. He seemed to take at face value the coon show acts he'd seen coming up, and no deed or feat could disprove his deep-grained notions about our inborn doltishness and docile dispositions. Why, that man took to feeding one of the stray camp dogs and, on account of it was black, named it Sergeant Sambo, saying it better deserved the rank than us real sergeants. He found this funny.

This left Backuss, who didn't have his own squad's confidence, much less that of the company entire. He remained standing afore me, and I wondered why. Did he wish to chat affably?

His cross-armed posture and unmoving face appeared to rebut the notion.

"Is there something else, Lieutenant?" I asked, looking up from the forms.

"No, Etheridge," said he. "Carry on."

He turned then, finally, and I watched him walk away.

As nine turned ten and still no orders, I surveyed the field, studying the company. Troopers dawdled about in a way that seemed dangerous. Restless anticipation can lead to disorder or mishap. I had my corporals circulate and inspect weapons and equipment, just to keep the troopers on something—all but Fields, whom I left to himself inside his pup.

The reading-and-writing requirement wasn't strictly observed of corporals, as book learning among colored was so rare. Fields had a little, what I had sneaked him when we were children, but not so much as to feel easeful composing official documents. What he lacked in letters, though, he more than made up for by the respect that others naturally afforded him. A sun-stretched face and a dead-eyed stare made a hard look all the harder, and he, like most Sand Bankers, tended toward the brusque and laconic—useful tools for leading men. Colonel Draper had recognized these traits right off and ranked Fields our first week at Freedom.

From where I sat, I could see General Wild standing under the eaves of Ferrebee's split-log store, speaking at Revere. Each stood eye-to-eye with the other, though Revere was much thicker of build.

The general's aide-de-camp, his brother Walter, was likewise there, nigh on a head shorter. The sad state of the African Brigade's officer corps was the reason Wild had drawn from the family pond to complete his command structure. Colonel Draper was following suit. I knew him to be seeking to have his younger brother transferred into the regiment, and likewise a number of trusted non-comms from his former unit, the Fourteenth Massachusetts—anything to build up the number of officers.

General Wild returned inside the store, and Revere rejoined our company. I watched Revere move broodingly among the men, here and there handpicking one or another. He plucked Bill Overton and Albert Banks from my squad, and my corporal Aaron Mitchell.

"He got four of mine, too," said Robinson Tynes, moseying over. Tynes had been recently promoted from corporal. "Only took boys from hereabouts."

I hadn't made the connection but saw it then. I knew Aaron Mitchell to be from a farm abutting the swamp, on the Virginia side. His knowledge of the neighborhood had assisted in guiding the column's passage down through the Great Dismal.

"Same with mine," I confirmed. "Three good troopers."

Leadership types whom I was vexed to see gone.

"What you think Revere up to?" asked Tynes.

"Whatever it is, the general appears to have ordered it. We'll find out in due course."

Revere and his detachment—twelve or so men, loosely ordered—moved up the Great Dismal road, opposite our direction, back into the pocosin. I will admit to chafing some that Wild had chosen that half-cocked fool for the special mission, whatever it was. I knew myself to be fully the man to accomplish any such assignment, just as much as he was.

On about noon, the general called a meeting of officers and sergeants, behind Ferrebee's store. As Tynes and I approached, I noticed that the few officers who weren't already at the fore of the assemblage moved there then, as the lot of us colored arrived. The night previous, wending my way through camp, I had likewise noted that they'd ordered built a separate fire to warm themselves by. Neither at Freedom nor thus far in the field had I yet to see an officer accommodate himself, or even share a brief respite, in the company of us non-comms.

The separate campfires, this separation now—it wasn't only to do with differences of rank. Would the Brigade's regular officers—Lieutenant Backuss, Captain Shurtleff, and the rest—regard us with equality when the Minié balls let fly, once we were bleeding side by side, man and man?

It was our duty as sergeants to hold to the conviction that they would, for the good morale of the troops, if not for our own commitment and spirit.

General Wild emerged from the store, followed by Lieutenant Colonel Holman and Major Wright. Wild bid us to press in closer, then commenced. "By some unaccountable blunder, our provisions have gone astray, down the wrong channel, likely."

He was referring to the canal steamers that were to meet up with and re-provision us. But "gone astray?" thought I.

Right. News of armed colored passed along quickly. It seemed just as likely that the bushwhackers had misdirected the steamers, or commandeered them and seized the cargo.

"These not appearing," the general continued, "we will advance, trusting in Providence and the country for the subsistence of the troops."

Old man Ferrebee, who lingered not too far away, giggled nervously at this, loud enough to draw Wild's attention.

The general addressed him with solicitude. "Loyal citizens need not fear any confiscation or loss. And thank you again, sir, for the use of your grounds."

Ferrebee appeared reassured. Or, at least, he struck up the weaselly look of over-enthusiasm that was meant to communicate reassurance.

Lieutenant Backuss waved Tynes and me over as the assembly broke up. "The company shall be required to forage for comestibles," he announced officiously, which, of course, Tynes and I already knew, for we'd taken part in the same briefing as he. "Instruct the troops," he told us, which Tynes and I were already setting off to do.

A spray of robins and mopes broke loose from the surrounding treetops with the first sharp notes of fife and bugle calls. There was the hurried pounding of feet as the men collapsed tents and crushed out fires, strapped on bedrolls and fell in, close order. I claimed my place at the top of F, behind Backuss. The general, a-mount his bay, trotted to the head of the column. He called the command to move out and we echoed it down the line, company after company.

The long roll set in. Getting one thousand men into coordinated motion is a sputtering thing, and we lurched forward, some companies immediately on rhythm, others shambling along. I shouted further reveille into the few troopers who looked in need of more morning coffee.

Though wooded hummocks loomed all around, possible positions for bushwhacker marksmen, General Wild was bent on making our presence known, a sort of provocation to the local citizenry. Still, in precaution, he rode over to Backuss and ordered F to the eastern flank, to bolster Company A, which was already out there. We would assist them in providing security for the column from attack. Tynes and I spread the troopers out in the neighboring woods, which were impossible thick. I threaded my way from man to man, all scattered through the trees, offering boosting or rebuke as needed, while the principal column of the African Brigade hup-twoed along the road, in the open and plain to see.

The first farm the regiment passed was still, unusually so for a work Monday. Then, slaves began to emerge from the chattel houses and the surrounding fields, a score or so of them, in groups and individual, old and young alike. All looked over at the legion of colored soldiers, amassing nearby.

General Wild broke free from the column, trotted over, and invited them to "fall in."

None moved. They all just stood stock-still, staring at the strange one-armed man.

"Collect your things," said Wild, "and bring along everyone."

No one yet moved, though the general was smiling.

A trooper came loping up from farther back, dropped his rifle on the ground, and took up an old uncle in his arms. The two spun and spun. The lot of slaves closed in around them, and there was an eruption of hollering, hands reaching for the sky, slaves and soldiers alike. Out where we were in the trees, too—Miles Hews and Zach Gregory and Drew Messer, huzzahing and waving their muskets overhead. Then Joe Gallop and Little Charley Brown started in on "Kingdom Coming" with a forceful piping and drumming. Some men sang along, and all smiled great smiles that lit up the already bright day. Me, too.

But none looked more pleased than the general himself. Wild put his horse's leather reins between his teeth, removed the slouch hat from his head with his one good hand, and raised it toward the heavens.

The slaves ran off toward their cabins and soon reappeared, toting whatever they could in burlap sacks and squares of cloth twined at the top, with babies on their hips and spindly children running after. They fell in behind the column.

It was like this at each farm we passed. Squads of troopers scuttled like fiddler crabs up to the dwelling houses as well as the outbuildings and burst through the doors. At one, what must have been the overseer, dressed as dingy as his colored, put up resistance, hollering and carrying on. The slaves meekly watched from the hemp field beyond, bent and diffident. Captain Bradbury of G strode up and "enlisted" the overseer into our service on the spot, prodding the man with the point of his sword to take up the loaded burlap sacks of two women whose arms were busy with little tykes. At another farm, Moses Cornick's squad found that the slaves had been locked up, down in a cellar. Like a bolted door might make some difference! They used a felled tree trunk to break through it, then helped the fifty-odd colored climb out. Cornick's men claimed a buckboard and hauled off lengths of dried beef and baskets of carrots and turnips, enough for his company's supper. Troopers took to commandeering whatever means of transport would roll and had livestock to pull it, hay carts, mostly, but also some landaus and a mud wagon, and this two-wheeled job that Backuss called a "cabriolay." He looked overmuch pleased to see such a thing in a place such as this, even if only from afar, given our position in the woods.

The region was thickly settled, so the column's advance was snail-paced but ever so distinctive. A clarion call of sorts, what with all the oxen and horses leading wagons, their gear jingling and rattling, and over all a generalized hymning, a hum of joy from the flood of folk who came away with us. I watched it all from the edge of the corps, joyous too.

Likewise General Wild. He sat atop his bay, beaming and saying little, as little needed to be said.

We didn't make it farther than a crossroads called Tar Corner, maybe two miles up the way, before the contraband train trailing the column came to be seventy-five wagons long. We stopped, then headed back to Ferrebee's farm.

The second column came into camp not long after dusk, six hundred men—five hundred from the Fifth U.S. Colored Troops, a regiment raised in Ohio by Colonel James Conine, who'd known

General Wild in Maryland, and one hundred more from the Fifty-Fifth, a colored Massachusetts regiment. The sprawling lot of us formed a sort of impromptu Negro city—much to the displeasure of old man Ferrebee, though he struggled not to show it. Cone-topped Sibley tents and row after row of pups; the din of sundry conversation and shared laughter among boot-sore soldiers and soul-leavened freedmen, with, just beyond, the nickering of horses; all of it alit by bonfires more glowing than Norfolk by night.

CHAPTER SEVEN

Where was the Home Guard? Where were the bushwhackers?

One day became much like the previous, with the column moving from farm to farm from dawn till dusk, steadily growing as it advanced, acquiring contrabands and varied means of transport to convey them in, my company out in the woods as flankers. Wild had moved our base of operations to South Mills, five or six miles beyond Ferrebee's. Though but a hamlet of twenty-odd houses without even a general store, it was the largest settlement between Fortress Freedom and Elizabeth City, and so a better site for our ever-growing encampment. All around was thick agricultural land, fields and fields of corn and wheat and flax, and full of slaves.

By night, we non-comms set our men on their end-of-day duties, brushing and oiling the barrels of their rifles or darning socks that had sprung leaks. Then we congregated about some campfire.

"Youall should have seen us today," said Gil Mezzell, of B. "Frye"—B's captain—"organized a squad of us to peel off and canvass a small farm out by the millpond's road."

Captain Frye had taken a ball in the thigh at Fredericksburg, and it still lodged there. The resulting limp had prevented his rise in his former company but not his transfer to the colored troops, and we were the better for it. As officers went, he was one of the good ones.

Men shuffled from foot to foot, blowing white plumes into the night, as Mezzell continued: "One mammy called to the heavens that we was a saving sight, and right off she and the others just fell in our line. They was eight slaves. With us, we did not count two dozen."

He took to chuckling, struggling to go on.

"The yard was filled with fowl, you see—turkeys and ducks and geese and such. I don't know, easy going on a hundred. Had us outnumbered five to one."

Other men joined in, tittering or bursting broad smiles. Likewise me, a release from the burdens of the day. Still, I noticed that Fields was nowhere about.

At a nearby bonfire, just within earshot, I could hear the newspaperman Tewksbury regaling the officers with his recent redaction, announcing that the article would be entitled "The Army of Liberation on the March!"

Mezzell resumed: "Well, youall recognize the DIE-lemma?" He mispronounced it for effect. "Here was fine feasting for two companies entire, and not a buckboard or a hay cart on the premises to convey them in. Meanwhile, the Mistuss of the farm, the only buckra about, is standing there straddle-foot atop her porch, glaring."

Mention of the woman caused some to pause their chuckling. I expect I wasn't the only one to wonder at the cravenly sort of white man who would leave his woman alone, what with us "brutish bucks" rampaging the neighborhood.

"Well, her Ladyship held her balled hands to her hips," said Mezzell, doing likewise himself, "cursing us with her eyes while Frye limp-stepped up and back, pondering the proper course of action."

"Get on with it, man!" said Cornick. "What did you do?"

"Frye ordered that we execute them prisoners."

"The barn fowl?" said Livian Adams.

"To the one," said Mezzell. "Frye told us they would feed the land pirates and feed them amply, was we to leave them."

"Ah, naw . . ."

It was in no way funny, yet all were laughing and laughing stout.

Mezzell said, "He didn't want to shoot them, on account of the noise and the waste of powder and shot. So here we was, chasing them birds about, catching some, but as many not."

"And the Mistuss?" asked Cornick, the question we all wondered.

"Her Ladyship did not leave the porch, just hectored us from there. Took to calling Frye the 'Officer of Geese.'"

"You making that up!"

"Said she had nary seen braver," said Mezzell.

We all busted up then.

Each day's confiscations were more and more joyous, and becoming the stuff of jokes. And where was the Home Guard? Where were the bushwhackers?

Flanking the main body of the regiment was not a thing to be breezy about, especially when the enemy was irregular and you in his country. But posted out in the woods day after day while across the fields the joyous notes of more noble activity resounded, some of my men began to surrender to easy distraction.

"Simpson!" I barked, a mite too sharp given our position on the edge of the corps. "Mind your watch and leave the buffoonery for camp."

He promptly ceased prodding his bayonet at Simon Gaylord's ample hindside and fell back to surveilling the trees for any signs of disturbance.

Keeping order was a thing I expected of my corporals, but Fields hardly reacted at my reprimand of Simpson.

As our picket line pushed forward, my squad came upon a simple house ensconced in the trees, obviously missed by the column.

With neither surrounding fields nor any sign of crops, maybe Wild had deemed that it lacked chattel or suitable provisions to merit a stop-over. Slaves were present, though—two men and a woman. Carrying their possessions in rolled-up blankets, they were clearly aware of the Brigade's presence nearby and of our mission out here.

"Please, please," an old gentleman cried from the porch of the house. He had flowing silver hair and sported a green velvet tailcoat. "You aren't serious, Jemimah. You cannot abandon me."

The three colored moved away up the lane, paying him no mind, though Jemimah glanced back over her shoulder. She looked resolved, if conflicted.

"Tom, Buck!" the old gentleman called. "Oh Jemimah, please! . . ."

I heard sniggering and, from one of my men, a scornful howl. The bondmen noticed us then, in the tree line, and along about the same time, I saw Miles Hews break our ranks.

"Buck Jones! Is that you?" he called, running over, and he and the man embraced.

The rest of us gathered around them. Hews said, "Sergeant, this here my mama's kin."

Buck Jones bowed, removing his hat—which left me feeling uneasy, somewhat abashed, as he was old enough to be my grandfather. I turned toward the porch.

The old gentleman dashed into his house, slamming closed the door.

Hews and Jones talked close, Tom and Jemimah joining them, and my men pushed in, too, some clapping the newly emancipated on the back. Then Hews worked his way out of the group, toward me.

"I'm told my mama's Barco people are nearby, out on a farm where they been bonded," he said. "Sir, may we . . . ?"

Backuss's squad was to our south. As the company's ranking officer, he should have the ultimate say, but I didn't relish having to ask his permission. The lieutenant tended toward diffidence when matters called for initiative and action. Would he allow a detachment to go after Hews's family when our assignment was to guard the column's flank?

"How far from here?" I asked.

"Not overmuch," said Hews. "Maybe a quarter mile through them trees."

How had the main body of the Brigade missed them?

Fields stepped forward. "I will accompany him."

And so it was decided. I would not deny Hews this opportunity to liberate kin, and perhaps Fields leading it was likewise just what was best for him, to put a peck of the hopeful overtop of his dour imaginings.

"Go, men," said I. "Take eight more with you. And be speedy."

They hustled off but did not return speedily at all. Thirty minutes passed. Nigh on an hour. The old gentleman not so slyly watched from behind the curtains of his front-room window, his expression ungenerous. I moved toward the tree line that Fields's detachment had gone into and listened intently. But for what? Commotion? Some sign of trouble?

Backuss emerged from the direction opposite, red-faced and striding toward me. I met him halfway across the yard, wanting to remain out of hearing of the rest of my squad.

"What is this, Etheridge? Why have you halted and disrupted our picket line?"

My men, who'd been lazing by the side of the house, rose to their feet at the sight of the lieutenant. The old gentleman gazed on purposefully, perhaps hoping for relief at the arrival of a white man.

"Only briefly," said I to Backuss. "Time enough to liberate one of my men's family, overlooked by the column." I added, deliberately choosing General Wild's words: "As per the Confiscation Act. Are we not to endeavor to emancipate every bondman in the region?"

He duly noted it, as I'd hoped. The heat did not drain from his face, though, and he stared at me harshly. "This will be documented," he said. "A record will be made of this." Then he turned and repaired into the woods.

It took over an hour and a half before Fields's detachment rejoined us. They were accompanied by a cart loaded down with a dozen men and women and tykes, singing "It's a Great Jubilee Day!" over and again.

All but one. A woman in a calico dress and holding a babe looked distraught rather than joyful. The light-skinned child appeared to be howling, though I could not hear it over the merry singing. It was maybe the baby's crying that provoked her distress, but Clapson's farm came to my mind—not the old mammy but Revere, cowhide in hand. This had been Fields's guidebook on confiscating when a defiant owner did not want it done.

I went to where he rested, on one knee aside a thick oak. "What happened out there?" I asked, likewise taking a knee so that we might speak eye-to-eye. "Wasn't any trouble, was there?"

"No trouble," said he. "The overseer thought himself still in charge. He was made to understand otherwise."

"Goddammit, Fields, what did you do?" said I, sharp but not loud, so as not to attract the attention of the others. "I'm accountable for what happens out here if things go too far. Me!"

"Nothing went too far. That baby be the overseer's, and the mama was of two minds about joining along. I decided for her, on account of the child."

I was picturing the force he might have employed against the overseer and whom among the detachment he might have enlisted to help him. "That's not how we do it, Fields."

"Ain't it?" I'd rarely known him to be deliberately mean, but there was meanness in his face. "Would you have me separate them, ma'am and pup? Or leave the baby behind? All them slaves is now freed."

I looked away. I recognized that, as his sergeant, I should press him—that I should get firm details and act accordingly. But then what? Write him up? Report him as Backuss was to do me? For freeing slaves?

I wouldn't do that, not under these circumstances especially— with what had happened to Riley.

But I couldn't have him making like Revere either, not when leading the men, and particularly not on behalf of me. So, what to do then about my old friend?

I knew Fields, and Fields knew me. I had to believe that my burst of anger had been heard. A lifetime of shared respect would check any more such impulses in him, should a like case arise. I had to trust this.

The joyous singing continued, the old gentleman still looking out from his window. We needed to move on, to unite with the column and deliver these contrabands, then rejoin our picket line.

As I rose, Fields said, "Do you think we will foray as far as Nixonton?"

He was asking on account of Riley and Lawrence. The Midgetts owned a farm at Nixonton, just beyond Elizabeth City, and Fields must have reasoned that his brothers had been taken there—a hopeful thought, as that place would soon be within reach of our column.

"I'm sure we will," I said.

In truth, I had misgivings that we would find them, should the Brigade venture out there. Some contrabands who'd come into our line reported on masters loading up their chattel and sailing off for Texas, where Yankee blue had yet to see any victories and slav-ery seemed a damn sight more nailed down and defended. I could imagine Llewelyn Midgett doing such a thing.

"Riley and Lawrence are all right," I said. "You will see."

I had yet to pen the letter to Sarah Etheridge, to attempt to suss out whatever information she might have about them. I wouldn't be able to see it dispatched, not until we'd attained Elizabeth City. But still, it needed doing.

"Form up!" I called, and to Fields, "Form 'em up."

As he did so, I pulled Hews aside. "You did right earlier, step-ping up for your kin." I was thinking about Fields's actions out there. "But know that you are always being seen."

He dropped his eyes, mistaking my words for a reprimand. I had meant them as instruction.

"You can be wearing stripes one day," I said. "You have leader-ship in you, Miles. So continue using good judgment, like you're doing. In everything, show your best, and the rank will for certain come."

He smiled broad, unmasking the child that he yet was. "Thank you, Sergeant, thank you! And so as you know, three of my cousins wish to enlist." He pointed them out.

"I will make sure you're credited for their recruitment."

That night, word came for officers and non-comms to meet at the general's Sibley tent. We gathered there and found Wild and, alongside him, Revere.

Also at hand was a party of colored that Revere had brought in, Negroes unlike any I had yet to see. I recognized them right off for Dismal Swamp Maroons, though before then I'd only heard tell of them without actually knowing their existence to be true.

They were said to be a colony of runaways that had holed up in the pocosin with the Indians, and some poor whites, too.

So this had been Revere's secret mission.

"What freaks," I heard Backuss hiss at another officer, and he laughed some Old World Dutchman's laugh.

His amusement rankled, but these men were indeed a strange-looking bunch. You would not easily confuse them with the colored we were emancipating, that's for certain. They numbered eight, all rough-hewn and unkempt, wearing trousers but overtop them, like cloaks, layers of homespun blankets, cinched at the waist with twine. If not for their woolly hair and sable complexions, for the thick lips and broad noses, I might have mistaken them for the Red Man you read about in frontier books.

I recognized my reaction to be twinning the one that Backuss had just expressed but could not help it. Even as these Maroons captured my curiosity, they likewise left me feeling unsettled, deeply so, for to my eye they looked more akin to animals than men and seemed a question mark on whether attempts at civilizing them would warrant the great effort that would clearly be required. It was an ugly thought, but one I felt just the same. I wondered if this was what we were like back in Africa-days, before they brought us here.

At the head of their group was the indisputable chief. He was small of stature but large of presence, with hair gone gray and smoking a curved pipe that looked made of white clay. One other stood out—a sight younger but of equal, chiefly bearing. His head was a riotous tangle of hair, twisting black sprouts that dangled from his straw slouch hat. It was natural, colored-folk hair but unlike any I'd seen on a colored.

The general's brother offered a camp chair to the Maroon chief. Wild sat opposite him. Major Wright and Revere stood behind the

general, and the Maroon chief's second—the young one, with rope
for hair—stood behind him. It was all very formal.

Moses Cornick, who was nearby me, threw his hands in the
air, not exasperated but in a sort of amazement. He whispered,
"Who in the world is this man who will sit down with bush-headed
swamp Negroes like he is hosting the king of England? What kind
of white man is he?"

Aaron Mitchell, anew among us, back from Revere's detachment, whispered in response, "Father Alick might not look kingly,
but he a legend hereabouts."

The general commenced then, making a show of portentous
introductions and suchlike—of himself and of the African Brigade
and of our mission. The Maroon chief, Father Alick, greeted this
with a stone face that conveyed neither awe nor dismay. Fifteen
hundred uniformed and musketed Negroes had little visible effect
on him.

Wild and Alick began an exchange between them that was
too low for us to hear. Someone behind me asked, "*That* old man
be a legend?"

Aaron Mitchell responded: "Sure enough. Folks call him the
Postman of the Dismal on account of his unhindered comings and
goings to-and-fro the pocosin. He ride an old mule said to be Nat
Turner's own and sell honeycombs to farms, and the white folks call
him 'uncle' and generally just leave him be."

"Honeycombs?" asked Orange Redmon.

"Yessir," said Mitchell, like that, as just one word, not so much
in respect of Redmon's higher rank but as a turn of phrase. "The
swamp men is bee gatherers, and white folk eat that mess up. Had
you tasted some of they honey, you would not ask why."

The night was colder than those previous. I buried my neck
deep into the collar of my greatcoat and drew in closer to Mitchell,

as did the others nearby, equally rapt. We all wanted to savvy more on these Maroons who had run off from farms and, despite slave catchers and bloodhounds, managed to evade capture.

"You say 'Father'?" asked Robinson Tynes.

"Yessir," said Mitchell. "The Postman be a minister, too. You would not think that white folks would permit it, but he ride up on old Nat's mule of a Sunday and preach to whoall will hear it."

Naws and general disbelief were the response. All, and likewise me, wondered at how this could be.

"I expect Mass would rather open his doors to the devil he know," said Tynes, "than try and keep colored from secret prayer meetings. Otherwise, Mass end up inciting conspirations and danger-gospel like that old mule's first keeper had schemed up."

Our group fell still with this last fraught wisdom, just as General Wild returned his voice to speechifying volume. "My brigade is here on a solemn mission," said he, "and I invite you to bring your people in. We will transport you to the freedman's colony that is established at Fortress Monroe."

"We already free," was Alick's reply. "How come we want to leave this home for another, unknown and uncertain?"

"Why, for safety, of course," Wild said. "For—"

He stopped, apparently unknowing how to go on, which was notable for the general. I had yet to see him at a loss for words.

"We already free," Alick repeated, "and safe as need be."

He turned toward his party, many of the other Maroons smoking clay pipes such as his, and spoke something so riddled with strange words that it could not properly be called English. A banter ensued among them that was sing-songy, with plenty of exclamations of "Eh!" and tittering.

Abe Armstead turned toward Mitchell. "And the young one there, with the misdirected hair?"

"I heard him called Osman Golar but ain't ever seen him before," said Mitchell. "Nor none like him, frankly. Must be part of some band set up deep, deep inside the pocosin."

That one, Golar, stood rigid and still, carefully surveilling what the surrounding bonfires would allow of our camp, and of us gathered around as well.

Revere, too. He stood by, silent but watching, much like the young Maroon. Even that Negro's calm aspect reflected a coiled anticipation.

Alick turned from his party back to Wild, and so we turned our attention back to them. "Naw," said he. "Sure, we got poison snake and mosquito as big as birds," to which his party laughed. "But no. For ain't no sun-to-sun travail in there," Alick explained to Wild, who listened, spellbound. "We got children ain't yet seen a buckra and wail salt tears the first time they do. You people call our home dismal, but that Black Mingo Pocosin be our paradise. Thank you kindly, General, but no thank you. We a feral thing, and we love this."

The parlay broke up thereon, the general gracious though snubbed, and we all made toward our companies. All except Revere. He followed the Maroons into the dark, out past the edge of camp.

Tynes, like me, watched him go. "Do you think Revere will be appointed regimental sergeant major?" He looked none too easy at the prospect. "If asked, I'd vote Adkins."

"Likewise me," said I, though I wouldn't have begrudged Tynes for voting Etheridge.

Revere, though, looked to be the general's prized dog. "It is Colonel Draper's regiment," I told Tynes, "but the general's command and vision. So we will see whom *he* favors. Only his vote counts."

Outside Tyne's tent, he bid me good night and I continued on, pondering. My duty as sergeant was to make my troopers fight;

Colonel Draper had taught us this. But it was not bad sergeanting if I could also keep them alive along the way. I shared a bond with my men. I took joy when they bested a challenge and felt myself aggrieved when they deviated from the assigned course. Whatever glory might be attained in this war, I wanted their names to be the ones sung out in song.

Our regimental sergeant major might not be of the same mind as me on most matters, but should he be a man whose battlefield judgment was guided by longings for vengeance rather than by a bent for survival?

"Split-tail or hung," Revere had said at the campfire our first night out, "all Secesh merit death."

"And so through the night goes my cry," he'd declaimed. "Evermore!"

Revere, our regimental sergeant major? He could lead us there, that seemed clear. But would he bring us out?

CHAPTER EIGHT

The Home Guard's presence was finally signaled the next day, our sixth one out, when we arrived at River Bridge, on the outskirts of Elizabeth City. The bushwhackers had got at it. All that was left was the charred tops of the pilings.

Paps Prentiss brought forward a recently freed contraband. "Mass," he said to Lieutenant Backuss. "This servant has got information on who torched the crossing."

Some of the men, old-timers especially, talked like this, calling our officers "master." (And Prentiss was as old as they came, fifty-one that fall, as likely as not the grandpappy of the Brigade.) It was a mode of address that we non-comms tried to get them shed of—and one that risked from the younger troopers mockery at best, and sometimes more. For those like Paps, the lesson did not take. He likewise carried the regrettable habit of being forever from ear to ear a-grin. Just then, he even removed his forage cap from his head, which Backuss appeared to welcome.

I hailed Fields forward, to accompany the contraband in.

Backuss waved him off. "No, Etheridge. You."

He turned and regained the top of our formation with nary another word.

I certainly did not mind the errand. Far from it. This offered me the too rare occasion of associating with the general directly. If greatness was communicable by proximity, I welcomed the opportunity to get close enough to share in some of his.

The contraband's name was Malachi, and I double-timed him forward as best I could. He moved gamely but gimping on unshod feet that, upon a closer look, were missing toes: the great toe and the minor on one, and the great toe on the other. The man was dour of disposition—on account of those feet and whatever dread history had prompted their misuse, I imagined. We arrived at the head of the column, and I presented him to the general.

Wild asked, "You have information, sir?"

Malachi was clearly unaccustomed to being formally addressed. He stared up at the general a long moment, not seeming to mind the courtesy, but not full-on trusting it either. Then he finger-pointed a nearby house.

"That there the domicile of Billy Drinkwater. Him one of Elliott's boys. They is the ones that shot Black Sanders."

"Black Sanders?" said Wild. This pricked his ear.

"The captain of them Buffaloes," Malachi explained, but this didn't appear to provide greater illumination.

I was surprised that Wild did not know of it—a Union officer shot down in the streets of Elizabeth City. The man's assassination had caused a stir throughout these parts. From what was told, Black Sanders had been to a frolic at the home of local colored, in celebration of the Emancipation Proclamation. A gang of masked men fired a volley as he was returning to his quarters later in the night, and Black Sanders dropped dead.

I stepped in. "Buffaloes, sir. That is what the Union Army volunteer company that was raised out here last year is called by folks hereabouts."

The name was not intended to convey fondness of feeling. Before relocating to Elizabeth City, the Buffaloes had been based on Roanoke and had recruited the Island. Captain Sanders had visited the Etheridge House to seek John B.'s assistance in the endeavor. John B. politely agreed, though I'd actually seen him do very little. Only a few Sand Bankers enlisted, and the Buffaloes moved on.

"White men then, these Buffaloes?" asked the general, bemused or amused, I wasn't sure which.

"Yes, sir," said I. "Organized by two brothers from up north, from President Lincoln's home state, I believe." I *knew*, in fact, but did not want to come off as too showy. "A Enos and a Nathan, one of flaxen hair, the other dark."

"Hence Black Sanders?" He smiled. "And the brother, White Sanders, I suppose?"

"Yes, sir," said I. "One a captain, the other his lieutenant."

The general's shifting facets showed his mind to finally recall the event. "Yes, yes, I remember the dispatch announcing the murder. The land pirates got at two others in the neighborhood, too, a Captain Newby and another named Dowdy."

Bone Dowdy, I expected, from over by Shiloh. Before the war, he did business in naval stores, and John B. often availed himself of the man's pine pitch for repairs on his boats or of his shake shingles after gales had blown through. A genial man. I did not know him killed and wondered if John B. did.

The contraband Malachi said, "If trouble been got up to around here, Billy Drinkwater either in on it or knows of it."

This seemed to rousen the general. "Well, then," said he, waving for his brother, his mount shuffling about beneath him. "Let us restore the bridge, then."

The general looked over at me. "Good work, Sergeant . . . ?"

"Etheridge, sir."

"Good work, Etheridge," said he.

A back-clap and well-done that I was gratified to receive.

The general turned to Captain Wild, speaking too low for me to hear. I said to Malachi, "You've done us a great service."

"It was my girl, Betsy, made me do it, elseways I would not have." He stared dead-faced at me. "I hope it not to cost us when you Union boys move on and we have to return home to here."

I fought my strong impulse to reply sharply. Instead, I attempted to alter his dim view of us. "How is it you ain't got shoes?" said I.

"Mass took 'em all up when word come of youall's approach."

"Let's rustle you up some new ones, then, Malachi."

It would take a special broad pair, I reckoned, on account of the bloated cast of his spoiled feet.

"That's Malachi, *sir*," he corrected me, and he smiled. "Due regard from white mens and new gunboats, to boot? A body could get used to such treatment."

A recruit in the making, thought I. "You know, you ought to consider signing up for service. Soldiering proper might not be possible." I glanced toward his feet. "But there is all sort of supporting work, cooking and suchlike. It'd provide a proper wage to buy all the gear you like or need, and you'd be pitching in your two bits to help emancipate others, such as we are doing."

His smile dropped. "I think not. I have plenty paid my fair share for the freedom of me and mine, working wageless for Mass Jepson on his crops and critters and what-all else he bid me to work these past twenty-nine years." He threw me again that dead stare. "Naw, I think I will leave broad-field emancipating and other such high-flown ambitions to youall."

He made a valid argument that I would not dispute. I took him for his shoes.

The quartermaster sergeant, Bill Berry, looked down from his perch at the rear of the supply wagon toward the spectacle of Malachi's feet. "You thought ten too many?"

Everybody was a jokesmith.

Malachi did not take it poorly. "I always thought myself deserving of a more distinctive look than the common lot. Mass Jepson decided to oblige me."

He claimed three pair of brogans, one for himself, another for "his girl"—either a wife or a daughter, I did not know—and the last for some other. Neither Berry nor I objected to the surplus. Afterward, I rejoined F.

Captain Wild conveyed orders down the line that all sorties were to cease and companies were to visit that man Drinkwater's home and secure whatever our engineers might need to rebuild the bridge. A thousand men swarmed the property, streaming in and out like ants on a hill. Some had at the dwelling house, others at the barn and outbuildings, selecting the best timber at first, but soon, whatever timber was left. It was all razed to nothing in less than an hour, with Drinkwater onlooking, in shackles for his bushwhacker pursuits, his wife and four children whimpering nearby. Hammers hammering, the back-and-forth whizzing of handsaws. The bridge went back up in less than six hours.

F was left out of the fun. We watched from the woods, as we'd been ordered to flanker duty again.

The column reached Elizabeth City just before nightfall and what we found left us-all mute. Desolation, the streets unpeopled and still. Windows shuttered or outright boarded with no sign of light or life beyond. The double-doors of the bank, broad open, one banging back and forth with each burst of wind, open then shut, open then shut, until the latch finally caught.

I'd sailed here more than once, accompanying John B. on some errand or trade, and old Elizabeth had been my London or Paris. I could not imagine more bustle and life than what my Sand Banker eyes had beheld of this city. Manufactories all about, and public houses for sharing chitchat and raising toasts, and ladies' garments stores and haberdasheries for men, and greengrocers with many-varied vegetables and fruit of lovely odor, staged in pyramids atop long tables. After the salt fat pork and hard biscuits that were our daily ration, I will confess to having joyously anticipated the prospect of foraging for provisions here. That hope now seemed dashed.

No sooner had we arrived in the central district, though, which had seemed completely abandoned, than there appeared colored of all ages and sizes, in every mode of outfit, streaming from those shops and other buildings. The brooding silence of the streets burst into jubilation and uproarious frolic as we were overrun, folks extending hands in greeting, others clapping us on the back, all waving hats and kerchiefs.

"We come in from over by Winfall, could not get here quick enough," an old uncle told me, his mouth more dark space than teeth, stretched broad in a grin. "Me and my old woman, and our grandchildren, too."

There she stood, wrapped in shawls against the cold and holding a tiny baby in her arms, two tykes clutching tightly at the skirt of her dress. All three little ones bawled, upset by the commotion.

"And likewise you?" I asked a girl in a red headscarf, clinging to their party. "You from Winfall, too?"

"No, sir," said she, taking up the smaller of the two bawling tykes, cooing the boy quiet. "Me be up in my Missie's cellar on Water Street, hiding there so as she could not find me, until they had finally left."

Such was the case all about. Some were local. More still had come in from the surrounding country. All had made their way here with freedom in mind, and they entwined with troopers, one soon indistinguishable from the other in the great throng of us. Over there I saw Simon Gaylord, smiling while attempting to retrieve his forage cap from the lively woman who had donned it atop her own gleesome head. And there, Valentine Dozier and Zach Gregory and Paps Prentiss in a ring dance with a party of bondmen. And there, Fields, a-smile and back-clapping, also caught up in it.

If the Brigade's presence had made of Ferrebee's farm an impromptu Negro outpost, then Old Elizabeth, the crown jewel of all northeast North Carolina, was now become a Coloredopolis! Emancipation City!

The mass of freedmen engulfed the general. Wild waved his stump over his head to the rhythm of their waving, waved and waved, his mount disquieted but unable to move in the crush of men and women and children closing in around them. The horse reared up, turned nervously to the left and to the right. But Wild—he didn't appear to mind one whit, keeping a-saddle as best he could, smiling full, and waving and waving his stump.

PART TWO

Babylon Is Fallen

Friday, December 11–Wednesday, December 16, 1863

CHAPTER NINE

In regard to its moral and political results, the importance of the raid cannot be over-estimated. The counties invaded by the colored troops are completely panic-stricken. Proud scions of chivalry, accustomed to claim the most abject obedience from their slaves, literally fall on their knees before these armed and uniformed blacks and beg for their lives. Never was a region thrown into such commotion before.

From Our Own Correspondent, *New York Times*

The order came down to billet by company in whatever building or clustering of them suited our needs, so long as we showed discretion in regard to the property of loyal citizens. Most white Elizabethans who remained in the city claimed loyalty, all the while scorning us black troopers with lordly glances or sharp words. Discretion was in short supply as a result.

The Riverside Boat Works stood abandoned, and we took abandonment to mean allegiance to the Rebel cause. The factory had four bunkrooms up top for its shipwrights, plus a broad and deep shop floor below, plenty sufficient for the troopers of Company F. Paps Prentiss found a larder off the main floor lined with shelves of preserved fruit in jars—whole peaches, mostly—which was a nice bonus. The four bunkrooms were divvied up thusly: our six corporals took two, three to a space (though each room had only one bed); Tynes and I took another (I allowed him the bed so long as he granted me free use of the small rolltop in the corner); Backuss had his own. Revere had yet to rejoin our ranks and thus was not allotted a place.

Six days in the field had made us-all ripe in only the worst ways. The December-wet soil had kept my brogans soggy, and my shell jacket and trousers and undergarments were stiff from the body oil I'd sweated with all our exertions. If the bushwhackers did not hear or see us, they damned sure would smell our position before coming upon it. So the first thing I did that first night was find a way to get clean. I left it to Fields to ensure that the company was properly kipped and occupied myself with warming up some water for washing. I then took a hand brush to myself like my ma'am would when I was a boy.

Though my clothes could for certain use it, washing them was out of the question, as others would follow my lead and our uniforms would likely not dry sufficiently in the winter chill, even with bonfires lit. What a sight that would make on the morrow, Company F falling in for inspection in long drawers, for those that had them, and less for those that did not.

After bathing, I strung up my pup tent in one corner of Tynes's and my room—more as a lean-to, really. It was less for privacy than to acknowledge that Tynes's and my rank deserved some regard, too. If ability was the measure, then we'd earned our own individual quarters all as much as Backuss had. The lean-to would have to suffice.

As our only remaining officer, Backuss was the company's effective commander. Yet the men of F treated me as leader more than him. And likewise me more than Revere, the other senior sergeant, whose hectoring style might prod a man to scale a mountain of horse's shit but would not inspire him to do so the whole day through.

The recruiting soldier on Roanoke had promised Fields and me only the opportunity to contribute in the service of freedom, and I'd understood this to mean wielding a spade and a pick, not a musket and bayonet, much less a sergeant's sword. General Wild had made known his aim to see colored in leadership, but could I imagine myself a Lieutenant Etheridge? Did I desire the pomp and tedium of officering—with even more reports to write than were obliged of sergeants, with more blame when things went differently from how those higher up expected that they should, yet little more say in the expectations? With more of what seemed the worst of soldiering?

That Wild wanted it for us meant something to me, as I held the man in high esteem.

Should ever such a thing come to pass, it would resound up and down the Banks, from Kitty Hawk to Chicamacomico. It would be heralded on Roanoke Island, and maybe even at the Etheridge House, too. This likewise meant something to me. I hated to admit it, but it did.

It was mere reverie, though, and nothing to do with my here-and-now duty. I stretched out under my lean-to, the wood floor less agreeable to my back than had been the winter ground, but a sight warmer.

Tynes's sleep was silent, but a low, rolling grumble echoed up through the floorboards from the vaulted warehouse below me, not so much a specific sound as an agitated rustling—men shifting about; hushed murmurs; snoring. I lit my candle and secured the tent flaps at either end of my lean-to so as not to disturb Tynes, then removed Sarah Etheridge's letters from my haversack. As before, I read the second one first. I wanted to ensure I'd not misread Fanny's cues. I wanted to know she was safe in the Aydlett house.

I went to the first letter after and lingered with it. I told myself that therein might lay some key to figuring out how best to secure

Sarah's assistance for particulars on Llewelyn Midgett and for whatever could be found out about Fields's brothers. In truth, my study
of it was as much for greater discernment into the uneasy thing that
was keeping me tethered to the Etheridge House and to that family,
even as I had lit out from it and from them.

Papa reared you an Etheridge, Sarah claimed in the letter, and
I found myself wondering at a memory—of John B. in the rattan
chair in the corner of the verandah, while Sarah drilled me in
grammar balloons and vocabulary, emulating the lesson school-
marm Mary Beth Scarborough had given Sarah's class during
the week. Sarah barked cues, which I countered with the right
answers: *"Ocean?"* "Noun!" "Synonym for *purchase?"* *"Buy!"* I was
so young at the time and could not now be certain that the next
part of the memory was actual or merely something wished for
but that had not truly been. In it—or in my recomposition of it,
whichever it was—John B. sat reading, yet also frequently glanced
over at us. At me.

Pride in you as well as me, Sarah had conjectured in the letter.
Perhaps, thought I. Perhaps pride.

I turned my attention to the postcard. Until then, I'd done my
damnedest to keep the puzzle of it in a quiet corner of my mind.
On that night, though, its disquieting implications would not settle.
The backside message:

> Patrick gave me this yesterday, with cryptic intimation. He said
> that, before, endeavors such as this pen-work were about all
> that he did better than you, but that soon this would no longer
> be the case. That was it, nothing more—cryptic, cryptic! He
> knows of our correspondence and it is clear he expects me to
> pass along his words. I wasn't sure I should, but here I have.

What was it that Patrick wanted me to know?

For him, all was rivalry and a childish drive to always beat my mark, regardless whether I was aiming to set one or not. Even now, Paddy, three months after I'd claimed my freedom?

Tynes rustled around on the bunk. The flickering wick and my whispering movements had become an annoyance. I blew a breath onto the flame and rolled over onto my back. The steady rush from the nearby Pasquotank River drowned out the eerie echoes from the shop floor below. I awaited sleep, a long and vain waiting.

Pups are likely to favor their paps, as things go—of appearance and bearing, if not also of humor and grain. Such was the case with me and John B. John B. never seemed to mind it, our shared resemblance—even when out together, among white folk. This wasn't but speculation on my part, of course, for John B. did not speak of his feelings, or much all else, for that matter.

My ma'am was of a different mind on the likenesses between my father and me, and I well understood the reason why. A constant reminder of one's suffering is no less suffered just because the bearer of the sad message is your beloved only child. But I could no more alter my disposition or the facets of my face than change the color of my skin, and she and I had settled on a middle road, unspoken but recognized. She would attempt to forestall casting sharp words or spiteful glares my way when I might inadvertently remind her of the man, and I tried my darnedest not to do it, inadvertently or otherwise.

Our make-ups are of a mind of their own and it was no small feat to control my very nature. I knew my ma'am's feelings on John B. and on the Etheridge House. I respected them. But a boy will seek out his father.

Lying sleepless beneath my lean-to, I found myself thirteen again. A Sunday morning—early, well before sunrise. I slipped lightly into the chattel house behind Midgett Manor and stirred awake first Fields, then Bill Charles, and bid them to join me. Neither much appreciated my creeping up on their pallets at that hour, yet both followed after, with little goading or much need of convincing. We were friends true.

It was our free day, made for sacking out for as long as was tolerated before whatever chores would be compelled by ma'ams and paps, then the weekly camp meeting after that. The three of us hauled one of John B.'s fifteen-yard seine nets over to the Croatan Sound. With Fields on one end and Bill Charles on the other, I managed the arced stretch in between. We dragged the shallows till the sun reached midmorning height, camp-meeting time, and brought in more speckles and red drum than we could carry. Fields and Bill Charles both took a share, precious bounty for families that never went unfed but were not quite fed enough. As author of the idea, I was allotted the two biggest drum. Each was nigh as long as my thigh and all but as thick. Hooking a hand in a gill of each, I lugged them up to the Etheridge House.

The fish were heavy, and it was a far hike.

I passed through the kitchen, greeting Ma'am Dinah, who was dishing broth into a ceramic serving bowl. She tossed up a silent hand as hello, then returned to her work, paying me and my load little mind, as my presence hereabouts was regular and never unexpected. I pushed into the doorway to the dining room and stood there, eyes lowered.

The family was at table after church, over at Roanoke Island Baptist, which John B.'s father, Adam, had built. John B. sat across from Mistuss Margery, Missie Sarah across from Patrick. Sarah saw me first.

"Hey there, Dick! What have you got?"

"I brung you a couple of drum," said I, raising my face.

"'*Brought* you,'" Sarah corrected. "I've taught you better than that."

"I *brought* you a couple of drum," I said, and extended my arms toward the table, though each one ached and trembled from the exertion of the trek over.

Patrick looked mightily impressed. But as he rose to inspect the catch, Mistuss Margery scolded, "Stay right where you are, Patrick! You are not dismissed."

I said to John B., "I borrowed your nets for the venture and expect I owe you something for their use."

There was a hint of a smile on John B.'s face. "You might ought to ask permission beforehand rather than assume my nets are for public purpose," said he. "But I appreciate your honesty, and the initiative."

"I wanted to show you what I can do when given the chance," said I, aiming for an assertive tone and not that of a question. "I'm becoming grown and thought maybe you'd give me a chance to run one of your fishing boats."

Patrick jumped in: "Me and him could run it together, Uncle John." He added, "Of course, I would supervise."

"I've seen how you supervise Dick," said John. B. "As for you"— he turned back to me—"you would do well to show a little less of these superior capabilities lest I have you out bright and early every morning before your duties, catching our noontime meal."

Mistuss Margery cleared her throat, though she maintained her focus platewise. "Does it not worry you, John, an industrious servant with his own program and aims, and maybe an ax to grind?"

The hint of smile quit John B.'s face. "Why should it? I've taught him his place."

"As I'm sure Goodman Turner up in Southampton County thought he had taught the nigger Nat his," said Mistuss Margery, moving carrot coins about with her fork.

No one seemed to suspect that I understood the reference. I left my eyes low so as not to give away that I did.

For raw spleen, John B. could match crossedness for crossedness. "Dick will one day be to our darky community what we are to the Sand Banks. Etheridge stock always shows its pedigree."

The strained muteness of the room portended the peril that might of a sudden befall me with this barbed turn. But I'd noted my father's words: he had spoken of my "pedigree."

The silence stretched.

"Take them back to Mammy Dinah," I heard John B. say, his words still sharp, though directed at me and no longer at his wife.

I slipped out of the room and left the drum on the kitchen counter and scooted out the door.

Later that afternoon, Paddy turned up at Ma'am's cabin. "Hey, Dick!" he hollered, calling me outside—boldly but not too bold. Whatever he might be learning about his station as white folk, every blessed soul on the Island knew his place with my mother.

I dragged myself to the door, and Paddy waved me over. He scolded, "Why didn't you tell me you boys was seining today? I'd have joined you."

"It's family Sunday, Paddy," said I. "Your place is over at Roanoke Island Baptist, then up to the house for dinner, with the family."

I'd meant the words to sting.

He went on about being left out of the fun, as was his right. I demurred but did not bow, as befit my blood—my "pedigree."

After he left, it was my ma'am's turn to scold me. "You got to carry whatever load he command you to, but not aught else." She wasn't talking about Patrick. She knew about the two big drum. Word travels fast on an island, especially among its colored. "He don't do for you, you do for him. So you don't owe him one precious thing."

My ma'am supposed that my attention toward John B. was a sign that I had no buck, I knew this. But it wasn't that, not ever. I had buck and then some. No, it was because the man was my father. It had been true then and remained so now. Those interested glances, chanced upon when John B. thought no one noticing—in those moments, I recognized that I was being looked upon as a son. Even had I hated John B. as my master, as the man who'd made of my ma'am a concubine and not a beloved, some feelings are inborn. I could no more quash my draw to him and to his family, to my fascination with my pedigree, than John B. could conceal his curiosity about me, who was of his own blood.

I told Ma'am that day, "Mass John B. say I got initiative and I got drive and might can run one of his boats." I didn't expect her to feel the pride from this that I myself felt, but I knew she would recognize its useful implication. "That be more catch and whatnot for you and me, and for everybody!"

"'Mass'?" she said. "His name Master?"

She awaited a reply.

I offered none.

"Not in my eyes, it ain't," she said. "And not in my cabin. No, son. That word is not permitted here."

Insolence wasn't ever my way, and so it was as though I was hearing some other self speak. "May not be for you. But for us-all else, it is."

"Pardon?" Ma'am said. "What did you say?"

I'd accomplished something with my sunrise venture and John B.'s acknowledgment of it, and it bore remarking. Me, the man of our household and head-in-the-making of the colored section entire. Me, Richard.

"For everybody else," I said, "Mass be the man's first name." I couldn't help myself, I added, "And he a pretty good one, too, I expect, as masters go."

Contrary words did not fluster my ma'am. They brought forth her rage.

"You think because he let you hang about his house that he think you special? That you different?"

The silence that followed commanded that I raise my face. It defied me not to!

I refused.

"You ain't sleeping in it, though, is you?"

I responded then, my voice as soft as smoke. "He taught me letters. Not to no slave boy other, just to me."

"It weren't John B. what taught you, but his daughter. All he did was not disallow it." She harrumphed fiercely, but only so as to catch her breath. "He allowed his daughter a pet to play with of a Sunday afternoon, a grinder's monkey on a leash."

Her silence went gentle then, and I realized that it was because my cheeks were shiny with wet. Ma'am didn't abide soft, but she sat in her sewing chair and pulled me into her lap. My body stretched almost as long as hers, yet I curled up small and sank into her breast.

I'd never known my ma'am's true age, only that she'd borne me when of about as many years as I was at that moment. She always seemed older. But curled up there, sobbing into her chest, I saw the beautiful girl she had once been, the face from my earliest memory—welcoming eyes, honey on a fingertip that I sucked at, hummed words that might be song or maybe just nonsense feather sounds.

"Making a baby don't make a father," she told me. "Remember that. Soon as you start to thinking elseways, you have forsook your own self. You got to understand, son: he *own* you, just like you had owned them dead drum."

I knew my ma'am to be right, as sure as day begets night and night becomes day. I'd known it back then just as I knew it now, lying beneath a lean-to on a hard wood floor. But pups will favor their paps. I knew this, too. A boy will seek out his father.

CHAPTER TEN

Colonel Draper had come into camp during the night and sent orders first thing the next morning for me to report to the regimental headquarters, at the home of a local Unionist, William Pool, down on Water Street. I knew the name Pool from hearing it spoken around the Etheridge House but could not recollect having ever seen the man, out there on the Banks or during a foray into Elizabeth City with John B. Although he was a Unionist, I knew Pool to own many slaves.

Fields had relayed the orders to me, and he lingered about the room as I dressed. "If you want," he said, "I can get down to the wharf and find a transport headed for Roanoke, to carry your letter."

I'd planned to rise early to write Sarah. Clearly, now it would have to wait. But I didn't want to disappoint Fields.

"I'll get it off as soon as I've finished with the colonel." To deflect from my tarrying, I added: "I expect the three stripes on my sleeves will put a peck more express in its delivery than your two."

He nodded but looked neither humored nor much contented.

The Pool residence put the Etheridge House to shame, boasting four imposing pillars out front and standing three stories tall. Lieutenant Backuss was already present when I arrived, gazing out a large bay window facing the water. The general, the colonel, and the general's brother leaned over a heap of maps on a desk, surrounded by Lieutenant Colonel Holman, Major Wright, and a few other officers. Only Backuss noted my entrance.

Seeing him there, coldly following me with his eyes, I wondered if he'd reported my conduct outside South Mills—*mis*conduct, according to him—when I'd disrupted our picket line to go after Miles Hews's people. Had I been summoned here for some sort of summary punishment?

"Sir," said I, broadly, toward all, so as to be noticed.

"Etheridge, good," said Draper, looking up, then back down, searching for something among the papers afore him. His whiskers had got considerable in the few days since last I'd seen him and his eyes looked rest-broken. When he found what he sought, he pushed a stack of envelopes in my direction. "See that these are delivered. As to their billets, I've cited those I know. The rest you'll have to make out on your own. Be sure to record them, though, for the regimental record."

"Yes, sir," said I, retrieving the stack.

Backuss's rigid posture did not release one whit. I awaited more from Draper, but he only added, "And with dispatch. This is pressing."

"Yes, sir," said I.

General Wild never even looked up. I headed out the door.

As Draper had forewarned, more envelopes than not had been left unaddressed. I noticed, flipping through them, that there was one for each of our company commanders. Tracking down their billets would be easy enough, by simple inquiry along my way. It was a Saturday, market day. While the city was nearly empty of business activity, its streets hummed with colored troopers and run-off slaves, families entire. There was joy all about, save among the few tight-lipped and jumpy-eyed whites out on the streets, who moved from A to B with distinct purpose and notable haste.

Delivering the letters took the better part of the morning. As I made my way through the various quarters of the city, I found that other companies had not displayed half so much fair-mindedness in their choices of billets as F had. The Fearing Plantation Guestrooms, a stately colonnaded establishment that was highly regarded throughout northeast North Carolina, had had the foresight to dispose of the Confederate States flag that was known to hang over its great front doors, but not time enough for much else that might have given the impression of loyalty to the Union. Sergeant Jeremiah Gray, who commanded D as its three officers were infirm and in the Moses wagons, ordered the lodgers run off, then freed the few slaves remaining and claimed the "plantation"—and the adjoining domiciles as well, by dint of their proximity.

Captain Frye, who'd ordered butchered all those yard fowl outside of South Mills, had apparently been more diplomatic in his acquisition of quarters. His company, B, commandeered the side-by-side mansions of a man by the name of Creecy. Creecy claimed neutrality of allegiance, but spitefully so. Frye allowed Creecy and his kin to retire to their farm, some four or five miles below Elizabeth City, along with an older house slave called Ellen, who, I was told, objected to her confiscation. I suspected that Frye would seek permission to pay them a visit in short order, though, to liberate Ellen, whether she wanted freedom or not, and whatever others might be out there. It was a military issue. Slaves left to Creecy might just as well be considered in the service of the Rebel forces directly.

I noticed Livian Adams on the far side of the Creecy mansion and made my way over. He was directing a group of men taking down a gazebo that blocked the possibility of drilling in the broad and deep yard. When he saw me, he offered his troopers a break.

We shook hands and exchanged the customary familiarities, then I said, "So you come up with Revere, did you?"

"I did. On the farm adjoining."

"And his people," said I, not quite knowing how to ask the thing I was after, "his ma'am and his paps. Were they about, too, or sold elsewhere?"

"His mama lived on the farm. Likewise his papa, given that it was his Mass."

Which was exactly as I had supposed! I knew not how I'd divined it, but I just knew, and not merely by dint of our similar complexions. His insistence on making of me a sort of rival, the barbed comments—these seemed the product of something that maybe struck too close to home.

"Well, a 'papa,' if you will, as those things go," Adams continued. "I expect some Masses take on colored gals because of feelings for them, attraction and such, or because of whatever be happening, or not, in the Mass's bedchamber. Not so Jonas Peters. He aimed to increase his slave stock, and this alone. That whole goddamned farm be peopled of Peters's mongrel weanlings—"

He stopped short then and dropped his eyes. "No disrespect intended, Etheridge."

"None taken."

But his account of Revere's upbringing explained much, especially the cause of the man's irascibility. It maybe also explained something about John B. and me. Revere's coming up would seem to have been in blunt variance to mine in the Etheridge House. The interest John B. took in me, his expectations about my place in the colored Banker community—these things had surely prepared me for my role in the African Brigade and reflected now in my style of sergeanting. I recognized them as a great advantage. And I had to believe that this early training had primed me to take on even greater responsibility.

* * *

Hustling about the city had left me no opportunity to compose the letter promised to Fields. By the time of my return to the Pool house, a short stretch on into afternoon, Wild and Draper had moved from the library to the drawing room, and the place was overrun with activity. Locals, some loyal and some visibly not, as well as a number of our officer corps and some colored sergeants peopled the space. The general oversaw the varied proceedings. He spoke at this person, then turned to that other, passing along orders to his brother, then asking Colonel Draper's opinion on a matter.

I noticed the rope-headed Maroon, Osman Golar, off in a corner of the room with three others. How I'd initially missed them I cannot know, for though silent and largely still, they drew the attention of everybody in the place, by either furtive glance or outright stare. It wasn't so much the Maroons' odd attire—as before, each one was wrapped in hides and furs—but the rest of it. Golar carried one of those old-style, short-stocked rifles with a mouth like the barrel of a bugle, a blunderbuss. John B. kept one mounted above the mantel at the Etheridge House, as a decoration, even though he, like all masters, locked up his arsenal. Yet, as antiquated as was Golar's gun, it was the only proper weapon any of them had. The other three were armed of bows, with quivers of arrows affixed to their belts. Each carried a long knife, too, and one a tomahawk.

In another corner stood Revere. He saw me and looked to be querying for the cause of my presence. I used this as an excuse to make my way over aside him.

"Sergeant," said I, formally, if cordially. I pointed toward the Maroons. "What's all this about?"

He offered only silence as a reply.

"Colonel Draper has me assisting in the organization of our occupation of the city," I said. "I could use a hand with it, relaying dispatches and such, if you're not on to something other."

Revere's face went as flat as that of the rope-headed Maroon. "I am on to something other," he said, though he did not suggest what.

It sounded like an excuse to me, to avoid the work. And further, I didn't particularly appreciate the surly cast of his gaze.

General Wild broke from the rash of citizens who were beseeching something or other of him then, and he and Draper crossed to the Maroons. Draper, noting me, curtly waved me forward. "Etheridge, Etheridge! Come here now."

I pushed my way through the crowd, though smartly—head high, chin forward—to counter the mortification I felt at his base summonsing of me.

The rest of the room closed in around as a parlay with Golar ensued. Golar removed his hat—in respect of Wild's station as chief, I supposed, and for some reason this surprised me. Other than this, though, he stood back-stiff, bearing unbowed. Up close, his head was a marvel, not untamed gnarls of rope but coiling lengths of it, with the texture of sheep's wool and falling nearly to his back.

Even from only feet away, his words were difficult to catch, as he spoke at a whisper—not submissive, just not overmuch concerned that he be full-on heard. "Two-score," I made out—his reply to the general's inquiry on the number of Maroons with him.

"With a detachment of our men, that would put you at about fifty," said Wild, turning for confirmation toward Draper, "an appropriate size for a scouting party, for reconnaissance and other such missions."

The colonel nodded in agreement.

Wild asked, "And for arms? Is this how you and your men are equipped?"

"Some has pistols," said Golar.

This seemed news to the local citizens present, and none too delightful.

"And in the usage of them?" asked the general.

Golar's whole face opened. "The fact of lacking guns don't make us lacking in their proper usage."

The general smiled, too. "I suppose not." He said to his brother, "See that they're properly provisioned." Then back at Golar: "As to mounts?"

"More would be welcomed."

Wild's glance toward his brother communicated all that needed saying.

"You organize your men as you see fit," said the general, directing his gaze now at Revere. "But the sergeant here will be my liaison to your unit and accountable for your actions. He will communicate to you my orders. Their execution is my sole motive in mustering and equipping your outfit. Are we clear on this?"

"Yes, sir," said Revere, stepping forward. Smiles were rare on that man, but just then he looked downright wolfish.

Wild looked to be about to dismiss Golar, but then bent in close to Draper and whispered some consideration. The colonel nodded.

To Golar, Wild said, "And you're certain your people will not come into the city, for transport to the security of the freedman's colony?"

"Black Mingo men gone do as they gone do," said Golar. "These ones here choose to fight. Them others hedging they bets."

Thus ended the parlay. Golar hatted his wild head, and the crowd parted to let the Maroons pass. Revere followed after them.

When they'd quit the room, the crowd engulfed Wild, and the din of protests and demands resumed. Draper moved toward Backuss, off against the wall. He noted me lingering in place and made an impatient wave that bid me to join him.

He said to Backuss, "Company F is particularly disorganized, so we will use your men in various detached duties." He turned to me. "And you, Etheridge, you'll move your billet here. I'll need you to serve as my aide-de-camp. Too much to do and not enough support staff to see it done."

Backuss's sour stare told he didn't much like Draper's choice of adjutant and would rather have seen himself in the position. Nothing seemed to be going his way.

I was no more overjoyed than he by the assignment, truth be told. "And my men, sir?" I protested. For I would rather have been with my company, soldiering, even if it wasn't but picket duty.

"Lieutenant Backuss will oversee your men," said Draper, and he said no more on it. He pushed back into the crowd, toward the general.

Backuss did not address me but rather exited at a clip. Me, I understood that I was to follow closely on the colonel's heels, which I then commenced to do.

More dispatches took me around the city the rest of the afternoon. One, in proximity of the boat works, allowed me to venture in and gather my kip. I'd also hoped to find Fields there, to apprise him of my new assignment, but the place was empty.

Hanging about headquarters at suppertime, I came to understand that the orders I'd earlier circulated were instructions for a public rally to commemorate our triumphant arrival here. (Not so different from what I'd boasted of to Revere, really.) The ringing of church bells ushered in nightfall, accompanied by the booming of a battery of cannon. The general looked up from the map over which he, Draper, Lieutenant Colonel Holman, and Major Wright had been conferring. Wild said, "We must go."

I followed them out the door, up Water Street, and over onto Main, to the courthouse square. A grandstand had been raised (just a scaffold adorned of company colors). The newspaperman Tewksbury was up there when we arrived, alongside the house-owner Pool and a few other local muck-a-muck Unionists. General Wild joined them, to oversee the proceedings, as did his brother, Holman, and Wright.

Colonel Draper kept himself nearby the scaffold but not atop it. He seemed to prefer this vantage point. I stood aside him.

The Stars and Stripes whipped lively from the flagpole above the courthouse. A crush of freedmen and women and children filled the walkways of Main Street, waving and cheering, as a combined corps of the regimental musicians—drummer boys and fifers and buglers, blazing "Babylon Is Fallen"—led the procession. Next was the principal body of the African Brigade, company after company after company. It was a rousing thing to see.

F was not part of the official proceedings. My unit was charged with manning sentry posts around town, as the joyous celebration could not be allowed to result in an unguarded enemy attack.

I noted Revere and the Maroons from earlier a short bit down the walkway from the colonel and me. Revere pressed closer when he saw that I'd seen him.

"Sergeant," I offered by way of greeting, only to realize that his approach wasn't meant for collegial banter. His eyes betrayed what was agitating behind: a puddle of dog shit would have been more warmly received than was my presence.

"Your proper place," he whispered near my face, nodding toward the colonel, "as a lackey and a lickspit. Let the men, bona fide and proved, have at the mission of soldiering and emancipating."

"Your proper place, too," I shot back, indicating Golar and his swamp men, "at one step's remove from wearing critter-clothes and living in your own filth."

It was an infantile retort and not especially clever—and none too well appreciated either, by Revere or the Maroons. Golar in particular threw me a notably evil look.

"How much you despise your own black skin," hissed Revere.

I don't know why I did not on the spot strike him, except to acknowledge that I was shocked into a sort of dazed paralysis, one over which I tortured myself later that night and on others subsequent. I didn't fear the man, not hardly. But his words had struck like a slaughterhouse hammer, with me the beef.

I watched as he backed his way through the crowd, glaring a hatred so profound that I puzzled at what could be its source. Golar and his swamp men followed.

Draper, oblivious, tapped a foot and bobbed his head to the *brrum-brrumm*ing of the passing drums. He had missed the entire exchange.

We would settle this score, Revere and I, and I could see by his expression that he relished the prospect of the encounter just as much as did I.

CHAPTER ELEVEN

Where Wild was, well, . . . wild, and predictably so, Colonel Draper was harder to figure. We all regarded the general as one of us. With the colonel, it wasn't always clear that he saw us truly. The very next morning, I arrived from my quarters in the Pool carriage house to find the colonel explaining to Tewksbury the method of effective leadership of colored troops. "The only course," he was saying, "is a kind yet steady and firm hand. You see, the Negroes are more ambitious of approbation than fearful of punishment."

He might have been describing a scent hound he was training to hunt. And just as though he was talking in front of a dog, Draper seemed to consider it no more likely that I would savvy his explanation than would the beast. He just went on about his point, even after noting my presence, the newspaperman enthusiastically scribbling the words onto a notepad.

It was clear he was different from Lieutenant Longley and his Sergeant Sambo camp dog routine. Yet and still, Draper maybe did not for real see us colored, all the same.

Though Wild forbade application of the lash in the African Brigade, regardless the offense, for respect of what we had known in bondage, Draper found ways to break even the most headstrong that would not or could not abide by his "steady and firm" regimen. The bark of the stump that served as a barber stool back at Fortress Freedom was worn smooth by the many men charged with hoisting

it as they marched the yard for poorly cleaned equipment or malin-
gering or dereliction of duty (charges which I learned were of easily
variable interpretation). And we all watched as Leon Bember spent
an entire October afternoon bucked and gagged atop a scaffold in
the middle of the parade ground for smart-talking Robinson Tynes,
when Tynes was yet a corporal. It wasn't a flogging, but it wasn't
far off.

It is unsettling to know that a man who is rooting for you to
overcome doesn't full-on recognize you as capable of rising to a
station akin to his own.

Once the colonel had finished his discourse with Tewksbury, he
greeted me with a military salute, accompanied of a warm smile—
oddly eager, even if stiffly formal. He then set me upon a series of
chores that heralded the routine and monotony that would characterize my subsequent days. The work of adjutanting a colonel was
largely administerial, I quickly came to learn. Wild and Draper
amassed abundant but sundry intelligence from the many freedmen who came into headquarters to offer it up. Once verified by
information otherly garnered—typically, from Pool or one of his
loyal acquaintances willing to speak with Wild and Draper, however guardedly—detachments would be sent to the four corners
of northeast North Carolina, units large and small, on canvassing
missions and for recruitment, to follow up on leads about the land
pirates or to forage for supplies. Me, I ran the orders that directed
these actions about the city.

Lieutenant Colonel Holman set out with a sizable battalion,
some four hundred men, to the west of our position, where there was
reportedly a large camp of irregulars commanded by John Elliott,
the bushwhacker who most vexed the general. Elliott's band was the
one that Malachi told us had shot down Black Sanders. The steamer

Frazier hauled Major Wright, leading two hundred, to the mouth of the Pasquotank River to scour the peninsula between Wade's Point and our base, where other guerrilla movements were said to be occurring. Each detachment was expected to return complemented of that neighborhood's slaves.

Beyond the contrabands carrying information, our headquarters was overrun from first sun till dark with complaints from local citizens. We heard claims of horses misappropriated by freedmen and of feed silos unjustly ransacked by troopers; we received white Elizabethans desiring to take the oath of allegiance or others requesting passes to quit the region entirely. This was all overseen by Colonel Draper. He dictated the unclassified directives to me. "Good practice for your literacy, Etheridge," he would say, as though my literacy needed practicing.

General Wild brooked no such assistance. He sat at a long mahogany desk in the middle of the room and worked at penning every dispatch himself. Having but one arm, and that one half lame, it was striking—honorable, even—but wholly inefficient. The New York newspaperman, who seemed always underfoot, was impressed just the same, which was maybe Wild's intended purpose.

"The General imposes very little office work on the members of his staff, doing nearly all himself," Tewksbury read aloud from his notepad one night beside the fireplace in the parlor, for the benefit of any who would listen. "This is especially laborious, but it is his way. Nothing, however trivial, escapes his notice, and he personally superintends everything."

Delivery of a satchel of correspondence for transport over to Roanoke took me to the docks that Tuesday afternoon, our fourth in the city. The weather had blustered since our arrival, making the Pasquotank choppy. But General Wild insisted on maintaining a steady communication and transfer of supplies between our position and the military camp back on the Island, whatever the conditions and despite the threat of ambush from the Rebels' so-called Mosquito Fleet. It was to the benefit of those of us from there. By this method, we could keep apprised of news from home—though none of it, so far as I could tell, was the information sought by Fields.

Before seeking out the steamer captain who would convey the current satchel, I gave myself leave to compose the overdue letter for Sarah so that I might entrust it along with the official correspondence before another day had passed with it yet unwritten. Duties called me elsewhere in the city, so I had to be brief. I took a seat on a piling to scribble hasty words, off a ways from the bustle of loading and offloading boats. It was hardly the "flourishes of plume" that Sarah had come to expect, just business: Did she have knowledge of Llewelyn Midgett and what had become of his slaves?

I heard myself hallooed and turned to find approaching me Joseph Etheridge, a cousin to John B., wearing Union blue and Navy insignia. He strode over and offered his hand to shake.

Such a strange gesture from a man before whom I'd always had to drop my eyes.

"How good to see you, Dick! And what a surprise."

"And likewise you," said I, forcing my mind to think only "Joseph Etheridge," lest lifelong habit, and thereby also my tongue, slip back to erstwhile titles: Master; "Mass Joe."

"So, you're part of this mission General Wild has struck up in these parts?" he said.

"Yes, sir" would have been the appropriate response, given his captain's patch and the scrambled eggs that embroidered his bell crown cap. But this too much recalled my previous condition, and I stood there mute.

He took my hesitant silence as a response in itself and continued: "It is a difficult but noble mission. Times are changing. We cannot live in yesteryear."

I supposed he was talking about our aims of Emancipation, but who knew? He was a slave owner himself. Maybe it was our operation against the bushwhackers to which he referred.

He pointed over his shoulder, toward the wharf. Disembarking from a steamer there was a procession of Zouave soldiers, bearded and mustachioed and sporting their Harlequin attire. "Me, I am piloting that paddle-wheel. It's my contribution to peace and union."

I found myself even more distracted by the Zouaves than by a blue-uniformed Etheridge, and not on account of their garishness. I didn't relish seeing those boorish white men arriving in the city. Were they just transiting through, or were they there in support of the Brigade? I very much hoped the former.

I hadn't asked about home, but Joseph Etheridge offered news. "All is well enough out on Roanoke. Cousin John is doing a healthy business with the government, supplying foodstuffs at just less than market price. Given the number of Yanks, he is cutting a tidy profit all the same."

And that was all—nothing about my ma'am or about the colored with whom I was kin or was known to be friends. The only bit proffered was of the singular part with which he was capable of associating me: my former master.

He smiled broad. "Your position in the army will be a great asset to Cousin John." He pointed at my stripes. "When you return home, your status will help to boost the family's business dealings with the runaways at the Freedman's Colony. They are more than you would believe or could fathom.

"And this would serve you as well, of course," he added as an afterthought.

His words rankled not inconsiderably, given his apparent assumption about where my loyalties lay. He struck me as being as much for "peace and union" as was John B.—which was to say, not much. The Etheridges were for their own stake, for siding with those who could aid in the advancement of family ventures and enterprises.

I said, "Thank you, Captain Etheridge. I'll remember that when I have done with fighting for freedom, should I decide to return to the Island."

He did not take it as I had intended or did not hear me, for he continued with his unspooling ideas on profiteering. "Yes, yes, your hand could be good in it. The Freedman's Colony counts nigh on two thousand darkies now." He beamed. "Hell, before the hostilities, the whole blamed Island didn't have but maybe six hundred people all told, nigger and white!"

He promptly blanched. "Forgive me, Dick. Habits of speech are not easily quit."

I did not concede that I would forgive it, but forbearance was somewhat inborn in me and I imagined that my face revealed this.

His humbling of himself seemed an opening for me to inquire after Fields's brothers. "Tell me, do you have news of the Midgetts? Of Llewelyn, in particular?"

Joseph Etheridge's face soured.

"Do you know what has come of him and his?" said I.

"The Island split much more than not toward Union, but a few have cast their lot the other way. Llewelyn figures among those."

I already knew this. I asked the more pressing question. "In our sorties into the neighborhoods hereabouts, we hear tell of folks taking their property and lighting out for Texas and suchlike, to keep as far away of our armies as possible. Might this be the case with Llewelyn Midgett?"

In pondering this as long as he did, Joseph Etheridge did not offer the quick dismissal of the proposition that I'd hoped for.

"The schooner *Erasmus* and the Midgett sloops are nowhere to be seen in Shallowbag Bay these days," he said, working out his thoughts. "I'd supposed this to mean that they'd loaded up what property they didn't want to lose to military seizure and transferred it down to Wilmington. But down there, seizure by the Confederate military is just as likely, and I suppose it ain't but a slight push past Wilmington on to Texas, when in exile already."

He paused again.

"It is possible, yes," said he. "I have not heard this specifically with regard to Llewelyn, but Midgetts have left in bevies. It sure enough is possible."

This was bad news. I didn't know what I would tell Fields.

"Llewelyn and his lot," said Joseph Etheridge, "they're not alone in slipping off in the night. Others have, too—nearer to home."

I didn't reply, as I was not following his intimation.

"Patrick," he said, and his face darkened further. "Patrick has defied his uncle and joined the Rebels."

"The North Carolina infantry? Patrick?"

"The irregulars," said Joseph Etheridge, glumly. "Jack Elliott's band, out here in Pasquotank."

"Paddy? A bushwhacker?"

"That is how I hear it."

And partnering with the worst of them, to boot. I asked, "From whom this information?" I needed to be certain.

"Bo Evans. He said Patrick come to his window one night and tried to get him to join along."

Evans was a boyhood friend of Patrick's, his closest one aside from me. He would not invent such a thing.

"Much ago?" said I. "When did he run off?"

"Two weeks. Maybe three."

Hence Patrick's picture postcard.

Oh, Patrick, thought I. Paddy . . . Was this yet one more attempt to rival me, only this time inspired of spite? Or was he acting on the cussed promise to ornament the gum tree on the square?

I turned my face so as not to give away what I was feeling. In that direction, I saw disembarking from Joseph Etheridge's paddle-wheel, after the last of the Zouaves, a huddle of colored faces I knew from home—six or seven, mostly men, mostly aged—and right there among them was Fanny Aydlett. My Fanny!

I ran toward her without offering Joseph Etheridge even a farewell, and she saw me then, too, and she ran to meet me. We were in front of colored soldiers and Zouaves and everybody there on the wharf, and she jumped right into my arms like it wasn't but us two in all the world.

"Oh, Fanny," said I, "what are you doing here?"

"Why, following you, Richard." She smiled broad.

"But here? How did you know I would be here?"

"I didn't." She let herself slip from my embrace and stepped back a pace. Pulling up her bonnet, half fallen from her head, and straightening her lambswool sweater, which had become disheveled in our entwining, she explained: "Pompeii injured his leg, helping construct the sawmill up at the Freedman's Colony."

Sure enough, there he was, off over her shoulder, leaning heavily on a crutch and on old Ebo Joe Meekins, who was helping him to stand.

"A kindly preacher from the missionary society said it could be saved with proper doctoring," Fanny went on. "He got Pompeii a dispensation to travel on to Norfolk. I secured passage as his attendant."

And then anew, her smile: the smile I so loved, beaming pride at her industry and ingeniousness.

Yet as happy as I was to see her, I wasn't at all glad that it was here, smack in the middle of our campaign in Confederate territory—a territory that was throughout troubled with murdering bushwhackers, at that!

"This ain't Norfolk, Fanny. How are youall to get up to Fortress Freedom from here?"

"They just put us on the boat. They told us the Union command would secure our passage on up."

This revelation set my stomach to churning. It would be Wild's and Draper's charge, another among so many, to get them safely there, and to keep them safe until it was accomplished. I tried not to let my worry show.

"Oh my, Fanny. I didn't have any expectation of seeing you for some time. Maybe not even evermore."

She grabbed me up into her embrace again. "I know it, Richard. This is why I was set on finding my way to you, wherever you was."

It was a tender moment, and I felt no compunction or embarrassment at tearing up right there in the street, my girl, Fanny, wrapped in my arms.

CHAPTER TWELVE

I'd known Fanny on about as long as I'd known anyone, excepting Ma'am. She was a part of our pack—of Fields Midgett and Bill Charles, Dorman Pugh and the rest, and Paddy, too, when he'd make himself a part of us. Depending on the season and our masters' moods, we might not find one another save for Sundays, but then for sure. Fanny was often the only girl, but none made a distinction. She was just Fanny. And, at most-all we undertook, she was tops. She swam better than Fields and knew whisper-tales on Island folk that we others did not and was generally first picked when we chose sides for chuck-farthing. Whatever the endeavor, she gave as good as she got. The only difference was that she wore a sack dress and covered her head in a bonnet where I and the others had on short pants and plaited straw hats.

She and I first recognized ourselves to be more than just play-mates one night out on Shallowbag Bay. I'd been left behind to unload John B.'s haul of terrapin from the *Margery & Sarah*, and Fanny was shelling a basketful of shrimp out on the dock. Night had fallen and she was late getting them to Ma'am Beulah for serving at suppertime. I left my chores and squatted aside her and helped her at it. Our knees touched as our hands worked in unison. We got the shelling done before trouble befell her for tarrying, and feeling as much joyful as relieved, I leaned over and kissed her, unprovoked. Just as easeful as that, a natural thing to do.

I would swear to this, at least, though my memory may have tailored the particulars. It may have been her who initiated the kiss. For that was Fanny.

It's said that, on account of unrelenting proximity, Island folk can sometimes fool themselves into believing an earnestness of feeling that isn't in fact true. With Fanny, it wasn't fooling. That first kiss confirmed it.

"How is it you did *not* know it until now?" she asked a few nights later, sitting alongside me at our secret spot over by Uppowoc Creek. "The top coons of the top buckras must surely breed the bestest pickaninnies, no? Why would I choose some other?"

She was joshing, of course. But not, too. We were children yet, but not children for long. Such was the life of a slave.

Even at that green age, I recognized that she was the one I would venture down the road with. I felt a great need to protect her, and though my ma'am was proof of the folly of the notion, I deemed myself capable of it. The more I knew Fanny, the more I allowed that she could take care of herself. What greater testament than that here she was, a lone slave woman conveying a party of old men on their journey to freedom.

Their baggage was minimal—all told, a few burlap sacks, not completely full, and one colorful carpetbag that I initially mistook as belonging to Fanny. (She had only what she wore on her back, it turned out.) Along with Pompeii and Ebo Joe were Ebo Joe's brother Kid (who had not been one in my lifetime, or even my ma'am's), August Dough (not of my ma'am's Doughs but an uncle of Bill Charles's), and his brother Wynne (I promise, that was his name—his erstwhile owner had a sense of humor); there were also two others from farther down the Banks whose names I could not recall. I drew Pompeii's arm over my shoulder, to replace Ebo Joe as a second crutch, then accompanied the group into the city, recognizing that my immediate mission now was to ensure that they were properly lodged.

I'd overheard General Wild instruct his brother that all contrabands to be ferried up to Virginia should be assembled in the
Cottage Point quarter, which was nearby the docks and largely
abandoned. We headed that way.

"You young bucks is heroes to us-all back in the Banks," said
Pompeii, smiling generously despite the obvious discomfort of his
bandaged leg. "They making tall tales of youall's exploits."

He was Fanny's uncle, and I'd known him my whole life, too.
"It's kind of you to say, Mr. Pompeii," said I.

The lot of them rifled questions at me about the Brigade and
about our doings, each of the old men much overjoyed and nan one
of them the least worried, as though they did not realize where we
were—surrounded on every side by unseen guerrilla Rebels. Fanny,
a few steps behind, was silent, her face down.

I led the group street by street through Cottage Point until we
came upon a house standing dark and still, one of very few that looked
to remain unpeopled by contraband families or shut-in whites. It was
large enough that each person could single up in his own room (though
not all in bedrooms). None of them had known such luxury in his long
life. Pompeii claimed the master's chambers, as Fanny would need
to share it with him, to tend to his wounds during the night (and, I
supposed, to forestall any temptation of wee-hour visitations by me).
Though Fanny would have but a pallet in the corner, the family that
had abandoned the house had done so in such haste that she could
avail herself of the many other indulgences that were left behind: a
closet full of dresses and such, including a proper coat; a body-length
mirror for apprising their fit on her fine form; and most importantly,
a separate and adjoining water closet in place of a night jar, so that she
wouldn't have to wander the grounds in search of privacy.

Despite this, Fanny seemed sour. She had since we'd quit the
docks. When the others were properly settled in, I found a way to
pull her to the side, out in the hallway.

"Girl, tell me! What is wrong?"

She shushed me with a look, then signaled that I follow and led me down the stairs, into the kitchen. There were unwashed dishes on the counters and a pot with rotting porridge hanging over the cold hearth. Fanny faced me and what I saw, to my surprise, was outright anger.

"I fear you are not glad to see me, Richard. Have I somehow vexed you?"

"Aw, naw," said I, and I pulled her into my arms, close, as much to avoid her sharp gaze as to offer a reassuring embrace. "I ain't vexed. I'm worried, is all. This is war, and we are in enemy country."

"I know that." She pulled back, forcing me to meet her eyes. "You don't think I know that?"

When I'd returned her look full-on to her satisfaction, she continued: "I had to get Uncle Pompeii out of there. There is just too much crookedness on the Island, that 'kindly' Northern preacher included, and I feared that, without being able to keep paying, Pompeii wouldn't get the help he needs." Her eyes glazed. "And I also wanted to be nearer to you."

"And I am glad for it," said I, and I kissed her mouth, properly, like a man should.

And she kissed me back, her emotion calming.

I asked, "Crookedness?"

"Up to the Freedman's Colony, yes."

"Joseph Etheridge told me things were doing well there."

This wasn't exactly what he had said.

"The Colony has grown," said Fanny, "but all ain't right. They is lots of new arrivals, but maybe too many. Numberless suffer as a result, living in lean-tos and under trees. We all try to do the best by them as we can, but the Zouave soldiers oblige us to continue working for our Masses if they have pledged loyal. It's real tough, Richard."

I knew a sawmill had been raised, along with a freedman's school and other betterments. But an unease was setting in as Fanny spoke about who was running things and how they were being run.

She pulled me by the hand to a set of seats by the hearth. "I haven't told the worst of it. The buckra in charge of the Colony store, a Copperhead sutler by the name of Streeter, has some side-door deal set up with the soldiers. He buys what they bring him, then sells it back to us, even if it was ours to begin with!"

None of this surprised, not hardly. Similar arrangements were common up at Fortress Freedom. Fanny's outrage about it, though— now that surprised. She was not naïve about the ruthless practices one man will enact against another. What slave could be?

"Them Northern soldiers, Richard! They break into our houses and do as they please. They steal our chickens and rob our gardens, and if anybody defends themselves against them, they are hauled off to the guard house for it."

She paused before going on, calming and seeming to gather herself. "Some of what Streeter takes in is ferried over here, I am told, to support the Rebel bushwhackers."

And just then, I remembered what Joseph Etheridge had informed me of earlier.

"Is it Patrick?" I asked. "Does he have some hand in this?"

"Yes, Richard," said Fanny, her face riling, with a furrowed brow and a sharp-set mouth. "The double-dealings with the Rebels, Patrick is in it. This is the general belief."

I found my rage mounting. "Does John B. do nothing? He's pledged loyal to Union, to what I am now engaged in . . ."

My mind had latched onto the wishful side of my memory of him, as though there was reason to believe that my father felt pride at the mettle and buck of his son. But it was foolish thinking. Just plain foolish.

"He tries to hide Patrick's involvement," Fanny said. "But I don't see him trying to stop it."

Just as he hadn't tried to stop mine. *You will do as you wish from here on, Dick,* he'd told me the night I announced my enlistment. And so, too, with Patrick, I supposed. John B. would reckon him free to choose the path he would set out upon, regardless of John B.'s own feelings on the matter.

And so, just as he was now doing with Patrick, John B. must have likewise attempted to conceal *my* involvement in the war, though for a different motive—for a different sort of shame. A son's buck, claiming his place, was not a trait that inspired pride when the child who displayed it was also your slave, emancipating himself. Strict obedience, I reckoned, was surely the only way that a slave-master father felt properly honored.

Fanny said, "You always put more stock in them Etheridges than anybody else ever has. Especially in that snake Patrick, when he has never done right by you that I know of."

She wasn't wrong, and so I didn't know what to say in reply. I said nothing.

"It's bad back home," continued Fanny, "real bad. All the loyalty-oathing has not changed a single person, maybe only made them worse."

"We got news that Llewelyn Midgett quit Roanoke with Riley and Lawrence," said I.

"With those two, yes, and all his others, too."

"Do you know where to? To Nixonton, maybe?"

"I cannot say. Only that he intended to remove himself to Midgett property in Confederate country."

It must be to Nixonton, then, thought I. I knew of no other place where Midgetts resided. But with us now overrunning the region and freeing every colored along our path, how long would he stay?

Fanny asked, "How is Fields holding up? It must be pure torture, he was always such a tender-hearted boy."

"Fields! Tender-hearted?"

"Much like you," said she, which I was loath to accept as a compliment, even though it had clearly been intended as one. "Family
matters to him, as it does to you, even in a world where all manner
of travail can come from this for a colored man."

Her hand had been on my leg, and she squeezed my thigh
now, hard.

"It is why I chose you, Richard."

And then her smile! The one that shamed the angels.

I lowered my face and asked the question whose answer I feared
myself incapable of bearing. "Have others aside Midgett taken to
using the lash? I mean, if Sand Bankers are now flogging feisty folk
just for sassing—"

Fanny shushed me, scooching her chair closer and pulling me
into her bosom. "Ma'am Rachel can take care of herself, you know
that." She patted my head like she might a child's. "I sought her out
when Uncle Pompeii and I got dispensation to quit the Island, asked
her to join along, but she said no. She and her sisters doing cooking
and such for the missionary society and tending to freedfolk. She
says her work for freedom is there."

This was a relief, and I found myself settling into Fanny's
caress and her warmth.

I left Fanny soon after, to return to headquarters lest my overlong
absence be mistaken for dereliction of duty or worse. Yet I was
deeply troubled the entire journey back. I longed for Fanny every
waking minute of every blessed day, but her unexpected arrival in
our ranks was an impediment.

Instead of fighting for the idea of her, here she now was, close enough to touch. With each step across the city, I wanted to turn back, to go to her, to be by her side—to protect her, yes, but also so that I might hold her in my arms. This, when the things that needed done to enduringly assure us such rights required that I be away, attending to my soldierly duties.

Quandaries like this one could prove dangerous—nay, deadly— especially if our success thus far was mere fool's gold, an overhasty belief that we were conquering our old home when the truth might yet bear out otherwise.

CHAPTER THIRTEEN

Upon my entering headquarters, Colonel Draper said, "Problems at the docks, Etheridge?"

It was not sincerely asked, only meant to remark my extended absence. But that was the end of it, too. He made no more of my truancy. He and General Wild had been engaged in some considered meditation, and he returned his attention there.

Listening in from my position near the door, I caught up on the particulars. With Holman's and Wright's battalions detached in the counties to the west and east of us, the remaining African Brigade in the city was at half strength. Six hundred troopers might seem sufficient, the colonel told Wild, but the Confederate regulars around Greenville, only fifty miles away, counted twice that number. He expressed concern that, should they be in the process of mounting a counter-attack to our invasion, we might find ourselves at considerable disadvantage.

"We must rely on our scouts," said Wild, referring to Revere and the swamp men, "to reconnoiter the countryside out there and alert us of enemy movements in a timely way."

He appeared much more reassured by this prospect than I myself was.

Wild then took up with a party of townspeople who'd been awaiting him in the adjoining room. Judging by the one-sided tenor of the exchange, they were not finding satisfaction to the grievances they had come to headquarters to convey. Before joining Wild, Draper handed me another batch of envelopes.

"See that these reach their destinations," he said, adding, "and promptly this time, Etheridge."

The next set of deliveries ate up my afternoon. Once done, though, I skipped supper in order to track down Fields, to let him know the little bit of news I'd learned. F was dispersed at various sentry posts around the city, so I had no idea where he might be. The best place to start was the boat works, where the men would return to for mess or to turn in for the night.

It was already dark, though barely past five, and cold, cold, cold—as cold a night as we'd had since leaving Freedom. As I entered, I found Miles Hews and some others seated around a small campfire they'd built right there on the shop floor. They were playing jacks with peach pits. Hews popped to attention, the others following suit.

"Where is Corporal Midgett?" I asked, suspecting he would be here or nearby, as these men were a part of his squad.

"Did you try his quarters, sir?" said Hews.

I began that way, adding, "Use your God-given good sense, Miles, and move the fire outside." Hews, of all of them, should know better.

Fields was indeed upstairs, stretched out on his bunk, fully clothed and also wrapped tight in a wool blanket. "Evening, Richard," said he when I poked my head into the doorway.

He sat up, and I sat beside him and got right to it. "I come by news of Riley and Lawrence—a little. Llewelyn has quit the Island for some family property hereabouts."

"That's good news!" Fields said. "They got to be at Nixonton, then."

Rightly, he wanted authentication of the source.

"How is it you come to know this?"

"Fanny landed with her uncle—"

"Fanny is here?" said he, appearing brightly pleased.

"With Pompeii and a few others," I replied. "She told me."

"Then the information is reliable."

A curious silence followed, his face shifting, his mind clearly going elsewhere. He asked, "You remember that time down to the Broad Creek marshes, Richard?"

Of course I did—and he knew that I would. The mere mention of "Broad Creek" always recalled the memory, and likewise always brought a smile.

He continued: "You and me and Riley, riding atop Syntax late of night when Mass John B. would not note the horse's absence. *All* of Roanoke asleep, save you and me and Riley, us thinking that that Lost Colony might yield up her treasures for us if we searched careful enough and with a mindful eye. And then them dead men's riches would be ours and ours only, not nothing we had to give over to our Masses."

"They come from nowhere," said I.

"Like the dark itself was birthing them. And so many all at once!"

"Who knew Russian rats to be so mean?"

Fields was laughing outright then, as was I.

"They rushed us from all around," he said, "and that damned horse reared up."

"And Riley shrieked and was unseated and on the ground. Syntax a-running, and poor Riley running after us, just slapping at them rats and running!"

It was in no way funny, not on the night in question—though we'd laughed then, too, in the excitement of it—much less right now. Yet here we were, Fields and I, sharing full-bellied laughs.

He stopped just as suddenly, dropping his face into the bowl of his cupped hands. "I feel as bad here as I did at the time, Richard. Like I have abandoned him yet again."

"Listen," said I in a commandful way, to reassure him of my ability to get done what I was about to promise to do. "I will gain permission from Colonel Draper for a sortie out there, for canvassing, and F will go out, tomorrow or the next day. I'll make the case, and we will go."

He did not raise his face. He didn't say anything.

"We'll get Riley and Lawrence, Fields, and whoever else Midgett has carried over to Nixonton, and we will bring them in."

He just sat there.

"Turn in now, get some sleep," said I. "I'll return after reveille."

I left him then, for I didn't know what more to say.

Downstairs, I ordered Hews to take charge of "Call to Quarters" and to make sure lights-out was enforced at the proper hour.

"Yes, Sergeant," he replied.

I pulled him away from the others. "Let Corporal Midgett alone for the evening, will you?"

I might have made it a command but thought it wiser to confide in this instance, to better communicate that the thing at issue was sensitive and that he should keep it quiet as kept.

He seemed to understand. "Is everything okay, Sergeant?"

"Okay enough," said I. "Keep it so, so that the corporal might have a taste of personal time this evening."

"Will do, sir," said he. "Will do."

When I entered the parlor back at headquarters, the newspaperman Tewksbury was cackling and saying, "They were calling the sortie the 'Great GO-rill-uh Hunt.' Gorilla! As though they'd been transported back to the wilds of Africa!"

He and maybe a score of men, a few of ours but mostly locals, stood about in what appeared relaxed conversation. There was General Wild, his brother Walter, and Colonel Draper, of course. Among the Elizabethans, I recognized the house-owner, William Pool. The rest were unfamiliar to me. A bottle of brandy stood open on a side table, though only Tewksbury, Pool, and the locals held glasses. Through the open door beyond, the long dining table was being cleared by two colored ladies whom General Wild had employed for cooking and maidly purpose.

He greeted my return with overmuch enthusiasm and waved me over. "Sergeant . . . ?"

I approached with a mite of caution. "It's Etheridge, sir. Yes?"

Wild continued, brimming with amusement: "Your timing is fortuitous. Mr. Creecy here questions the Negro's capacity for instruction and military service." He gestured toward a doughy man in an everyday brown sack coat and tie, where the others in the group wore more formal tails. "He contends that you follow blindly and do not even properly know the target of our mission."

"Sir?" said I to the general, for I knew not what he was driving at nor what he expected of me.

But I then remembered this man Creecy. He was the one whose side-by-side mansions on South Road Street had been taken over by Company B, the man with the mammy who refused emancipation.

Creecy in no way found the subject matter amusing. He said to Wild, "I admit my judgment to be tainted by the indignity of seeing your Negroes in the streets of my home—of my place of birth!—in uniform and armed. I will admit this. Still, it doesn't change the simple facts. The Negro will always be true to his instinct as a faithful servant. He blindly follows. But do not confuse it, sir, for other than what it is. This does not a soldier make."

Given his cross tone, I didn't mistake Creecy's informal duds for an oversight.

Wild jumped in: "Blind following *does* a good soldier make." He wore a foxly grin. "Still, you underestimate the capacity of these men." He turned toward me. "Etheridge, tell us. Who is it we're down here to ferret out?"

"The Partisan Rangers, sir."

"And they are . . . ?"

The answer was obvious—too plain. I didn't know what he wanted. "Land pirates?"

He waited for more.

"They call themselves 'Home Guard,'" I continued, piling it on for the general's benefit. "But we know them for criminal murderers. Unmustered and ununiformed villains who have no honor."

Wild smiled archly. Tewksbury and the others, too.

Not Creecy. His cheeks beet up, and rage stormed his eyes.

"They are guerrillas, yes," said Wild. "Now spell it for us."

"Sir?"

"Spell the name of our enemy."

I wasn't sure which man I most wanted to shoot right then, my commanding general or the self-professed "loyal" citizen with blood flaming his cheeks. Maybe Tewksbury, for having raised the matter and found it the basis of a joke.

I noted that Draper looked to be attempting to make himself small. I began: "G-U-E-R- . . ."

Wild spoke over me as I finished. "He well knows one from the other and has no misapprehension about wild African animals being the target of our mission." He directed this first toward Creecy and, after, at Tewksbury, and appeared downright pleased with himself. The satisfaction beaming in his face reminded me of the expression I'd seen John B. wear when I'd mended a fence without needing to be asked or some such thing—not just unsurprised but smug, as though some doing on his part had been responsible for the achievement.

I tipped my head in quiet salutation and briskly made for the door without asking to be dismissed before Wild ordered me to cake-walk or sing "Jump Jim Crow." I felt in that moment more a dancing bear than a soldier—no more truly seen than I ever was back home, by John B. or Patrick or any of the Etheridges. I was out the door in a few quick strides but heard it open and close behind me before I could get out of the foyer. It was Draper.

"Please don't retire, Etheridge." He said it like a question—like I had a choice in it. "I may need you yet, once this *gathering*"—he put emphasis on the word, aimed to be heard as disapproval—"has broken up."

"Yes, sir," said I. I stood at ease but made a point to remain out in the corridor.

He did not re-enter either. "It was the general's idea," he said, "this dinner with the leaders of the loyal citizenry." His tone remained oddly casual, confiding almost. "From my view, not all who came seem necessarily Unionist, regardless their professions of allegiance."

If this was meant as an apology for the earlier scene, I aimed to push it to advantage. "With your permission, sir?"

"Please, Etheridge, speak."

"I'd like to lead a detachment from F into the neighborhood nearby the city."

He considered the request a long moment.

"I'm only figuring on going as far as Nixonton, sir," I added, "maybe five miles away."

His reply disappointed. "It's imprudent. The Rebel militias are stirring and organizing, they're burning the bridges." He paused, anew considering, but then stood firm: "No, it's not possible. A platoon without support is at great risk, even in relative proximity to the city, and the entire company can't be deployed, as they're needed for sentry duty."

I hadn't expected resistance, particularly on the grounds of our safety. But in the service of family, *our* safety could not be a concern, only that we be allowed to ensure *theirs*.

"It's Corporal Midgett," I explained. "His brothers are being held out there, and I got word that his owner plans to flee with them farther south, so as to keep them in bondage."

His face softened, looking something like what it had when first he'd followed me out of the parlor.

Just as quickly, he drew in a sharp breath. "It's imprudent, Etheridge—really. Too, too dangerous."

He placed a hand on my shoulder, a curious and unexpected gesture. I had no recall of any physical contact between him and me, ever, not a clap on the back or even a handshake.

"I'm sorry," he said. "Some battalion or other will sweep them up at some point. If they are nearby, then this is certain."

"Yes, sir," said I, though it didn't seem at all certain to me.

"I should go back in now," Draper said, but he didn't move. His hand remained on my shoulder. He asked, "Tell me, what do you think of the general?"

What did I think? . . .

This felt like a trap. "I expect it's not my role to opine on the general," said I, "nor upon you."

He smiled. "You're right. In fact, it's your duty to execute orders without pondering too carefully their source or rationale. 'Yet and still,' as you lot like to say . . ." He drew nearer, as though we were friends, or even just friendly, which before that instant we had never been. "I see you men observing General Wild, his eccentricities. What do you lot make of him?"

My lot?

His manner, much like the general's earlier behavior, made me uneasy. I questioned the wisdom of responding. *Yet and still* I said, "You and he have armed us and permitted us to take the field to fight this fight. Rare are they that would. We colored troops appreciate this, sir, and do not ponder much beyond it."

Draper searched my face as though some other, truer response might reveal itself therein. From years of practice, I knew that none would.

Perhaps in his brief time with us, he'd learned it, too. For he renewed his smile and removed his hand, then turned and went back into the parlor.

I got a plate in the kitchen and ate heartily before returning to the parlor myself. Only a fraction of the original party remained. General Wild and a few others sat in a circle in high-backed chairs— Pool, Creecy and one other local, and the general's brother and Tewksbury. The colonel had retired for the night.

I kept by the door, unsure whether, with Draper's absence, I still needed to be here. No one seemed to notice me, so I didn't leave.

The tenor of the conversation had changed. "I've been a Whig my whole life, and it's not these troubles that will alter it," Pool was saying. "I've also been a slaveholder my whole life. Where do men like me fit into this new world that you are set on ushering in?"

Wild no longer smirked, as he had earlier, and there was no play in his voice. "On the side of right, or on the foul side of my sword."

"A centuries-old practice is not easily revised," replied Pool. "We've been striving to change our labor system—"

"Not quickly enough," said Wild. "Not willfully enough. For tell me in all honesty, how many of your own slaves did you free before we arrived at your doorstep? Would we be seeing any compliance at all were my men and I not here?"

"We are many—the prominent Unionist families here—and we're doing all that we can," pleaded the other local, desperately if not altogether convincingly. "I've offered my servants wages and freedom of movement on Sundays, to no avail!"

Wild said, "We pay their ladies five dollars a week to work as laundresses and to cook. Soldier recruits earn ten. If my offers outshine yours, then maybe you need to better compete for their services."

He looked stern, his brother worse, and Tewksbury scribbled. The three locals turned away, each in a different direction.

Pool was the first to speak again. He looked conflicted between sadness and resignation. "Our way of life is changing. This is perhaps as it should be. I only pray that you'll be measured in your application of justice, sir, because the rules of civilized society no longer apply as before, and we, the local Unionists, suffer it on both ends."

Creecy, the one in the informal sack coat, jumped in then. "Emissaries of the Partisan Rangers are everywhere—everywhere!" He did not speak timorously, like Pool, but spat it out as he would a boast. "They roam the country freely, threatening with fire and sword all who dare to defy them. Their tactics are severe, and readily applied."

If being a prominent Unionist had been the ticket to sup with the general, this one, Creecy, would seem to have forged a counterfeit chit.

Wild looked to have noted it, too. "It is incumbent on the local citizenry to root out the criminals," said he, "just as you would any other lawless element or gang of miscreants."

"Criminals, you say?" replied Creecy. "You, who see it fit to imprison innocent women?"

He was referring to the three locals Lieutenant Colonel Holman had conveyed back to Elizabeth from his sortie to root out the guerrilla leader John Elliott. Holman reported that he located Elliott's camp but found it abandoned of men. Two women there, though, were said to be the wives of notorious bushwhackers. They, along with a youth who lived nearby, were being held under guard at a house not far from our headquarters.

"They aren't prisoners," Wild corrected him, the mirthful grin returning to his face. "They are merely in temporary custody."

An artful turn of phrase, even to my ear.

"You are called a cousin to Beelzebub in my quarter," Creecy said, "and worse. They say the deeds of spoliation inflicted upon our home are unexampled among the many atrocities heretofore practiced by any man upon another, even by Attila the Hun!"

"And what say you?" said Wild, all the more calm-seeming for Creecy's outburst.

Creecy paused, as though to gauge the degree of ire that it remained prudent to express. "Me?" he said. "I say that this boy Daniel Bright who was brought in with the women is an honorable soldier on leave from his regiment. A simple company musician. He's not a member of the Home Guard as has been alleged. And it can be proved."

But then, as before, he just let go what he was feeling: "He's a good boy on leave and, by the laws of armed conflict, a war captive, then! Not an irregular—not a criminal 'miscreant,' as you would characterize him."

Creecy's particular interest in the boy, even over the women, was curious.

He leaned forward, toward the general—a gesture of entreaty, I supposed, though his face hardly conveyed any humility, nor his voice any tone of appeal. "I've known his family all my life," he continued. "They're corn farmers, I've employed some at Cloverdale. And I've known Daniel since he was a babe. It was me that appointed him to our community militia on his sixteenth birthday, and he served honorably and well."

Wild stiffened. "The 'community militia'?" He looked as much amazed as outraged. "Your infamous slave patrol? This is your defense of his character?"

Creecy did not immediately respond. "The militia is necessary for public safety," was what he finally managed to get out.

The general's brother spoke the first I'd heard him say all evening. "That you think service as a slave catcher and a Rebel soldier is an indication of a *noble* boyhood casts doubt on your professions of loyalty, sir."

Captain Wild was no more capable of disguising his anger than was Creecy. And bully for the man's blunt candor!

Pool and the other local sat very still, each one blanching visibly. Creecy stood to leave but had a few last words to offer.

"Say what you will about the South and our labor practices, General. You're an officer with two ruined arms and no other options for command than this dusky horde, and yet, do you accept them as equals any more than I? Where are your nigger captains and majors and colonels?" He glanced my way. "Hell, your nigger aide there is more lackey than soldier."

Captain Wild rose now, too, abruptly, the metal of his saber and scabbard clanking. "You use that word with neither pause nor compunction and have maybe chosen the wrong audience for that particular vocabulary!"

This did not moderate Creecy in the least. "You Yankees fuss over our niggers—over our *Africans*. You, men who had heretofore never seen one in your lives. Ha! It's only someone who was not raised alongside and daily rubbed elbows with them that would apprise them fit for soldiering. You stand in judgment of the South, but I know the African in a way you never could. I know his capacities and deficiencies and what makes him go. You'll begin to learn these things yourself once your 'men' are challenged under fire."

He moved toward the door, and General Wild placed a hand on his brother's arm, to forestall whatever it was the captain seemed bent on doing. Then Wild said to me, "Sergeant, will you escort Mr. Creecy home?"

"I do not need an escort in my own damned city," said the latter.

"If you're caught out past curfew without a laissez-passer," replied Wild, "you'll be arrested."

The general insisted on the French term; he'd had to spell it out for me when first I heard him say it. The alternative, "pass," he explained, had such a terrible connotation for us who had been slaves as to warrant its suppression.

Creecy sneered. "And a 'laissez-passer' is not an option, I suppose?"

Which was likewise my own question for the general, as I did not relish having to spend time alone with this man.

"It would be incautious," said Wild, his arch smile returned. "As you yourself noted, the all-seeing land pirates roam the country freely and are terrible to those who show loyalty to Union."

Creecy left the room without bidding good-bye or thank-you, nor giving me the chance to get my coat.

He walked at a brisk pace, a few strides ahead of and completely ignoring me. He didn't pause at either sentry post we came upon, but I calmed each set of troopers with a raised hand and the day's countersign.

Creecy stopped abruptly when we arrived afore his stately manor on South Road Street. The gate to the yard stood open, yet he did not pass through it. I heard raucous laughter and saw shadowy movement through the unshuttered windows in the main house, where Company B was presently billeting.

His back to me, he said, "When this country is retaken, you niggers who've betrayed it will not fare well."

I didn't know whether he awaited a reply or just stood there for effect.

I said, "I suspect you are right. Still, I'll take my chances on freedom."

I left then, as my duty to him was now fulfilled.

CHAPTER FOURTEEN

I headed to Cottage Point, where Fanny and the others were bivouacked. The streets were dark and mostly quiet on account of the curfew, until a few minutes along, when I heard the crack of gunfire in the distance. I asked myself should I go toward it. It was medium far away, maybe out by River Road, at the city's edge. A short volley from what sounded like Harpers Ferry muskets (our weaponry) was offered as reply, then silence.

After several minutes, there was no further gunfire nor signs of an organized response, nothing that might necessitate my aid.

All was still at the shelter-house, so I let myself in. I removed my brogans for lighter footfalls, climbed the stairs, and made my way to the master's chambers. There, a determined goose honk trumpeted through the closed door. This had to be Pompeii, for it was unimaginable to me that my narrow little Fanny could bellow such a big noise.

Would she be able to sleep through it? Could anyone?

Fanny was lying on a pallet only feet from me, perhaps unsleeping also, but safe. I slipped down the wall and pulled my knees to my chest, then sat my chin onto them. My tired mind longed for sleep, but restless thoughts would not permit it. They circled back to the gunfire from minutes before, and I wondered, Had Patrick been the author of the initial potshots? He was out here somewhere—a Partisan Ranger, a sneak-murdering bushwhacker.

I removed the postcard from my haver and by the glow of the moon through the nearby window reread Sarah's coiling script: *He said that, before, endeavors such as this pen-work were about all that he did better than you, but that soon this would no longer be the case.*

The desolate beach, the crumbling hut. Paddy, wretched Paddy! What had that boy gone and done?

A memory came to me then, vivid and strong. It was of the day I'd told him about Fanny—maybe a year past, after the fall of Sumter but still months before Roanoke was overrun, before anyone understood the full meaning of it all. Few knew about her and me. I hadn't even told Fields. Patrick and I were in the barn, grooming John B.'s stock. Patrick loved those horses nigh on as much as did John B., and he often joined me in carrying out horsely duties. The *scree-scree*ing of cicadas from outside the open barn door was a music we worked by. Even if, with age, we occupied diverging stations, we still talked much, too, open and free. We were debating how best to treat Syntax—she was the prize of the stable but had been favoring her hind leg. Patrick wanted heat but I knew cool to be better, to keep the swelling down. It went my way, as Patrick tended to trust my judgment on such things.

As I cool-wrapped the leg atop the fetlock, he showed me a picture he had drawn. It was nice, right nice, of a shipwreck, with Sand Bankers on the dunes working to salvage the lumber and sails. He'd titled it *Graveyard of the Atlantic* and had captured justly the ominous look of the dark, heavy surf. I was no judge; all I knew of fine arts and picture-making were illustrations in books and the portraits of famous Etheridges that lined the walls of the Etheridge House. But to tell by Patrick's drawing, he had a flair for it.

He said, "You're pure hell with a horse, you boat well and fish even better, but here's something I'll always best you at. I can draw the hairs on a fly's arse and get the shading just right."

Patrick could crow with the best of them.

I told him, playful, "Mass John B. thinks it impractical and not a good use of your time."

I'd cast the words jokey but meant them as a caution also, to forewarn of John B.'s inevitable outburst of anger. He had little patience for Patrick's interest in art.

But Patrick retorted: "Uncle John thinks that whatever I do, if he did not bid it done, is a poor use of my time. I'll make my fortune one day on my skill with pen and ink, with oil painting, and Uncle John will see that I'm all the man any Etheridge ever was, and me, by my own path."

I reached the picture back at him.

He smiled broad and would not take it. "Go on and keep it. You can be my first customer."

"But I ain't paid you aught for it," said I.

"Well, you can still be my first customer, so long as you don't tell anyone I gave it away for free. Tell them I made you muck out the horse stalls for it or something."

"Smokes, Paddy-boy, I got to do that anyway."

It was moments such as this one that recalled our closeness coming up, fondly, with a regret hardly befitting a soon-to-be full-grown man, and none too wise of a slave ever, no matter the age. And so I wanted this now rare feeling to last. I wanted Patrick to know about Fanny, about the thing that had blossomed between us—about our fugitive midnight moments together at Uppowoc Creek, about her tenderness and heart, about her bewitchery and beauty.

I said, "I think I might make a gift of your art-piece to Fanny."

Not asking permission, mind you, just confiding.

"Annie Aydlett's handmaid?" he said. "You got something going with her?"

It wasn't joy for me that I saw in his look, but something other.

"Well, let me tell you," he continued. "You ain't the only bull in the yard sniffing after that heifer. I tried to get her into the woods myself just the other week."

Crowing again, raw and ugly. He was not done. "She wasn't having none of it. But you know it's just a matter of time. A nigger gal ain't keeping nothing from nobody."

Even then I gave him the benefit of the doubt. I tried to teach him better. "Is that what you think of me, Paddy? Am I just a nigger, too?"

"I've known you all my life," he said quickly, seeming dismayed, as though he'd not recognized his words to be cruel and the knowledge was only now dawning. "It's different with you, we come up together. You're like family."

"*Like* family? Patrick, you and I *are* family."

My defiance brought on his anger, which was always close at hand and ignited high-hot. "Nobody ever whipped you! You tell me one time you was whipped, maltreated. Hell, we learned you letters. You sleep well right here beside us, eat well. What more do you want?"

I dropped my eyes—not out of deference, no!—but because to not do so was to take the next step in this rising encounter, and that could only end poorly. I understood just then something about the source of his constant rivaling with me. If I bettered Patrick at most-all, it was because overseeing me and the others rather than working alongside us had softened him by comparison. I was sure he fared well when with other whites. But when with me or Fields or Dorman, when with Lawrence or Riley? Not hardly.

To see his face—clenching, even as his eyes darted elseways—it was as though in that moment he recognized it as well.

Silence blanketed the barn, so thick that it smothered the nature noises beyond the open door.

He said, his voice subduing, "We ought to take Uncle John's sloop over to the Alligator River come Sunday. Black bear is pesking this time of year. I bet you if we laid some traps we could get us one."

"Yes," I said. "I'm sure we could."

"It'd be fun! And well worth it—for the hide and claws."

"Yes, sir," I said, "if you wish it." All but calling him "Mass Patrick."

He realized I would not join in his empty banter. Pointing toward the stalls, he spat a command about me mucking them once I was done with Syntax, then stormed out. And I did so, making sure to leave his sketch among the droppings and chips that I carted off.

He said that, before, endeavors such as this pen-work were about all that he did better than you, but that soon this would no longer be the case.

I'd read Patrick's picture postcard so often, I now knew the words from memory. But where, before, I'd interpreted them as a tortured admission of his decision to join the bushwhackers, a new meaning began to present itself. In the barn that day, I'd made known to him my love for Fanny, its full worth. And so I'd assumed that the one time he'd tactlessly blurted out about trying to get "that heifer" into the woods had been the whole of it. But had there been more, later advances after that—even *after* he knew she was my girl?

Surely not, Paddy. Surely no . . .

More back-and-forth gun banter distracted me from the distressful considerations. I sat in the house at Cottage Point, knees pulled to my chest and chin sunk onto my knees, listening for signs of an organized response. I would have felt better out there in it, doing something other than this. There was no response, no apparent need of succor.

CHAPTER FIFTEEN

I worked my brogans back on the next morning well before Pompeii had ceased the steady sawing of deepest sleep on the other side of the door. Outside, the city streets had yet to awaken. I headed for the boat works, as I hoped to catch Fields before F set off on some duty or errand. I didn't yet know how exactly I would convince Draper of the need of a mission out to Nixonton, but I would, for this day or the next. We would save Riley and Lawrence from Llewelyn and continued bondage. We would *not* leave them behind. I needed Fields to feel assured of this.

I arrived at the boat works, which were quiet yet. Nights on the broad shop floor seemed little different from sleeping out in the field. The sharp cold blustered in through the loose-jointed board-and-batten walls, and troopers had wrapped themselves up in whatever clothes were available, their heads completely covered, mouths breathing out plumes of frost air. Backuss, Tynes, and I hadn't considered this drawback when choosing the billet, nor had Backuss and Tynes seemed to care enough to move the company after it had been noticed.

I saw Stewart Bell descending the stairs—to rousen the men, I assumed. I crossed to him and asked where Corporal Midgett was.

"Sleeping when I got in last evening," said Bell, "and already gone when I awoke a short time ago. I assumed on some official matter. Is this not so?"

I didn't reply. I did not want to compromise Fields if he was doing what I feared he might be doing.

Miles Hews, who wore a second greatcoat overtop his own, rose from his place on the floor. "I saw the corporal leaving. He rode out on a horse, maybe . . ." He thought on it. "Not half an hour past."

"Your map," said I to Bell, who, as a corporal, should have one. Had I still been here with my men, as I should have been, my own would be at hand or nearby. Instead, it was at headquarters.

He handed his over. I felt fairly certain of being able to find Nixonton without the map but I wanted a fallback for my memory, as Fields and I would officially be deserters if found out before I could reach him and get us back to the city.

"Have you received orders for the day?" asked I of Bell.

"Only to report to the lieutenant up to Sentry Post G after reveille."

"How many are you?"

"Forty-one," said Bell, "less Corporal Midgett."

"Thirty-one for the morning," I corrected him, to which he nodded, consenting.

I turned to Hews. "Organize a detachment of ten and report back here, and on the quick. Make one of them Gaylord." As always, I was supplied of my sergeant's sword but no other weapon. So I added: "And find me an available musket."

Then to Bell: "Report to Backuss as planned." I leaned a little closer. "Unless he asks for an accounting of your roll-call, do not offer one."

"Yes, sir," said he without pause, which indicated to me that he understood.

Men were rising and mustering, from Hews's prodding of them or just the general activity in the room. I took a sheet of stationery and my pen and inkwell from my haversack and squatted right there on the shop floor. After pondering what best to say, I settled on:

Colonel Draper,

    Am detained on an urgent errand.

Respectfully,
Richard Etheridge, SGT

Simple and vague. Nothing that might offer clear indication of my movements.

I passed the note to Simon Gaylord and ordered that he deliver it to Colonel Draper at headquarters and to no one other. (Having left Bell undermanned, I wouldn't also saddle him with one of our lesser soldiers.) I told Gaylord, "Do not linger upon completion of the mission, and if queried, do not offer any information that you don't with absolute certitude know. Do you understand, Simon?"

He nodded.

I told him, "Wait until nine or thenabouts before setting off."

"Yes, sir."

The men before me, from Bell and his squad to Hews and our detachment, recognized that something was amiss. They didn't know what, but I appreciated that they would follow me without question or pause whenever I called it urgent. They believed in me, as Fields had once. I must not let them down.

If we were to overtake Fields, we needed horses. There was a stable on Jones Street, one street over, that would have mounts enough for our group. I figured Fields to have procured his own from there, and the stablemaster confirmed my suspicion.

It hadn't occurred to me to have Hews compose the detachment of men with experience with the great big beasts. He and Single Phillips and Josh Land turned out to be pretty good horsebackers, but the others, well . . . The rest were not cavalry and showed no disposition toward it. They rode unsteadily, managing the reins

with two hands while barely keeping their rifles balanced across
their laps. Along with Hews, Phillips, and Land were Harvey Hill
and Zach Gregory, fine privates who I knew would one day rank,
and also Briscoe Young, plus three more whose names I could not
on the spot find.

I didn't need to order my troops to maintain silence, as our
susceptibility to attack was generally understood. Only the beat of
our horses' hooves made a sound. We endeavored to keep some semblance of military formation, with me at the head and two abreast,
staggered five-deep behind, on the chance that we might encounter
a guerrilla band—or worse, a large unit of Confederate regulars.
A week into our foray, it wasn't unreasonable to imagine that the
regulars had organized to challenge the African Brigade's incursion
into the neighborhood and were out here somewhere.

A brush with Rebel irregulars wouldn't portend much better for
us, truth be told. Wild's military escalation—sacking John Elliott's
camp; taking hostages, for that is what those women were, and
holding them under colored guard, prominently, for all to see—was
having the effect the general desired, that of rousening the bushwhackers to greater anger. Last night's increase of enemy gunfire
evidenced this. It wouldn't play to my detachment's favor, as Draper
had forewarned. A modest-sized band of vengeful-minded men
would wipe out the ten of us before support could arrive.

Crossing Trunks Bridge over Newbegun Creek, I recalled having come this way before, on an errand with John B. This gave some
comfort, though there was no logic to it. We were no safer on the
road for me recognizing it.

The more distance we gained from Elizabeth, the more my
mind cleared. I realized that my object, once we overtook Fields,
was not to stop him or attempt to turn him back. It had maybe
begun thusly, but ceased to be so the farther we got from the city.
No, Riley and Lawrence were out here, likely other Midgett colored,

too. I would see them freed. But I wanted it done by a proper unit, not just one man run off, absent without the leave to be. If we were found out, punishment by Colonel Draper was guaranteed. I remembered bucked-and-gagged Leon Bember atop that scaffold on the parade ground at Fortress Freedom, imagined a similarly contorted Fields on display on the square in Elizabeth City, disgraced and humiliated. This way, if punishment was coming, it would fall on me. I hoped the rightness of our undertaking might take some of the edge off it, but if we were caught, it would be me who was in dereliction of duty.

A little ways up, we came upon a cluster of three homes being canvassed by Company B, Captain Frye's unit, maybe fifty men total. It was a confused scene. The troopers, looking more sheepish than sure, were in the yard, keeping at gunpoint a batch of women, while Captain Frye stood on the porch in brash dispute with some gray-bearded rusty guts.

He wasn't no "Officer of Geese" on this day. Frye was shouting, "Are you loyal or disloyal?" to which one of the old men shouted in response, "This is the grossest goddamned outrage!"

"We are loyalists," cried another. "Loyal!"

"We took Phoebe Munden and Lizzie Weeks not far from here," shouted Frye, "on account of the transgressions of their men. Do you think your own ladies immune from us?"

"The grossest goddamned outrage," repeated the first. "They are but ladies and girls!"

The ladies and girls referred to numbered nine or ten. All were pale and looked as skittish as the skittish soldiers guarding them. Most held on to some other one nearby, save a youthful girl who, on her knees with arms outstretched, prayed skyward, the white skirt of her dress mud-streaked.

Two-score barn fowl, a couple of hogs, and a piebald pony with more hump than haunches were also under Company B's supervision, yet nary a slave in sight.

My detachment had not the time for pause, but the scene struck me queerly. Spotting Mezzell among the guards, I signaled my group to sit their horses, then rode over. The usually jovial sergeant did not look so right then.

"Gil," said I, dismounting.

A first-name greeting seemed most apt to the situation, though I couldn't explain why. Perhaps in hopes that a show of familiarity might help calm things a touch—on our side, at least, if not among the locals.

Mezzell commenced to explaining without my having asked: "The first man there says that upon entering his home, we uttered insulting language and threatened foul treatment of his daughter and her girl."

I peered over at Mezzell. "Did someone?"

"On neither count, no," said he. He then scanned his men. "They all said they didn't, anyway."

Why Captain Frye didn't just leave the porch and quit this chaos, I did not know. There appeared to be no slaves to emancipate and so, little advantage in lingering here.

Why I didn't leave either, and on the spot, was equally a mystery, as Fields was still unknown lengths ahead of us. I supposed it was seeing Mezzell, discomfited as he was—an unease that looked to match a thing that had likewise been troubling me. I questioned these new tactics. The taking of women as hostages was maybe the new strategy of provocation, but it threw me.

For one, it didn't fit. In all my life, I never knew of colored men hatching schemes of outrage toward Southern ladies. If anything, the rageful Negroes I knew were of the mind of old Nat Turner. He did not linger in any of the bedrooms he visited; he got on about the business at hand and moved along to the next farm.

And after all, were we not, in fighting this fight, aiming to disprove the terrible tales that were concocted about us? If the general intended to use this method of combat against the Rebels—menacing the men by the threat of terror to their women—it put us colored soldiers in a tight spot. For would we not be seen as the lustful brutes that Southern men already believed us to be in the first place?

On the porch, the screaming tangle took a strange turn. One of the old men was saying, "I purchased the damned horse legal, for his use!" to which Frye replied, "But if this son of yours is in the Confederate Army, then you're abetting his service to their military. So how can you claim loyalty?"

"I have sworn my loyalty," retorted the old man, "and signed the oath papers, too. Yet you call me a liar!"

Mezzell whispered at me, "I offered earlier that we ought to just confiscate the farm animals and leave off with the fractious argumentation."

"It's what I would do," said I.

The focus was momentarily diverted from the women, at least—a minor victory in a needless battle. Or so I'd thought.

The girl who had been praying rose up then. "Even if Pawpaw won't claim Secession, I sure as hell will!" said she, shouting it out, curse words and all. "I'm a Secessionist through and through like my brother Sam. And I wished I had forty brothers more just like him!"

She wasn't but ten, maybe eleven years old. A woman—her ma'am?—took to pulling roughly at the girl's sleeve to try to get her to shut it up. The girl would not.

"I expect you niggers will march back to Norfolk when you have done with your abuses here among my family. Well, by God, may you meet a Manassas on the way!"

It was a rich taunt, and I found myself liking the girl for it. Others of us, too, clearly, as here and there I heard chuckles. Even Captain Frye. He beamed a smile and moved in his limping way off the porch, ignoring now the protestations of the old men.

All would be right soon enough. I considered requesting escort from Frye to better assure the safety of my detachment's passage through the enemy country. But his company would severely slow our progress, given that his troopers were a-foot. Plus, how was I to explain to him our unauthorized sortie without lying, which would only increase the offense?

I nodded to Mezzell, mounted, and heeled my horse's ribs, proceeding up the road. My men followed.

The farms we passed over the next stretch were quiet, too much so. I had the men keep a keen eye on the tree line and moved us at a gallop, even though it spread out our line.

Hews and Phillips pulled abreast of me. Hews said, "The incident back yon, Sergeant. Some of us were wondering what to make of it. Is our mission now to be bullying women as a way to spook their men?"

He was a sharp one, Hews.

"We'll do what we're ordered to," said I, not quite liking my response. So I added: "Yet and still, a good soldier will give some consideration to what is being asked of him."

I'd made up this last bit and wondered if Draper would approve of it.

"I know some of them boys back there from B," said Phillips. "They're not the sort to commit outrages."

"Sergeant Mezzell either," said I, "nor to watch them being committed."

"And Captain Frye?" said Hews.

"It is the reason for sergeants. We're the go-betweens. Trust in us."

Draper would approve of the latter response, this I knew for certain, as he'd previously instructed us non-comms this very thing.

We came to Meadstown, a hamlet of eight or ten houses. As we trotted down her center, the silence felt off. The lane seemed narrow and tight, all the windows dark and unmoving. Eerily so. I only then realized we should have bypassed it altogether, ridden the long way around. It was what any competent commander who was short on numbers would have done. I signaled the men to be attentive, peered from one window to the next for signs of movement, for the muzzle flash that would herald the ambuscade.

It did not come. Nothing stirred at our clomping passage.

A half mile or so beyond, the way forked onto the Nixtonton road. These environs were of a sudden very familiar. I knew that soon, to the left, we'd find the lane leading to the Midgett farm—Hollybrook, I now remembered it called.

Turning off the road onto the lane, I heard a pounding of object against wood, and Fields's voice, raging, before the plantation was even properly in view through the trees. I spurred my mount. She'd been panting hard plumes of breath but promptly dashed forward. The property came into sight—Hollybrook Manor, the two-story colonnaded house of Leonidas Midgett, Llewelyn's cousin (and John B.'s, too, once removed). Fields was at the great front doors, kicking at them.

I leaped from the saddle upon arrival and went and grabbed Fields. "What are you doing, man? Calm yourself!"

He pushed away from me harshly. "Mass Llewelyn might be in there, and they will not open the door."

"Calm yourself, Fields," said I, calmly myself, firmly holding his shoulders so that our eyes might meet.

The other men had gathered around, near, though not too near. If they'd not known it before, they by now surmised that this mission was personal and urgent, yet not properly assigned and maybe not even approved.

I said to Fields, "If Llewelyn is here, we will find him. If he's gone, then we'll interrogate whoever remains and get information on when he left and where he has left for. But we must do it soldierly. More flies with honey, right? With respect and a firm examination. Your way is failing to even get opened this door."

And just then, it did open. Before us stood Leonidas Midgett. He was a portly man, his jacket straining tight over his shoulders and chest, and older than I remembered, with thick, grayed hair and sagging features. He leaned heavily on a cane, seeming completely unperturbed by the violence recently unleashed against his door.

"Ain't you one of Cousin Lew's niggers?" said he to Fields.

Fields stiffened but did not respond.

"And you, you're Cousin John's?"

"Was," said I.

"Indeed," said Midgett, sneering. "I suppose you're right."

All was still behind him, off in the house.

"We come after Riley and Lawrence," Fields said. "My brothers. We have intelligence on them being out here. We have heard this."

He seemed to struggle with how to address this man who'd been family to his master and thereby a legal master of him—and who, despite the circumstances, still behaved as though this were the order of things. This surprised me of Fields.

But Midgett appeared to enjoy Fields's struggling. "Your *intelligence* was correct but has since lapsed." He said it spiteful more than mocking, though with some measure of both.

The other troopers, in a semicircle behind us, looked to have noted it, too.

A wheat and flax farmer of some renown, Leonidas Midgett had once counted two-score colored as his property, but there was little noticeable activity on the grounds. The barn stood open, with a still-ness inside, and there were no carts or livestock anywhere to be seen.

Holman's column must have come by here, or some other unit. It was impossible to know if this boded well or ill for Riley and Lawrence, given the Midgett men's excitable natures and proneness to rash action.

This one took our silence as a prompter for storytelling. "When your confrères besieged the farm yesterday morning, my people—pickaninnies as well as chambermaids—feared that niggers in uni-form were an augur of the Apocalypse. Dear old Aunt Betsey threw her hands up and shrieked that it was Biblical end-times now set in upon us."

He smiled at the memory of it. Then his smile passed from smirkly to wan.

"Every last one followed after them all the same," said he. "And now you want more? I've got nothing more to give."

A woman dressed in finery such as I'd rarely seen and young enough to be a daughter appeared in the doorway behind him, though she laid a hand on his shoulder in a way that no daughter would. "Dear, please, let them have whatever they've come for so that they might leave," said she, spiteful like her age-lamed husband, only without the bonus of mockery.

I could sense Fields tensing up, an angry tensing. I jumped in: "Riley and Lawrence, then. Did they go off with the others?"

Midgett ignored me. "For all I know, it's *you* they've come for, dear," he said to his wife, truculently, defying us to act in any way that might confirm his words as true.

The woman leered at us. Contempt, when it's pure and plain-worn, makes a fiend's mask of even the most beautiful face. She took two steps forward and spat on the stretch of ground at my feet.

Fields shot forward in a blink, and I was just able to restrain his advance, the woman scurrying behind her husband, who'd raised his cane above his head in preparation of swinging it at us. Fields said with a venom I'd not known him to have, "You will tell me where my brothers are, or you will lose like I have lost."

Midgett backed into the doorway, the cane still raised, but did not slacken his imperious, scornful air. "Cousin Lew had already departed well before my niggers quit me, and he took his dusky drove along with him."

"But they *were* here," said I, "Riley and Lawrence?"

"I don't know Riley and Lawrence from Tambo and Bones. All I know is that Lew brought all his niggers with him, and he and his overseer carried them off from here as well."

His overseer? Few were the Sand Bankers to employ an overseer, and typically only for temporary usage. Overseers were known to be the most base and cruel sorts of men. What cause would Llewelyn have for one?

"Where was they off to, then?" said Fields, no less riled than before.

I was in my mind devising the words to get from Midgett truthful particulars on how they were being treated, given the presence of this overseer, when from the far side of the house I heard the clop of hoofbeats. Around the corner appeared Revere, Golar, and several of the swamp men. I would have thought them farther afield than this, scouting out Confederate movements, but here they were.

They numbered some twenty and looked an awful sight for anybody who might prove of a contrary bent to their way of seeing things. Wrapped in their hide and Indian-blanket attire, the swamp men carried the rifles General Wild had outfitted them with, hanging over their backs from slings fashioned of braided hemp. Many had also come by revolvers. Some carried two or more, tucked into their belts or in pockets sewn into their outer garments.

Midgett and his wife looked particularly disquieted by their chance arrival. Where my men hadn't rousened in the Midgetts fevered visions of bloodthirsty brutes come slinking unannounced from out behind the woodpile, these ghoulish smokes for certain did. Midgett stumbled hastily backward into her, all evidence of spunk drained from both of their faces.

Golar and his men hung back as Revere, who remained properly uniformed, ambled his horse forward. His imposing stoutness seemed to bow the creature's back at the middle.

"Etheridge," said he—notably equably, given our last encounter.

"Revere," I replied. "What's your business here?"

"Same as our business everywhere." He nodded the bill of his forage cap toward the Old North State flag, hanging limply from a pole. "This is not a loyalist outpost. Clearly."

Only Old Glory signaled loyalty. Most anything other, the opposite.

I said, "The mission is to confiscate the property of disloyal citizens. My men have matters in hand. You can move on."

Revere took me in, eyes probing my own, his horse inching forward in small easy steps. "That's *your* mission, sure." He turned his gaze toward the porch, toward Midgett and his wife. "Ours is to suss out bushwhackers and their patrons, and to bring them to the general or to heel."

The incident with Frye, from earlier, came into my mind—the new tactic of terrorizing the women—as did Revere's hot words at the campfire the week before, on wanting all Secesh dead. Split-tail as well as the men, he'd said.

Split-tail?

I wondered at his intentions.

Likewise at those of these swamp men—armed as they were like outlaw marauders rather than proper soldiers, some dismounting now, moving out of sight around the side of the house. Two sidestepped me and pushed past Leonidas Midgett, blanketed over his quailing wife, and they strode indoors.

"We have things in hand here," I said to Revere. "Move on!"

He moved nary a shiver. Quite the contrary. Golar clopped forward, his face framed by the Medusa hair but otherwise blank, saying nothing yet in complete collusion with Revere.

With me aground and them atop those horses, I felt small and at disadvantage.

Revere said, "Your man seems of a different mind." He nodded toward Fields.

Had they been spying from the trees before making their presence known? And why show up now, when there was no need of it?

I strode up on Revere. "It doesn't matter what my corporal feels on the issue. I'm in command here."

Directly afore him now, I was even smaller by comparison. His horse bobbed its enormous head up and down at my aggressive advance, but then held it lazily there aside mine. It watched me with the one dull eye, then smacked its lips.

Revere's hideous face did not shift. Golar's either.

And the scene of a sudden paused, everything seemed to cease to move. I found myself puzzling over what it was precisely that I aimed to do. For whose benefit this confrontation? For Leonidas Midgett and his spite-eyed wife? Did they merit this attempt at defense from Revere, from Golar? Or was it Fields I was attempting to protect—from the course Revere would set him upon, toward the impulses of some lesser self? Maybe it was just the idea of right that needed safeguarding. How much would be too much?

It was as if Revere could read my thoughts. "You think me capable of this, Etheridge?"

He looked from me to Midgett's wife, crumpled in a heap in the doorway, body jerking with the effort to suppress her tormented sobs.

Revere's face then took on a look not at all expected from him. Something like hurt. "You worked the big house, didn't you? Eating scraps still warm from Massa's table and sleeping in the kitchen by night beside old Aunt Chloe. Tell me, were you given tails to wear when serving company?"

His horse capered right, but Revere did not quit me from his leer.

"You were told something shiny about yourself and you believed it, word for word. That you were the top-dog nigger. You took from this mostly just the 'nigger' part, that you were top among your *breed* but less than them, regardless. And so you think you have to prove something to good ol' Massa. What will you not do to keep your place on top of the heap?"

His horse nickered, as though agreeing with his assessment of me.

"I pity you, Etheridge. You're not fit to lead colored men. I ain't sure you're fit to breathe."

He double-whistled then, sharp and sudden, and the swamp men came together, those gone inside the house and likewise the ones disappeared around the side. Without him or Golar saying a word, the band of them turned their mounts and set off at an easy pace, across the field, toward the trees.

I did not dare look at my men—into their faces. I couldn't reckon what it was they saw of me, or would from then on see. What had Revere exposed, which even to my own ear registered a whisper of truth?

"Thank you, Sergeant," I heard Leonidas Midgett say, "thank you for . . ."

"Shut it, goddammit," said I, "and tell us the whereabouts of Llewelyn and his men, Riley and Lawrence."

He was unaccustomed to being thusly addressed, but his chastened face appeared to allow that, from here on, such would be his lot. "Lew was only here two nights before setting sail again. Bound for Roanoke, I assumed, but did not ask."

His wife fiercely sobbed, unabating. He took her in his arms and held her fast, as though this present show of protection might in some way blot her imaginings of things gone another way with the swamp men. He then pushed into the house and closed the door. I heard the metal on metal of locks securing into place.

Fields glared at me. "Why did you keep me off him?"

He wanted a repeat of Clapson's farm: not just information, but retribution.

"I need cleansed, Richard. Working they vegetable plots and tending they beefs and cleaning up they shit and no choice but to do it. I need rinsed of the stink, man."

He went to his horse and took the reins from Hews, who was holding them. He mounted, then faced me.

"But you?" He shook his head. "God damn, Richard," he said.

I couldn't distinguish Fields's reproach from Revere's earlier one. It all recalled pups and paps and pride in pedigree, and it felt shameful. Hide-your-face shameful.

Fields *haw*ed and heeled his horse's ribs and set off up the lane.

"Hews!" I called. "You, Phillips, and Land, catch up and keep apace with him. Make sure he gets back safely."

They set off.

I mounted my horse and led the others, silent and uninviting of the least query.

CHAPTER SIXTEEN

After returning the horses to the Jones Street stall, I aimed to make sure that the men who'd accompanied me could without hitch rejoin their squads. I hoped to avoid Backuss, and it proved easy enough, as he was neither at the boat works nor at the sentry posts.

I likewise hoped to avoid Fields. I wasn't yet ready to face him. And luck went my way. Like the lieutenant, he was nowhere about.

At headquarters, I slipped into the drawing room, attempting to attract as little attention as possible. Only officers and a few sergeants were present, no citizens protesting this or the other, nor freedmen with intelligence or services to offer. Yet it was bedlam all the same. Orders were being sharp-spat about, men jumping to in fleet response.

Colonel Draper, standing with the general in the center of it all, noted my arrival and with a flick of his finger indicated that I meet him in the corridor. I proceeded out and awaited him there—a long-dreaded moment.

In my three months in the Brigade I had yet to hear him shout, even at his sternmost. Yet, here he was, shouting at me before having even closed the door behind himself. "Absence without leave is a grave offense in the army!"

"Yes, sir," said I, snapping to attention.

"The gravest offense in the field, akin to treason!"

I repeated, "Yes, sir."

It was from then on a belittling dressing-down, insulting, telling me things I already well knew. "We establish a hierarchy of rank
in the military, and those who are esteemed worthy of it are favored
with stripes and are meant to take orders from more highly ranked
men, and to effect the execution of said orders among those below.
This is leading."

He stood there, hands on hips, glaring. I didn't know if he
expected some excuse, more stock to tear into, but I offered none.

"Do you not understand the responsibilities of rank, Etheridge?
Has my instruction been so wanting that you see fit to subscribe to
your own daily program?"

He paused, glaring some more. And just then I realized that he
wanted me to cower, like a hound whose nose he'd cuffed. "Ambitious of approbation more than fearful of punishment," I'd heard
him tell Tewksbury.

But I'd had enough humiliation for the day. What did this
white man know of lickspits and top-dog niggers? Revere's words
bit all the more for Draper's oblivious invocation of them.

So I stood at rigid attention afore him—shoulders back, face
high, eyes raised. I would not lower them, just as, on the docks,
I'd refused to submit to calling Joseph Etheridge "sir." No, not like
this. Not when I'd done what I had to do. It was wrong, sure, by a
military standard, and I'd known it. But it was right by the standard of lifelong friendship akin to brotherhood. Fields and I had
been boys together, and slaves, and we were now soldiers together,
non-comms leading a company on a mission of Emancipation, and
by God, whatever had happened out there, it was not a white man,
Abolitionist or no, superior officer or not, who would shame me
for tending to mine. Buck and gag this nigger if you must, but no!

Draper found my eyes, and in his own I noticed something of
what I'd seen there the night before, after he'd followed me out of
Wild's abasing spelling bee.

"I rely on you," he said evenly, no longer shouting. "If I could have my way, you'd be a lieutenant and Backuss not even part of this regiment. But we make do as best we can. I recognize that it is your home country and that you have ties here, close ties. But we're surrounded on all sides by a vicious enemy and you're a soldier, and a sergeant at that, before you are a father or a son or a friend. Your first duty here in the field is to this regiment, to the United States Army, and thereby to *all* of your people."

This turn confounded as much as it surprised.

"Are you with me, Etheridge?"

I felt rebuked, yes, but uplifted, too. This was not punishment, a nose-cuffing. It was another lesson in leading.

"Yes, sir," said I.

Not punishment for me, anyway. I'd thought that Fields was also being spared but now came to understand otherwise.

"Corporal Midgett's unauthorized leave, however justified, put lives at risk," said Draper. "Who was supervising his sentry post in his absence? A greenhorn private? And you and your rescue party—how were you to be seconded had your detachment come into contact with the enemy? It's a serious offense."

I didn't know how he'd come up with so many particulars of our expedition in such little time.

As though reading my thoughts, he said, "Infantrymen are puzzle pieces in a larger picture. Empty spaces are quickly noted and immediately accounted for."

"It wasn't his fault, Colonel," I pleaded. "I promised him we'd go after his brothers."

"And your request was noted," said Draper, "and would have been fulfilled, too—safely. If those men are in the neighborhood, then some unit of the Brigade has been assigned to canvass the farm where they're being held. They will be found. Each trooper must trust in our judgment and know that we have a plan."

A plan, sure, thought I. But Riley and Lawrence were already gone by the time whatever unit had arrived at Hollybrook Manor.

"There must be consequences," said Draper. "Misconduct cannot be tolerated, especially in the field, and your company must be shown the penalty for it. As for you, your penalty—and your duty—is to assist in the punishment of Midgett."

He turned and went back into the hubbub.

I was to follow after, but I took a moment. Fields disciplined, and me carrying it out? The worst of outcomes.

Draper was again aside the general, surrounded by officers. Of the sergeants present, most remained off by the bookcase, standing silent. All but Adkins, who stood behind the cluster of officers around Wild and Draper. I made my way toward him.

He greeted my arrival with a nod and a whisper. "They got one of ours."

"What?"

He gestured that I be quiet, that he would fill me in when the timing permitted.

Just then, General Wild said, "Read it again."

His brother raised a sheet of paper to his face. "My little force is doing all we can to hold Wild's villainous army in check but cannot operate successfully against so large a force, as we count only three hundred fifty and are dispersed about the district. Skirmishes with their pickets and now one of their number captured—this is all to little effect. If they are not speedily dislodged, the Confederacy need not expect to get any more provisions from this section of country between the Pasquotank and the Chowan. But if they are driven off, the quantity of pork and bacon that will come to the Confederacy will be truly incredible."

Captain Wild paused for a breath, and Adkins used the pause to whisper: "It's a letter captured by Major Wright's expedition, from the Rebel commander out here to the general in charge at Raleigh."

"Who is it they got?"

He looked me dead-on. "Cornick."

Moses? The airy and jovial corporal from Company K?

"Naw," said I.

But Adkins's face confirmed it.

Oh, poor Cornick.

Captain Wild continued reading: "Wild's plan, evidently, is to let loose his swarm of blacks upon our ladies and defenseless families, to plunder and devastate the country, committing all kinds of excesses, in the most tantalizing manner. Against such a warfare there is but one recourse—to hang at once every black captured belonging to Wild's expedition."

A tight silence befell the room, the officers solemn but appearing also confounded, and this surprised me as much as the news of the capture. Well, not surprised. In truth, it left me dismayed. What else did these white men think Southerners would do with rebellious slaves? For this is how they regarded us. Our military uniforms counted for naught with them.

General Wild said, "They are bandits and behave as bandits and have not defended nor are they capable of defending their state or any portion of it. They can only harass us by stealing and burning, by stopping Negroes from reaching us, and by terrifying Union citizens and now murdering one of my men."

He looked particularly vexed, but also bedazed, his lecture spoken more to himself than to us others.

He snapped to then. "Walt, take this down." Wild rarely did not do his own writing, and he never publicly addressed his brother by a pet name. Yet here he was. "We will have it delivered to that scoundrel Elliott who holds our man, as well as copies to General Pickett and Governor Vance at Raleigh."

Reclining against the bureau, he began dictating, his voice Sunday-morning certain: "To John T. Elliott, Captain of Guerrillas. Sir, I still hold in custody Mrs. Munden and Mrs. Weeks. Concerning the colored soldier taken by you, as he is treated, so too shall they be, even to hanging."

And I thought, really? All of my heart was with poor Moses Cornick—but to hang the women?

No one else seemed startled, much less discomfited, by Wild's pronouncement.

"By this time, you know that I am in earnest," he continued dictating. "Guerrillas will be treated as land pirates. You will never have rest until you renounce your present course or join the regular Confederate Army." He leaned toward his brother, who was steady scribbling. "For the valedictory, add no salutation or other courtesy, just 'E. A. W., Brigadier General, Volunteers.'"

Wild looked notably pleased with the letter. "*Similia similibus curantur*," said he—Latin, I have since learned, which translated to "likes are cured by likes."

With this, all was again still in the room.

Then, of a sudden, not. Officers began relaying orders and positing questions and dictating dispatches.

Lieutenant Colonel Holman spoke over the thrum toward the general. "With this, then, sir, do we carry on with preparations for our withdrawal from the city?"

Wild replied with a brisk nod, but I thought, Withdrawal, already? It felt like we had just arrived and more was yet to be done. And what about Cornick?

All was moving too fast. I asked Adkins, "Where was Moses taken? What can we do?"

He waved me silent, as I'd unwittingly interrupted his council with Wild, Draper, and Holman. I heard Holman saying: "They gave us invaluable information and assistance on our mission out to Hertford. We wouldn't have had any success at all were it not for them."

I knew not of whom he spoke.

Wild turned to Draper. "You shall keep them as scouts for your column when you set off tomorrow."

And then I knew.

"Be sure that Sergeant Revere has been resupplied," Wild continued, to his brother now, then he moved on to the next business, this time with Draper.

The back-and-forth between commander and commanded went on like this, with the general inquiring and others replying, all to ready our departure on the morrow. As for me, my mind had turned to Revere. I dreaded the idea of him and the swamp men attaching to Colonel Draper's column, for this meant that he would thus be in proximity of me.

"Dying on the field of battle is one thing," said I to Adkins, out on the back steps of the kitchen. "But this?"

Though the meeting had paused for grub, I had no appetite. I sat hunched up in my greatcoat, shivering, while Adkins, a-seat beside me, dipped a chunk of bread into a bowl of soup. The others remained inside.

Poor Moses Cornick, thought I. A good man condemned to a bad end.

Had things gone otherwise on our sally out to Hollybrook Manor, it might as easily have been Fields taken captive, or one of the men I'd brought along, or all of them. Or me.

"Dead is dead," said Adkins between chews. "We don't have a choice in how it comes."

"For us?" said I, incredulous. "For colored, dead is dead?"

He didn't appear to get my meaning.

I'd forgotten that he was from the North. New York must be different for colored, I supposed. I said, "Down here, dead ain't necessarily just dead. Getting there can be a real Calvary."

I recalled Clapson's Jenny's back, Malachi's spoiled feet. This was what Cornick was likely being subjected to, or worse yet, before the relief of the Final Sleep.

Adkins, feasting yet, and with spirit, seemed incapable of envisioning the terrible particulars. It made me hunger for a world where there weren't Jennys or Malachis or now Moses Cornicks.

"What's it like," said I, "up where you're from?"

He finished slurping and swallowing before answering. "Different from here, but similar, too."

"Similar, shit!"

I wasn't the sort to utter oaths gratuitously. That one just came out on its own.

"Why does this leave you disbelieving?" he asked. "You think the North a paradise?"

"A heaven next to here, that is certain."

"A heaven next to what we're undertaking here at war, okay. But a paradise? Ha!"

He tipped the bowl at his mouth to get the last drops, then set it on the step at his broganned feet.

"I was born free," he said, "never knew shackles. Likewise my folks. They wait on an old-money family, the Caulfields, as their butler and cook."

Waiting on whites, that was similar, sure enough. But the manner of it? I expected that to be a mite different.

"I grew up around their children," he went on. "My parents' patrons' children, I mean. The Caulfields live up toward the top of the island, and my mother and father—and I, when I was yet there—come to occupy the carriage house behind their house, refit from a lodge for coaches to one for humans." He smiled at this. "This was their gift to my parents, you see."

He stared at me, as though waiting for some sign that I recognized a sameness between his previous condition and mine. I did not still—though I found myself distracted by the thought of New York being an island, like Roanoke, as I had not before then realized that it was. I wondered if this shaped how Adkins saw things, as it did for us Sand Bankers.

"When I was six, maybe seven, one of their boys called me a nigger," said he. "Not at me directly, but making reference of me to his older brother. The boys were amusing themselves at Scotch-hoppers out back of the house while I sat on our cottage's stoop, and I heard Tommy say, 'Willy, should we include the nigger in our game?'"

He paused again, awaiting some sign of epiphany in me. But getting called "nigger" by white folks wasn't exceptional down here. It was every colored man's middle name, if not the proper one outright. I knew a Nigger Joe, an Old Nig Maxie, others too.

"Tommy was trying to be kind, offering to include me," he continued, "and I'd taken it in this way. But then I heard the crash of furniture and saw his father as only a flash, flying off the porch. I hadn't even known he was there. He ripped off his belt and whipped Tommy—heartily so! And that man wasn't the whipping sort."

Now this intrigued me, for I couldn't envision John B. acting thusly on my behalf toward Patrick, though I must confess to having more than once wished it.

Adkins said, "He was a Radical Abolitionist through and through, and his son's words had betrayed his highest values. A man knows no greater disappointment than this, a contrary son. Because it looks to him like his own failure at fathering."

Bushwhacking Patrick? Run-off me? I wondered which of us was more greatly disappointing to John B.

"For a long time, the episode brought out a pride in me, at my good fortune and that of my parents—that we were in a place where equality was right there for the taking. After a while, though, I took to noticing how I never got called into the house for a glass of water when Willy and Tommy and me had been running about. I drank from the pump by the carriage house. Likewise other things. Mr. and Mrs. Caulfield offered my parents baubles at Christmas but never a seat at their table, not even the kitchen table. My folks and me, we were among them, but not *of* them."

This rang familiar—and more still, as he wasn't kin to the Caulfields, like I was to the Etheridges.

"I joined the American Colonization Society the day I turned sixteen"—I didn't know what this was and did not interrupt him to find out—"and began preparing for my emigration to Monrovia."

Monrovia was in the country made by Abolitionists, over in Africa, a place to send freed slaves. I'd heard other troopers speaking about it, as a place of possible destination after the fighting ended.

But Africa? thought I. I remembered Father Alick—the Maroon chieftain—and the other swamp men, with their crude style and primitive manner. *This* was what the Abolitionists would have us aspire to and what some of us now desired? Backwardness and want worse than what we already knew?

I said, "And yet you come down here to fight instead of setting off for there?"

"I am American, full-on one hundred percent," said he, rising, "not African. This was the realization that brought me down here.

My service in this army will prove it to all those who dare attempt to view it otherwise."

In this he was dead right: Fighting to break loose the shackles was but the beginning of it. We colored would have more struggle to undertake to attain our full share of the rest.

He offered a hand. I took it and pulled myself to my feet.

Still, I wondered at Adkins's experiences. He and I were alike and not alike, and I would have enjoyed more time to jaw on it with him, to help me better puzzle out my thoughts about this place that was my home yet home no more.

Only not right then. Right then, nary a bit of it mattered, for Cornick was still captured and all but condemned, and we were still in enemy territory—not merely us but the contraband families, too, and Pompeii and the Roanoke elders, and my Fanny—and things were getting hot. With the general's escalating tactics, they seemed sure to get hotter yet.

Back inside, the work of coordinating and planning had recommenced. Major Wright was saying, "Can we know for sure, sir? Those that claim neutrality, or even just sympathy with us, are typically—and reasonably, I'd argue—afraid on account of the guerrillas."

"With Pool's assistance and the intelligence collected from the freedmen," Wild responded, "we've compiled a reliable list of the genuine Union citizens out here."

This seemed to please the officers around the room, as though they didn't yet understand that such things were slippery and adjusting, depending on who held the gun and at whom it was pointed.

The general added: "We've also made a list of those from the region who are known to openly consort with the irregulars, supplying them and offering other support."

The officers looked even more pleased by this.

Captain Frye asked, "And is it reasonable to assume that we have achieved our goal of removing all the bondmen from the region?"

"We've confiscated upwards of twenty-three hundred, by our best count," said the general's brother, "not including whatever slaves we will encounter in Currituck and on Knotts Island on the return. That is most, if not all, of them. So yes, it's a reasonable assumption."

General Wild aside, everything was "reasonable" and "reasonably" with these men and never better.

Still, twenty-three hundred! This great figure surprised me. I hadn't known that we numbered so many slaves hereabouts, nor that near all had come away with us. So, reasonable? From my view, the African Brigade had sacked the devil's house and taken his pitchfork, too.

Wild asked his brother, "How have our efforts at recruitment among them fared?"

"Reasonably well. I should think the enlistment rolls will swell once they and their families have been safely conveyed back to Virginia."

Major Wright said, "And what of the captives?"

The general didn't immediately respond, though it seemed clear that options had already been discussed and all that remained was his decision.

The afternoon went along in this manner. I remained on the edge of it, running whatever errand I was bid to. Near dusk, Colonel Draper pulled me aside and ordered that I rejoin my company. By his grave look, I understood the reason why.

When I arrived, F stood at attention in parade order, on the yard to the side of the boat works, Little Charley Brown and Joe Gallop afar side them, at the water line. Torches had been lit and outlined the square. I searched the scene for a scaffold onto which had been set up torture tools—a thick stick and twine for bucking and gagging, or a log to be heaved overhead and sustained aloft. There was none of this, and I felt relief.

Backuss, at the top of the company, called out as he noticed my approach. "Etheridge, hurry up! We have been waiting."

I put a hint of peck into my step, but not overmuch. I didn't like being addressed thusly in front of the men, nor the occasion for which I was being hastened forward.

Fields stood at attention, facing the lieutenant, without his greatcoat despite the sharp air. The reason was at once apparent, his blue corporal's stripes prominent on the sleeves of his shell jacket.

Regardless my pace, it felt a long, long walk to the fore of the assembly. Once there, I took a place behind Backuss and immediately made to meet eyes with Fields. I had to, imperatively needed to, as he was my friend, my entire-life friend.

He would not grant it. He stared steadily ahead, avoiding direct engagement.

Backuss waved me forward, to his side, yet didn't deign to face me as he spoke. "The colonel advocates for you. He judges this a minor lapse on your part and states that you and Midgett here have promise. Me, I understand better."

He turned to me then, hissing. "You are responsible, Etheridge— you! You should have overseen this man's behavior and actions. It is your duty, and you refuse to do it."

Overseen? Like an overseer?

I disliked his word choice but did not dispute its aptness.

"If it were up to me," Backuss said, "it would be the strap, and be damned your sad history."

I refused to shrink even one bit at his bile. I stretched as rigidly tall as my frame would allow, looking out over the men, all assembled in taut lines.

Backuss signaled the musicians, and Little Charley Brown set in with an unceasing drum roll. Backuss let it persist, on and on. Then he strode abruptly forward and grabbed at the blue cloth stripe on Fields's right sleeve and yanked roughly. He yanked and yanked, frenzied now, wrenching Fields's shoulder downward.

My old friend did not flinch, though his forage cap shifted awry atop his head.

Finally conceding that the cloth would not give, Backuss removed a penknife from his pocket. The shriek of tearing sleeve was miserable to hear. The insignia came away, but it left a long, torn strip. Backuss repeated the procedure on the other side.

He righted his greatcoat and returned to his position. Then he turned to me.

"Dismiss the men."

I sought Fields's eyes. He still would not meet mine.

Little Charley Brown and Joe Gallop set in on "Call to Quarters."

I called, "Company! Dismissed!"

Tynes and the corporals gave me a wide berth. I lingered near the doorway, and as preparations began among the men for our next-day departure, I left.

I headed to Cottage Point. I needed to be near Fanny. I needed her help to make myself right with this thing with Fields. I also needed to be sure that she and Pompeii and the rest had secured passage on one of the transport steamers bound for Freedom. If not, they would have to make the voyage overland, in the wagon train of contrabands, which would be so much more dangerous.

But there was more. An elusive, ugly realization had been dredging itself up in my mind over the course of the afternoon, as I was aide-de-camping Draper. In brooding over my failure at protecting my lifelong friend, dreading the arrival of the impending dread assignment of discipline, it dawned on me that maybe I had failed far worse, and long before—failed at protecting Fanny. The bitterness and gloom sketched onto Patrick's picture postcard, Sarah's foreboding words about his changed humor, his joining up with the bushwhackers. Oh, the things a man will do to another man when he feels pushed past what he thinks he can rightly tolerate! My enlistment heralded the end of everything Patrick had ever held as true. Finally recognizing this, its full weight, I knew how hard he would push back, just how far he might go. He'd once boasted about trying to get "that heifer" into the woods when things were good between us—between him and me—and then they were no longer good, so how could that have been the only time?

I remembered my ma'am, her venom toward John B., and I remembered Fanny's venom toward "that snake Patrick." One seemed much like the other.

Fanny, my dark angel!

It was so plain and clear: she had been set upon by Patrick. I remembered Livian Adams, what he'd said about Revere's master and his mongrel weanlings. And so how many times, Patrick, and how recently done?

Fanny's precipitous departure from Roanoke into a theater of war, her pat explanation of the need to accompany Pompeii—just evasion to spare my inevitable hurt. And I knew her capable of lying to me. She'd masked before so that I might not fully grasp something she wished me not to understand. Because of this, I was now all the more certain.

So it was with great urgency that I strode across the city. I would likely be going into battle before she and I would see each other again, and thus we might not, in fact, see each other again. I needed to know what I needed to know.

I knocked and entered and found in the parlor beyond the front door Pompeii and the others, discussing the details of their departure, all save Fanny. They had passes for berths aboard the steamer *Three Brothers*, bound for Fortress Freedom at first light. This news, at least, was to my great relief.

I said, "I must speak with Fanny. Is she about?"

Pompeii finger-pointed the kitchen, and indeed, she was there. The space had been properly cleaned since last I'd come, surely her doing. She stood at the hearth, leaning into a kettle, preparing what smelled like seasoned pinto beans.

Finding myself now afore her, though, words would not come. It was fear, it was anger, it was hurt gumming up my mouth.

"Richard, I'm so glad to see you," said she, looking up. "I need to talk with you."

Me, I looked away.

"Oh, what is it, dear-heart?" she said, crossing to me. "Is it Riley and Lawrence, is it something terrible?"

I finally managed, "He did it, didn't he? He did . . . something to you!"

I didn't know how to finish it. And when she looked confounded, I added: "Patrick."

She backed away a pace, puzzlement undoing the facets of her face.

I said, "This is the true reason you quit Roanoke so of-a-sudden, ain't it?"

"I quit it like I told you. To be with you, and because Uncle Pompeii needed me to."

I wanted to believe her but could not, the rage within now rising, a blazing that surged through my whole self.

Yet if I expected that she might drop her eyes, grieved and mortified, and confess something at me—mister, that was not my girl. She erupted. "You don't think I can take care of myself agin that hateful Patrick Etheridge? I've told you why I left! You may imagine me some broke-winged bird that you can cup in your hands, but this don't make it so."

Her aspect was awful to see. Awful. Like Leonidas Midgett's wife, out at Hollybrook Manor: a fiend's mask where before had been her beautiful face.

She said, "I am no such thing, nor do you want me to be."

Pausing then, her face released, the blades now gone from her voice. "Or if you do, then it's not me truly that you want, Richard, and that is no better."

Which did not confirm whether Patrick had broken her wing or not, just that she did not desire my help in mending it.

Or maybe even *need* my help.

I loved the fire in this girl—and her great big heart. In that moment, though, none of it eased the disquiet knelling inside my head. Quite the opposite.

She said, her voice still flat, "I needed to speak with you tonight, Richard, because I've hired on to work on your general's wagon train, and I wanted you to know it."

"You did what?"

"I've hired on to cook for the wagon train returning to the Union fort," said she. "If this is to be the last I will see you, then I will see you to the last, till the day you are felled or I am. But I won't sit in some freedman's camp away from you, not knowing your fate. This is who I am truly."

"Goddammit, girl. What have you done?"

"Do not curse me, Richard Etheridge," said she, the blades returned.

"You just don't know! We are likely to meet terrible resistance, bushwhackers like what killed Black Sanders, or maybe even a Confederate column set on putting us down."

"I know plenty well what I know, and it is decided."

The thing was settled. I recognized it by the look in her eyes, a look I'd seen all my life, on Ma'am. There was nothing to say to counter her or . . . just to say! For whatever I said would have little import or weight.

I turned and left.

PART THREE

On to Freedom

Thursday, December 17–Thursday, December 24, 1863

CHAPTER SEVENTEEN

At the commencement of the war General Wild was practicing medicine in Brookline, Massachusetts. That he understands the guerrilla pathology, and can give a prescription that will cure every time, I think the Pasquotank bushwhackers will acknowledge.
                From Our Own Correspondent, *New York Times*

The rain drummed down the next morning. The African Brigade marched up North Road Street out of Elizabeth City, company after company, to the beat and fifing of "John Brown's Body." Behind the main column, the wagon train wherein Fanny rode; behind them, Company K, our rear guard. A large group of citizens followed despite the cold and wet, curious about the notices we'd posted announcing the day's courts-martial, or maybe just eager to assure that we were truly leaving.

Our great assemblage didn't travel far—maybe a mile—before stopping at River Bridge, the hamlet where, upon our arrival the week before, we'd razed the house and barn of the bushwhacker Billy Drinkwater to rebuild the crossing that he had destroyed. Intelligence gathered from contrabands who'd come into headquarters confirmed that many dwellings hereabouts were peopled by irregulars or by folks who supported them, and so the general's choice of location was plainly deliberate. Orders came down to form up on a makeshift parade ground afore an unfinished post office on a knoll. At the front, a scaffold had been raised with wood from the construction site.

The Brigade, more than a thousand strong, filled the rain-slicked field. I called F to order. My corporals—Fields, of course, no longer one of them—relayed the command to the various squads. Most officers pushed toward the fore, but Colonel Draper made his way back toward us. He took a place aside me, with Tynes on the other side. The musicians had quit playing and rejoined their companies, all but the drummer boys, who formed up in two parallel lines afore the scaffold. Under guard aside it were the twenty-odd prisoners who had been taken during our forays into the surrounding countryside. All were shackled, save the two women.

General Wild and his brother climbed the scaffold. The general addressed the congregation afore him, soldiers, citizens, contrabands, and prisoners alike.

"We convene this drumhead court-martial today to review the cases of the men and women arrested since our arrival on the eleventh ultimo." His voice was clear and strong, even to us standing several rows back. "If these accused can prove their legal status as regular soldiers of the armies of the Confederate States, then we will attend to their various offenses committed while in that service."

Two cider barrels had been established up there, a plank in between to form a sort of table, and the general and his brother took seats behind the makeshift judicial bench. Case after case was heard. Captain Wild sounded officious in his reading of the charges. Nearly half the captives managed to produce papers that the general judged sufficient to warrant immediate release. Most of the rest—men wearing random pieces of butternut duds or forage caps or both—had documents to attest to their enlistment in the Confederate service or orders proving they were on furlough from it. Wild declared these ones prisoners of war and announced that they would accompany our return to Fortress Freedom, where they would be jailed.

Next came Phoebe Munden and Elizabeth Weeks. They offered up no defense, neither speaking a single word. Each stood stiff and tall, with a wool shawl over her shoulders and a bonnet atop her head, hands manacled in front. Wild concluded that, being women, they were obviously not members of the Confederate Army. Yet, on account of their associations, they would remain detained.

He had decided against execution. For the time being, at least.

The sun was full out now, having burned off the clouds, the sky sheening blue. General Wild had kept for last the case against Daniel Bright, the boy whom the dinner guest Creecy had advocated for, and it quickly became apparent why. Wild proclaimed: "Lieber, in his study of the matter, clearly and succinctly distinguished a combatant from a common bushwhacker . . ."

"General Orders Number One Hundred," whispered Colonel Draper, leaning into me, explaining, "what's called the 'Lieber Code'—the regulations meant to guide proceedings such as this one. Section Four, Article Eighty-Two is the one concerning the irregulars. 'Men, or squads of men, who commit hostilities, whether by fighting, or inroads for destruction or plunder, or by raids of any kind, without commission, without being part and portion of the organized hostile army, and without sharing continuously in the war, but who do so with intermitting returns to their homes and avocations—"

I nodded thanks and cut him off—"I did not know it"—upon which he quit his schoolmasterly recitation.

What a queer bird, thought I, wondering how long he would have gone on, or been capable of going on, had I not stopped him.

Up on the scaffold, Wild turned from the documents laid out afore him toward the boy. "You say that you belonged to the

Sixty-Second Georgia, yet you wear no uniform, nor was any found at your domicile."

Bright was stringy, in a long wool coat and what looked like farmer coveralls beneath it, and he had crab-apple cheeks that stood out against his bleached face, even from my vantage point, a bit of distance away. Though barely younger than many of us in the Brigade—and likely older, in fact, than ones like Miles Hews—Bright did indeed look only a kid. He hung his head at Wild's words and didn't respond.

"If you were a deserter as you've claimed," said the general, "there should be some evidence somewhere of your enlistment. We've held you in custody for going on a week and where is it? Where are the papers or orders, or even a tintype of you in uniform?"

The boy looked puzzled, bewildered.

Wild went on. "Quite the contrary. Since your arrest, your cohort has kidnapped one of my men as a retaliation"—Moses Cornick—"further evidence of your being in league with these armed prowlers, with the vile bushwhackers."

Bright hung his head anew as General Wild rose from his chair.

"I shall not be held hostage to the *lex talionis*!"

I turned toward Draper for translation, but none was forthcoming. He just watched now, no longer in a teacherly mode, most-all transfixed.

"The crimes and enormities to which we've been subject since our arrival have included the destruction of property, pillage and bridge-burning, and provisioning the larger guerrilla force. The punishment for any one of these activities is summary execution. Absent a single shred of evidence to the contrary, you, Daniel Bright, are found to be guilty of Articles Eighty-Two through Eighty-Five of Section Four of the Lieber Code, and are hereby sentenced to death."

The boy dropped to his knees at this and commenced what sounded like prayer, a Sunday camp-meeting invocation. "O merciful Father! O merciful Father!"

Major Wright led a handful of troopers in stripping the unfinished post office of still more wood. With this lumber, they set to fashioning a gallows. The banging of hammers overlaid the "O merciful Father!" but could not drown it out. The rest of the field was quiet—soldiers, citizens, contrabands, prisoners.

"Shurtleff!" cried Wild, and the captain of H emerged from the parade assembly. He was long like the boy and strode to the fore and climbed onto the scaffold. He leaned over Bright, his shoulders hunched forward in what looked like a gesture of easement.

It did not calm the boy one whit. "O merciful Father! O merciful Father!" He repeated it a hundred times if he uttered it once.

"He was a seminarian before the war," Draper said, indicating Shurtleff with a glance.

I already knew this, as Shurtleff regularly held Sunday morning services, though none of us colored were ever welcomed to join in.

"The general wanted that it should be me," confided Draper, "but I'm not suited to it." He looked genuinely unsettled. "Ministering to souls? No, no."

The hammering ceased. The judge's bench had been disassembled and one of the cider barrels rolled beneath the gallows—a standing post with a crosstie up top, which called to mind the spar of a schooner. Captain Wild handed Major Wright a halyard, and the latter tied a hangman's knot, then secured it to the joist overhead. Captain Wild placed a wooden wedge under one side of the barrel, such that it tilted forward.

"O merciful Father, look down on me!"

Shurtleff grabbed the boy by the lapels and gave a sudden shake. "Stop it, son. Stop it now!"

Bright did. They faced one another, the condemned and his make-do spiritual counsel.

Shurtleff helped him to his feet and up onto the chair that abutted the cider barrel, and from there, up onto the barrel itself. The captain held him steady by the elbow, as the wedge made the barrel wobbly. Major Wright climbed onto an adjoining chair to put the noose into place. General Wild leaned in and spoke something at Bright, discreetly, and Wright looked at a loss an instant, overhearing. Wright then unwrapped the red scarf from his neck and secured it about the boy's head. It left more of his face uncovered than not.

Wright quit the chair and then the scaffold. Only Wild and the make-do chaplain and the boy remained. The boy's mouth moved over and over in a rhythmic way. *O merciful Father, O merciful Father* was what I supposed it said, but he spoke it too low now and I was too far to hear. Shurtleff bowed his head and looked to be praying. I strained for his words but only caught the final "Amen," which was on the spot accompanied by the general raising his leg and landing a hard kick at the wooden wedge below the barrel, triggering the gallows.

The barrel crashed over with a *thunk* and rolled off the side of the scaffold, and Bright's long body dropped a few feet and snapped to a stop. His legs scissored back and forth and back and forth and back and forth, setting his body to slow spinning like a pocket watch at the end of a fob.

It took a while. His neck would not break. The red scarf sagged on one side, no longer blinding him, and he reached his foot out for a toehold against the nearest upright post. His boot-tip attaining, he pulled his body as best he could toward it, to relieve the pressure of the rope, and he found a pinch of air. His foot slipped off then and thus recommenced the slow spinning. He once again gained purchase. Five seconds. Ten.

Finally, he tired of the effort and let go. His legs jerked up and back, but not fighting now, his body stretching. I wanted that they had thought to use a hood rather than Wright's insufficient scarf, as the boy's whole head was revealed and going the color of his cheeks, and his tongue poked from between bulging lips, and it was impossible not to look.

"That nigger Wild," I heard behind me, only with what sounded like dismay. I thought it Hews's voice but did not look to see.

Tynes said, close to my ear to keep his words from reaching the colonel, "Them buckra soldiers back at Freedom, the night before we left. They called the general a lunatic, and it ain't so clear that they might not be a little bit right."

"Killing boys not yet fuzzed of cheek and chin?" It was Gil Mezzell, the sergeant of B, not at all tempering his loudness of voice. "Is this now our mission?"

Colonel Draper glanced over, but his look did not reproach or admonish us to be silent. It confessed that he likewise was unsure of the answer.

I'd seen death and knew that, unless my own precluded it, I would see plenty more. But as it did the others, the boy Bright's slow spin sickened me.

I scanned the crowd of townspeople, off to the rear, searched and searched for that man Creecy. I didn't find him. I would have liked to, and liked for him to see me seeing him, for him to know that I would not shrink from what had to be done, no matter how raw. None of us would.

I turned toward the wagon train then, to the section where were posted the hired-on helper women, and sought out Fanny among the faces there. I wanted her to know, too—that this was what we were into, that this was what we were in for. The cost of freedom. I found her and saw that she was looking back at me. I saw that she knew it. How had I imagined that she wouldn't?

General Wild spoke at his brother, and the captain leaned over a piece of flatwood the length and width of a guidon. He used his kerchief as a makeshift brush and, with ink from his well, made a placard that he then affixed around Bright's neck with a length of twine. I read it as F marched past the scaffold, shortly after:

THIS GUERRILLA HANGED BY ORDER OF BRIGADIER GENERAL WILD.
DANIEL BRIGHT, OF PASQUOTANK COUNTY.

It might as well have been Cornick's body up there slow-turning in the wind.

The African Brigade made its way up the road with the boy left hanging there. The message was plain. The ante had just been upped.

CHAPTER EIGHTEEN

General Wild split the African Brigade into three battalions, and each column headed out on separate routes to Currituck Courthouse, a rallying point some five or so miles below the Virginia state line. Major Wright and Companies A, B, and D, about 150 men, were paddle-wheeled down to Powells Point, at the tip of the peninsula overtop of the Sand Banks, from where they would march north through the hamlets of Grandy and Coinjock and Barco, canvassing along their route. There weren't but so many farms out there, so Wild estimated that Wright's number should be plenty sufficient for taking in the bondmen of that region, and also for countering any of the few irregulars thereabouts, should they be set upon. Wild himself led another battalion, much larger at 500, Companies C, E, H, J, and K. They were taking the more direct course, up the Sligo road, leading the wagon train of contrabands. Colonel Draper, with F, G, and I, was to wend his way alongside the pocosin that bordered the North River, where the main guerrilla camps were said to be located.

It was us who would engage the bushwhackers. We marched four abreast on the Old Trap road at a rhythmed pace and awesome to see—250 men, a dusky legion. Colonel Draper rode up and back along our line, a silent and tall presence in the saddle. Me, I marched aside Backuss at the head of F, which was at the head of the whole of the battalion. No need for calling cadence. Our phalanx was of a single mind, one unified beast. We meant solemn business.

The bushwhackers of the surrounding neighborhoods were spread out into various bands. Should they unify, they would out-number us significantly. No matter. We, Draper's battalion, were to be the next dose of Wild's vicious medicine. The colonel had made this clear to us before quitting River Bridge.

He'd stood on the back of a buckboard on the bank of the rip-pling Pasquotank, Bright's body still visible in the distance, over his shoulder. "We will be in the enemy's country, men, so look sharp and bring pride on the African Brigade." He was a sight calmer than Wild in his speechifying but no less inspiring, with a fire in his face and a charge in his voice. "We will engage in a more vigorous style of warfare, and they will know that we are here. We'll picket every crossroads and every stand of trees till we catch the guerrillas. And we will catch them. Of this there can be no doubt."

Draper then gathered his command staff—one captain, two lieutenants, and nine of us sergeants—to inform us that we aimed for the hamlet of Shiloh by nightfall. We recognized this as a daunting task. Setting a large body of men on an eleven-mile march after a noontime hanging was getting a late start. We would arrive after dark, that seemed certain.

We were all right with it. This was serving as soldiers true—finally! Not parade and drills nor court-martialing and summary executions, but action in the field with the likelihood of Minié balls tendered, which we would return in kind.

Who among us knew what to expect?

None seemed the least distressed by our shared ignorance.

Me personally, I was most glad for our column's tasking. I had something to prove. Revere had called me unfit to lead in front of my men. It was an insult that had deserved violent rebuttal on the spot. Having let slip the chance then, I would show my mettle now, to my men as well as to myself, for I regretted not having defended my honor.

*   *   *

Skirmishers in small, detached groups snaked in and out of the surrounding trees, protecting our flanks and probing the woods for the enemy. Revere and his swamp men, they were out there, too. Colonel Draper called me to his side early on in the march. Leaning down over the pommel of his saddle, he said, "You'll need to do double duty, Etheridge, leading F alongside Backuss and also seconding me. I still require your services."

"Yessir," said I, the one-word way.

It wasn't a promotion. In fact, sort of the opposite—twice the work, twice the responsibility. It felt like getting ranked all the same, a testament of Colonel Draper's belief in my worth and indispensability.

Double-timing to my place back atop the column, I spied Fields, marching along with his squad. Though this was the sort of thing I would have typically hurried to share with him, I did not. The absent insignia left discolored stripes on his sleeves that were a humiliation to him and evidence of perfidy to me, with me the Judas. Because of the weather, we wore our greatcoats overtop our shell jackets nearly all the time. Thusly was I spared bearing constant witness to my shame.

He'd rarely met my eyes since his demotion, only by accident, it seemed. I understood why. I'd failed him, and he'd suffered as a consequence and suffered yet. Riley and Lawrence were lost in bondage worse than what we'd suffered when bondmen ourselves, and here he was, roving the countryside freeing others, doing nary a thing for them. My raised position in the battalion did aught to alter this.

Being down a corporal and recognizing the possible consequences of it out here in the field, I found Miles Hews and pulled him from the line. "I do not have the authority to rank you a corporal," said I, "but know that I rely on you like one."

"Yessir," said he. He couldn't hide his smile.

And on down the road our battalion advanced, brogans beating over packed dirt, the air sere and the sunlight sharp. Each farm we passed was already empty of colored, many emptied of livestock and conveniences, too, and no one stepped out onto his porch to observe our passing, as had been the case the week before, upon our emergence from the Great Dismal Swamp.

Revere and his band sat awaiting us at Areneuse Creek, a mile or so above Shiloh. We'd beat the sun's set to our destination, an improbable feat, but I hadn't anticipated the swamp men to be our greeting party. Backuss and I each raised a hand, and the order "Relief, halt!" was barked down the line. Draper rode forward, and he and Revere conferred.

Where before, the swamp men had been bedecked of homespun blankets or strange hide wraps, I noted that now many wore more proper attire, if somewhat improperly—layers of waistcoats and sack coats of fine cut, most with abundant wool scarves and one with a new-fashioned Derby hat. Some carried bulging sacks hooked over the pommels of their saddles. These men were looting, this was certain, but Draper did not notice or did not care. He remained in intense negotiation with Revere. I would have liked to know what it was that was being exchanged, for the colonel looked pensive and grave. Yet I kept my place, some fifty yards back, as he didn't call me forward.

Watching the trees, I saw sudden movement but quickly realized it to be our own skirmishers. The sudden rush of fire in my veins got me thinking on Fanny. I knew her to be relatively safer in Wild's larger column than if she'd been out here with us, as she'd desired. Still, this did not feel nearly safe enough.

Before leaving River Bridge, I'd sought out Adkins. "My girl is in the wagon train," I'd told him, as serious as I knew how. "Make sure that she arrives at Freedom."

He'd replied, "If she doesn't, it will be because Heaven has rained hellfire down on Earth and none of us could get back there."

I trusted I could hold Adkins to this.

When Draper had finished with him, Revere returned to his swamp men, and they heeled their mounts and moved off into the woods. Draper rejoined the column, keeping his own counsel, offering nothing on the recent proceedings.

"Forward, march!" echoed down the line.

We entered Shiloh at day's first dusking, and it looked as abandoned as the other villages we'd passed on our route, with shuttered windows at its twenty-odd domiciles and little apparent movement within. On the northern edge was Shiloh Church, which was famous hereabouts, for it was the first Baptist church in the state, 150 years old, it was said. She was a sturdy, white batten-board building, little adorned, with a row of four tall windows along the east and west walls, and a modest steeple at her foretop.

We sergeants called, "At ease, at ease," and the men fell out of line, squatting on their hunkers and leaning against trees. The colonel went to the small dwelling house beyond, which by its proximity must have been the home of the preacher, and banged on the door. There was no response. He banged again, then went to a window and looked inside. No light nor sign of life within. He returned, calling for his command staff to gather inside the church.

Men sat in the choir section and the colonel stood afore them, with me standing aside him. Revere had made his way into camp; he leaned against a windowsill off to the right and refused to even edge his face my way. Colonel Draper advised us that the guerrillas were near. He nodded toward Revere as the source of this intelligence.

"They're rogues and sneaks," said he, "so *we* must dictate the field of battle, not them. We will greet them according to their own custom, as bushwhackers."

He laid out his plan. With the remaining light, we were to pitch tents and set up camp around the church, as would be expected. But at full dark, each company would move stealthy-like out into the surrounding woods, F to the west, G and I to the north, in a sort of upside-down L. Draper gamed that the bushwhackers would approach the camp from the east, which was thick-wooded and closest to the pocosin. To draw them in, a small group would be holed up inside the church, making noises such as a large body of men at ease in camp would make. When the bushwhackers opened up on them, revealing their position, the rest of the battalion would respond, catching them in a crossfire.

It was a sharp plan, and plain that all of us were pleased by it.

Revere rose and addressed us. "Be sure to demand strict discipline of your men. No bugle calls, no talking or smoking. Anything that might clang or jangle must be tied down tight."

"Excellent point, Sergeant," said Draper. "Meanwhile, you keep your horsemen on the perimeter, but within easy gallop to the scene. Once they've shown themselves, circle around and attempt to force the guerrillas toward our fire."

The colonel turned to me.

"Etheridge, you'll take charge of the unit inside the church."

"Yes, sir," said I.

It remained as dandy a plan as before, only my assigned role in it took a bit of the luster off. Just common scad, baitfish on a hook.

Colonel Draper dismissed us.

*   *   *

Tynes was every bit as good as I at prompting proper soldiering of poor soldiers. But in the middle of a fight with irregulars, in the pitch of night, was not the best time to have to do it. In consequence of this, I picked my group of fifteen from among the men I judged lesser, so as to keep their defects from encumbering the rest of the company. Paps Prentiss, on account of his advanced age; Simon Gaylord, who tended toward hesitancy—men of this ilk. I needed two or three good ones to take up the slack for the second-rates and considered Fields, but then thought better of it. Being chosen for this particular assignment would not be read as a gesture of conciliation, but the opposite. I enlisted Miles Hews instead.

None of the chosen looked particularly happy at having been selected.

The companies outside went about preparing a campsite around the church as the colonel had instructed, expecting that watchful eyes were all about. Meanwhile, I slipped my men inside. Where her outward look was plain, this church was a shiny gem and contained unsuspected treasures. Alongside the various paintings of the Trinity and the Crucifixion, the walls featured portraits of the succession of preachers. The first in line looked the model of a Plymouth Rock Pilgrim like you see in books, with a sugarloaf hat in the crook of his arm and a dour expression veiling his face. The plaque inscription below the painting read: PAUL PALMER, ABOLITIONIST WHO ORGANIZED THE SHILOH BAPTIST CHURCH, MOTHER CHURCH OF NORTH CAROLINA. And I thought, I'll be! An anti-slavery preacher, and one who was well thought of hereabouts, to boot.

Paps Prentiss, who was probing the wall shelves, came upon a Bible as big as a strongbox, with the date September 27, 1729, inscribed inside the front cover in a fancy and flowing script. I read it at him, and he replied, eyes agog at his discovery: "This place was raised well before the war for freedom from the king!"

It pained me some to have to blaspheme a site such as this. I didn't tell the men to be gentle—wasn't no place for gentle in war and soldiering. We pulled down the purple velvet draping that lined the walls behind the pulpit and cut it to usable size, to fashion curtains that would obscure the view of whoever might be attempting to spy inside. We then upset the pews and constructed a rectangular redoubt in one corner of the nave, behind which we might find cover from the onslaught of Minié balls that, if all went as Draper hoped, were likely to rain in upon us.

Once that was done, we turned up the lanterns so that they burned bright, then positioned ourselves inside the makeshift fortress of overturned pews. It was quiet beyond the walls of the church. Our task was to make the opposite within, to create a ruckus like more than was actually our number and thus give the impression of being the bulk of the battalion. My task, as commander, was to keep us alive once the ruse had had its effect and the shooting began. Hews had found two long sticks, used for cleaning the upper reaches of the windows. He took one and I the other, and at regular intervals, each of us reached out to rustle the curtains and create the semblance of movement. Past this, the men sat hunched up, largely silent.

I asked Zach Gregory, "How are your feet?" He'd complained to Corporal Mitchell of painful blisters.

"We are blessed for having shoes," said Gregory. "But two weeks marching in them! Lordy, Sergeant. Mine just rub me raw."

Paps said, "It's the constant water. Damp makes the leather go tight."

"It give me foot-swell such as I ain't ever had," said Gregory. "And believe you me, Mass made sure my feet had plenty of occasion for puffing."

I took up the long stick and gave the window curtains a shake. "Have you got socks?"

"Replaced my holed ones in Elizabeth City, but it don't seem to make a difference."

"Raise them up," said Gaylord. "Raise them such that they are overhigh of your heartbeat. It's good against the swelling."

He spoke it with an assuredness that I was not used to hearing of him. Nor was anyone else, for that matter, judging by the general silence that followed.

Gregory readjusted himself and kicked his feet up onto a laid-over pew.

Paps looked slyly toward me then and slipped a small home-crafted clay jar from his haversack. "This here help the swelling a mite bit as well."

The others turned to see my response.

Paps was a good man, but too old for soldiering such as we were doing. He marched well and fired a musket better than many, but his old-uncle ways made him over-wary and slow to react. Yet in this mission, he was proving a benefit.

I reached out my hand, and when he placed the jar there, I uncorked it and turned myself up a sip. It felt of fire but tasted of grape. I passed it to Gregory.

"But only the once and not too deep a pull," I cautioned. To the others, I added: "Just enough to help keep out the cold."

They all laughed.

Around our circle the clay jar went, working its way back to Paps. He took his turn and replaced it in his haver.

The old man then produced a deck of cards. "I ain't one to push idolatrous diversions on true believers, but my specie don't spend out here in Jeff Davis country and my change purse is getting awful heavy to tote."

The men seemed to perk up at this, but I quashed their keenness right away. "We may be but decoys in this operation," said I, "but let us be attentive ones all the same, lest some sign or signal be overlooked, to our detriment."

The group fell still. I reached out and gave the curtains another shake.

Single Phillips said, kind of smirkly, "This'd be a fine site to meet your Maker, eh, Hews? That would show her good."

Others sniggered.

"What's this?" asked I.

Hews dropped his face and said, "Barbery, Sergeant."

I knew not of what he spoke.

"His wife," explained Zach Gregory.

"His *was*-wife," Single Phillips corrected, and the sniggering was general then and grew to outright laughter.

"I thought it known about the company," said Hews, more angry than embarrassed, though a bit of both. He had at the curtains with the second stick. "She was owned by Judge Winston, over to the next farm beyond the one where I was worked. By and by, she took up with another boy, from her own farm, and she would not have me visit no more. It's what spurred my running off to join up—to be fully shed of her." He gave the curtains another vigorous shake, and he smiled broad. "But I have met Miss Anna Lipscomb, over in Norfolk, and we will be married in the church there upon our return to Freedom."

I looked about the group. "And youall find this funny?"

There was silence.

Phillips said, "Well, a mite, sir. The Anna Lipscomb part—that this nigger would be such a damn fool all over anew!"

And all yawped and chortled. Me, too.

Zach Gregory said, "This task we on, Sergeant . . ."

His pause stretched overmuch.

"Go on, speak up," said I.

"It ain't the best of tasks. The colonel has us as targets for Rebby rifle practice."

"Who would you have do it?" said I. "Fields Midgett? Josh Land? Them brothers Ephraim and Leon Bember?"

"Well, maybe Leon Bember," said Paps. "I ain't heard a worser mouth than the one that boy has got on him."

Hooting and titters broke the tightness that had befallen our group.

But I wasn't done. "This here is soldiering, son," said I, insistent, "what we signed up for. Someone has to stand elbow-to-elbow in the front row of a battle line and take the enemy's volley. There is no victory without that some of us do this. And without victory, we are all of us for certain doomed to worse than what it was we fled in the first place."

Their silence seemed different now, anxious still, yet glowing of the honorable feeling of self-sacrifice. It was my duty to instill this in them, either by fear, as Revere would do, or by a shaming logic, as was more my wont. All the same, I hoped to pull each and every one of them through to the other side of it.

Paps seemed as despising of silence as he was of passing two seconds without beaming that coon-show smile of his. "I was a shantyman before joining up," he said. "Did youall know this?"

We all did, for he had on many and many an occasion told it. Hews gave the curtains to one side a shake, and I those to the other.

"Shantymen the most hardy men they is," Paps said, and the others offered piqued protestation.

"You boys care to know the reason?" He spoke overtop them. "Because of our beauteous voices and not just our foredaunting brawn."

He kicked into song then before anyone might retort:

"Hey, Capt'n, Capt'n, you must be blind.

Look at your watch, it's quitting time."

His lyrics were met with chuckles, but the old man indeed had the harp in his mouth, his singing voice full and bright in a way that his speaking voice was not. It was a joy to hear.

I likewise recognized another usefulness to his song. Though we were but fifteen, to the darkness outside, our back-and-forth booming would sound like an army.

"Hey, Capt'n, Capt'n, how can it be? . . ." sang Paps.

The others called back: "Hey, Capt'n, Capt'n, how can it be?"

"Whistle keep a-blowing, you keep a-working me . . ."

"Whistle keep a-blowing, you keep a-working me!"

Then began the banging—just thunderous!—so many guns popping off at once, firing in from what seemed all sides.

"Get down, men! Get down!" I cried. "Bellies to the floorboards, flat as snakes!"

Windows shattering and the makeshift curtains come down, splinters of glass and batten wood zinging just over our barricade or thudding into it. Minié balls ripping all around. And outside, yipping and Rebel-yelling.

This was my first test under fire, and I did not feel fear like I'd thought I might. My heart raced, but my head was calm, steady.

The volley of musketry of a sudden worsened, but not the spray of glass and wood. In fact, inside the church went still.

Outside, there was higgledy-piggledy commotion and roars instead of the yipping. Another volley, sounding from another direction. It went on for several minutes. Then echoed a command to cease fire, and there was huzzahing.

I rose up, cautious at first. Took a hasty count of my men coming uncrouched around me. "Phillips, Gregory," said I, "is everybody okay? Paps?"

"Yes" and "Yessir, Sergeant" came back.

Many of the lanterns had been shot out, but in the shimmering penumbra that remained, Hews appeared, silent, his face streaked red. The wetness coursed from beneath his forage cap. Paps, the others, agitated toward him, and me likewise. This caused him to reach for the wound, his facets gone from dazed and blank to of-a-sudden distressed. He ran a hand through his crop of hair.

"Aw, it ain't nothing, youall," said he, slapping away the others' reaching hands, though he was clearly relieved himself. "Ain't but a nick."

We all settled, laughing now.

"Dang, Miles!" said Single Phillips. "I thought you trying to chagrin your old Barbery after all."

"By my own death!" said Hews. "Getting shot just to shame her treachery? Naw, son. I will live long for Miss Anna Lipscomb."

We laughed some more.

My men were all accounted for. We'd made it through the skirmish at Shiloh, though the church had not. She was shot up something terrible, with every window destroyed and chips and holes peppering the walls.

The great front door burst open and in strode Colonel Draper. "Etheridge, are you and your men all right?"

"Oh, Mass Colonel, sir!" said Paps, forestalling my reply. "Lawdy, our hearts is gladdened to see you!"

I added, for official confirmation, "We're all fine, sir."

Draper, his smile a-beaming, clapped me on the back—not very colonel-like. He turned in the doorway and faced the night, bellowing at the top of his lungs. "Run, you poltroon Elliott! We know your tactics better than you. Run, boy, for we are coming!"

All of us broke into huzzahs now, inside the church and out, then took to singing "Babylon Is Fallen!" We were 250 strong—less the skirmishers, and Revere and the swamp men, still out on our flanks—and we crowded around the church's front door. After twice belting "John Brown," Paps led the men in ribald shanties that cursed Johnny Reb and the cowardly bushwhackers. Colonel Draper did not discourage it. The opposite. He removed his hat and, standing between Paps and Robinson Tynes, caterwauled to beat the band. I even saw Backuss's lips moving heartily, his voice lost among the rest. We sang and sang, shanty after shanty, deep into the night.

CHAPTER NINETEEN

The next morning, Draper, with me by his side, learned from Revere that it was a band of seventy-odd bushwhackers that was driven back. "Any casualties?" he asked.

"The tracks show there was likely some wounded."

"No dead?"

Revere did not reply. His protracted stare was his answer.

The three of us stood just inside the doorway of the church. "Is there something more?" asked Draper.

"It's said a detachment of the Gray Ghost's men have come down from Virginia, along with what's left of Clapson's bushwhackers, and joined up with the raiders hereabouts, under Cy Grandy. They were the ones last night."

"Not Elliott?"

Revere's dead face was again his reply.

Elliott was Draper's target, but for me, this news was a consolation, as it meant that Patrick would not have been among our attackers of the previous evening. Joseph Etheridge had said that he'd joined up with Elliott's band.

"The Gray Ghost?" asked I, and Revere offered not even a flinch my way.

"John Mosby," Draper explained, "a notorious guerrilla captain who has harassed our forces ceaselessly between Richmond and the capital." He turned back to Revere. "Down here? Are your sources sure?"

"Nothing is sure," said the other, adding, "but guerrillas are guerrillas. Does it make a difference?"

Draper dismissed Revere, who rejoined his detachment, awaiting a-mount on the edge of our camp. The colonel said to me, "Etheridge, take this down." He paused until I'd loosed some paper from my haver. "'To all citizens,' new paragraph. 'Anyone harboring or otherwise abetting in the least ways any guerrillas, either local or from abroad, shall not be spared,' end paragraph. Signed, 'Alonzo G. Draper, Colonel, Volunteers.'"

I finished my scribbling, thinking about that fool Revere and half mumbling to myself: "And so through the night goes this cry of alarm . . ." Revere would heartily approve of this public warning. He'd maybe even see it as license to unleash his swamp men to loot the hamlet and commit other such depredations.

"Pardon?" said Draper.

I didn't realize I'd spoken loud enough to be heard. "Nothing, sir."

"The poem?" His smile broke up the tangle of beard that had, since our departure from Freedom, spread over his mouth and cheeks.

I recited what I recalled of it:

"And so through the night goes this cry of alarm
A cry of defiance, to every village and farm . . ."

I had to think on it a moment.

"A knock in the darkness, a knock at the door,
And a voice echoing . . . evermore!"

"Ha!" said Draper. "I suspected you for a literary man, but didn't know you were a devotee of Longfellow."

"Sir?"

"Longfellow," said he as though I should recognize the name. When it was clear that I did not, he set in:

"Listen, my children, and you shall hear
Of the midnight ride of Paul Revere,
On the eighteenth of April, in Seventy-five:
Hardly a man is now alive
Who remembers that famous day and year."

He went on at some length, much more than Revere had offered up, until he arrived at what must have been the very, very long poem's end. It was an impressive display.

He looked sheepish then, as though embarrassed. "I have a gift for recall."

A gift for recall? This was understatement. I remembered his unending recitation of the Lieber Code. He seemed to retain word for word whatever was put before him.

He removed his slouch hat and ran a hand through his topmost crop of hair, a deliberate gesture, to deflect the focus elseways than on himself. "And you," he said, "how is it you've come to know and love books so well? I thought them off-limits to slaves."

"I had a mistress who didn't like to be told what to do."

"Well, bully for her, then."

Sure, why not? And likewise bully for me, for I had played along with Sarah's safe rebellions. Sarah and Patrick and me—John B.'s ungovernable children.

I said, "The poem, though—it was Sergeant Revere I heard to recite it. Me, I don't properly know it."

"Sergeant Revere either, really, though what I heard was a close approximation." He paused, pensive. "Revere, eh? . . ."

"Sir?"

"It's called 'Paul Revere's Ride,' by Henry Longfellow. I wonder if Revere is truly his name or one he chose once he joined our lines, in regard for the poem."

The former Obediah Peters. And so through the night, indeed!

"Back to the task at hand," Draper said, returning his hat to his head. "Find material with which to make broadsides." He pointed toward the portraits on the walls, some of which had slipped slant-wise. All were in one way or another spoiled. "The backs of those paintings, if you must. Then post a few about town. Keep the rest for farther along our route."

He moved through the door.

"And leave off the literary flourishes," he added, smiling. "Just the directive, as dictated."

I enlisted Tynes and Sergeants Merritt Pool and Thomas Artis of G to join me. By halving the portraits with Artis's penknife, we had sufficient stock to make some twenty-odd posters. Miles Hews took charge of seeing four of them put up around Shiloh. We kept the rest for other places upcoming.

Colonel Draper consulted his list of abettors of the irregulars, . compiled from the captured enemy reports. He found two names that were cited as being from here. We located their residences. They stood side by side, as it turned out.

With our companies at attention afore them, Draper had me take a squad and evacuate the dwellings. "You, not Backuss," said he. "I want the Rebels and anyone of sympathetic inclination toward the Rebel cause to see Negroes exacting the cost of disloyalty."

Though he was no longer ranked, I ordered Fields with ten men into the house on the right, hoping the gesture might take him and me a first step toward reconciliation. His face didn't register appreciation. It did not change one whit, remaining as blank as the canvas of a sail. But he hopped to and executed the assignment.

I led ten others into the house on the left. I knocked harshly, then burst through the door, hustling in and thereon hustling the inhabitants back out—a man my age or thereabouts, his wife and young son. Fields's squad had found a larger group, with what appeared to be grandparents alongside a husband, wife, and three young tykes. The entire bunch was held at gunpoint in the lot beyond the houses.

After taking one last turn through the first domicile to make sure no one remained, I spread fuel from their lanterns overtop of whatever looked like it might readily catch—under the ticking of the sofa, on the window curtains, all such as this. I then scooped lit coals from the hearth into a long-handled pot and distributed it about. Flames jumped up quickly. I repeated the procedure next door. It was all efficiently done.

Draper announced loudly: "Citizens of Shiloh! The penalty for disloyalty shall be severe!"

Within minutes, smoke billowed from every opening left ajar. Glass panes burst out on account of the crackling heat. The men of the two families screamed protest, and one rushed toward the flames to attempt to snuff them out. Fields and Hews forced him to the ground and used their knees to keep him there.

No townsmen turned out of their houses, though the curtains of the neighboring windows shifted to allow for viewing.

When the flames had grown to where no amount of water might douse them, Draper turned toward the battalion. "We move out, men! Forward, march!"

He led us out of the town.

"Damn you!" cried the man whom Fields and Hews had restrained. "May God damn you all to Hell!"

I heard Fields's retort, though the man himself could not: "I am already there."

The **bushwhackers** took to potshooting our march up the Indiantown road. But their here-and-again sniping didn't accomplish much beyond displacing our pickets, who would rush toward the position only to find it abandoned, not a soul in sight. After the first few times, the battalion hardly even slowed with each crack of rifle fire.

"They're probing our line," said Colonel Draper, "feeling us out for exposure."

We made periodic stops along our route. At each house from the colonel's list, fire was applied as rough medicine for poor association. Draper varied the sergeants to lead the procedure. "To assure that morale is kept up equally across the companies," he whispered down to me from his saddle.

He was generally such a reserved and composed man. It was odd to see him derive such pleasure from these doings.

His tactic worked, though. As we paraded up the road, our men boomed "Go Down Moses," a song most-all knew from bondage times. Our voices echoed into the trees, all the way to the pocosin beyond.

At the third stop, a stately manor not a mile south of Indiantown proper, we found eight bondmen but no masters. A blanketing drizzle had settled in. The slaves, who were mostly very old women and men, confirmed to Draper that the house's owner was in league with the bushwhacker gangs hereabouts.

"More than just this," said one old pappy. "Mass Sanderlin be currently raising his own outfit of Partisan Rangers."

Draper assigned Thomas Artis, G's sergeant, to take charge of the torching.

The battalion had been collecting contrabands as we'd progressed—maybe thirty, including these new arrivals. Most were aged like these ones, or terribly crippled. All would have difficulty traveling. General Wild had believed the country to be mostly empty of colored, given all the canvassing in the neighborhood during our occupation of Elizabeth City. He was wrong, though, and this was proving a problem. Where Wild's large column was meant to be a sword thrusting toward Currituck Courthouse, our smaller one was to be its cutting edge, striking at the irregulars who peopled the region. The new arrivals threatened to compromise our mission by hindering our mobility.

I ordered Hews to confiscate what carts and draught animals he could find hereabouts and join them to our ambulance wagons, which were already full of previously chanced-upon colored. I found the colonel and let him know what I'd done.

He nodded but seemed distracted, looking off toward the Sanderlin house.

He then made a gesture toward the unceasing drizzle. "Be sure to keep your sword dry of the lingering moisture," he said. "Otherwise, it'll rust."

This was an obvious thing to a colored man raised to domestic duty, what I myself might tell a tyke, to begin teaching him the oversight of things.

"Done, sir," said I, though it was at times like this that the obligatory "sir" felt bitterly akin to saying "Mass" to me.

He remained preoccupied, notably so. Further, his horse had taken to whinnying and pawing at the ground with a foreleg, its ears flicking back and forth. I'd seen Syntax behave such as this back home, when anxious.

We were being watched, and by unfriendly eyes. The horse clearly sensed it.

Our battalion had tarried here too long. We were disorganized and now vulnerable. Captain Smith and the bulk of Company I were spread out among the chattel houses. Likewise G, in the neighboring domiciles.

"Colonel, sir—" said I, aiming to forewarn him of my apprehension. But he stared fixedly at the manor house yon.

He dropped then from the saddle, grave of countenance, and strode toward its front doors.

"Sergeant Tynes!" I called, and he came forward. "Take your squad and form a battle line along that fence."

It faced the pocosin, two hundred yards distant.

"Yes, sir," said he.

I chased after Draper. Passing into the house, I found him in the great room, his pistol drawn, staring at the entrance to another space. He waved curtly to bid me to be quiet. I made my way to him. In the room beyond, a dining hall, were Sergeant Artis and three of his privates—Shadrach Keyes and two men I didn't recognize—stuffing silverware and varied ornaments into pockets and havers and knapsacks, whatever would accommodate their treasure. One half-wit was trying to wrestle a candelabra into the sleeve of his greatcoat.

This was what had caused Draper's unease, passed along to his horse, not bushwhackers in the tree line. He took two strides forward and fired his pistol—at the half-wit's arse-end, I thought, but in fact just near enough so that the man felt a proper warmth there.

Startled, Artis and the rest stopped their doings and looked up.

"Sergeant, what's going on here?" said Draper.

No one spoke. All looked pained.

Me, too. I was outraged at them fool Negroes, looting such as they were.

I also felt a tinge of guilt for finding myself on the side of the white man in this incident. It somehow recalled the night of the discipling of Fields.

"Sergeant!" said Draper, echoing his earlier inquisition, only more sternly now.

Artis said, "It would all be spoiled in the fire, Colonel, sir. So what difference that we take us some?"

"What difference?" Draper looked genuinely flummoxed, if not by the question itself then by Artis's audacity in asking it. "We will abide by military order and discipline, this is the difference. You, of all men, should know this, Sergeant."

Lieutenant Backuss and Captain Smith burst into the room, other troopers following.

Glaring yet at the guilty men, Draper said, "Were we encamping here, I'd have the lot of you traced up by the thumbs on the village square." He turned then toward the officers. "Place these *thieves* under arrest. Manacle them and strip them of their uniforms. If they have on undergarments, bully for them. If not, they shall march without. But they are not fit to wear the Union blue." Draper added, again facing the guilty ones: "Keep them on the column's flank for all the others to see, until we can transfer them to General Wild's column and they join the other miscreants and prisoners."

My heart was gladdened that he'd saddled the officers with this dour chore and not laid it on me.

As to Backuss and Smith, neither appeared in the least bothered by the order. Smith asked, "Their brogans, too? We've a ways to go, sir, and their marching barefoot over frozen ground may slow the battalion's advance."

Draper turned toward Artis and the other three. "Let them keep their shoes."

I sought Artis's eyes, to ask of them with an earnest look: Why, Thomas? Why would you do this? . . .

He faced the floor and would not look up.

Backuss waved over some nearby troopers. They took the guilty ones roughly by the collar and shoved them out of the room. Backuss seemed to derive pleasure from it.

When it was just the colonel and me, I said, "Is it wise, sir?"

"Pardon?" He again wore an expression of bafflement, like the one at Artis's earlier attempt at justification.

I let it all out in one long breath to preclude him from interjecting or otherwise interrupting: "The punishment, sir, this shaming punishment. They've been treated—we *all* have been treated—as less than men our whole lives. As beasts of burden, no better than the ones we were made to drive out in the fields. Humiliation was our daily course. Artis and them, they know they've done wrong, they were caught red-handed at it. Punish them with extra duty or reduction in rank—or imprison them if you must. But don't publicly shame them like you might an over-eager dog that has wet the front-room carpet. Do not rub their noses in it. Leave them their dignity, Colonel. Especially out here in the country we all heretofore come from, in front of kinfolk as well as former owners."

It occurred to me to, but I chose not to mention Revere's swamp men and their suspectly-got new costumery.

I merely added: "It'll go a long way with the men, sir, to know you're capable of understanding our previous experience, of seeing things as we do, from our view."

He didn't on the spot respond, and I didn't give him much chance to. I saluted and left, as that was all of this conversation I cared to partake in. What I'd said had needed saying, and if there were consequences for me, then so be it. Draper had taught me things on leading. This time, it was him that needed teaching.

The battalion passed through the center of Indiantown, a hamlet not so unlike Shiloh, in size and also in the shuttered-up disposition of its domiciles. Artis, Keyes, Green Whitfield, and Washington Darby (as I learned the other two thieves were called) were confined to the wagon train at the rear—bound at the wrists but fully clothed—not off to the side of our column as some spectacle to behold.

I will confess to appreciating this—the colonel's effort at understanding. He'd heard what I'd said.

The neighborhood was hardly empty of slaves, as Wild and Draper had anticipated it would be, and bondmen continued to attach themselves to our column. Ten more came away with us at Indiantown, one, a ma'am with her four tykes. For the transportation of themselves and their things, they chose the ornamented buggy of their erstwhile owner, not for its practical purpose—the five of them barely fit along the single bench seat—but for its style. They sang ditties, and the children attempted at dancing in the tight space of the buggy, wearing what had clearly been the Sunday clothes of their masters.

Not far along the road to Sandy Hook, our next destination, Draper hailed me forward. He didn't give me an order to relay as I'd expected. Instead, he dismounted and, leading his horse by the reins, ambled forward. He seemed to want me to join him.

"You know, Etheridge," said he, thoughtful, facing the ground rather than the route afore us, "I'd never met a Negro before my enlistment in the service."

"Aren't there any up in Massachusetts?" said I, though I knew full well that there were.

"Some, sure, but not many." He glanced toward me but beyond, at the North River pocosin in the distance, on our flank. "Not enough to note in Lynn, anyway, where I'm from."

I let the silence ride, as I didn't know what he intended with this.

"I'm an Abolitionist," he said, quickly, "have been my whole life."

"I do not doubt it, sir," said I. And I didn't.

"I've always seen my mission as to the downtrodden. Back home, before enlisting, I led the journeymen shoemakers—cordwainers, cobblers, and the like—on a workmen's strike, to earn their fair due. Did you know that?"

How would I? I didn't even know that he'd been a shoemaker. I had heard that he was read in the law.

"The rights of the common man must pertain as much as those of the gentry," he continued, speechifying now, as for effect, "for how do we, by spurious notions of natural right, deny fellow men a decent wage with which to feed their wives and children? I launched a well-read broadside to achieve this end and canvassed most of New England and New York, drumming up support. Even those opposed to my positions praised me, in speeches and print alike, as someone who always 'invariably counseled moderation' and 'deprecated, at all times, any resort to violence.' These were their very words, Etheridge."

I found myself unsurprised by the things he was telling me. Sure, he tended to keep a certain distance from us others, as a commander should. But unlike so many officers, it didn't seem from scorn or mistrust.

He looked me dead on then, confiding again as he had at the Pool house back in Elizabeth, and it felt equally odd now. "Making hostages of women? Burning and razing property? Me, the 'man of moderation,' undertaking these sorts of behaviors?"

I, too, had been surprised by the Brigade's descent into the terrible. Still, I felt a need to defend the general.

"When bushwhackers lurk about in every direction," I said, "and are irreconciled with the message that we carry, maybe moderation isn't what is called for."

This didn't appear to ease his mind. Nor did it mine, really. For I was also finding the general's actions increasingly difficult to stomach, as with the boy Daniel Bright.

"Maybe comes a time when we are all new people," I went on, trying for better, "unfamiliar even to our own selves. When seraphim become fiendish and lambs lupine, we do what needs doing because the times dictate it."

He smiled. "I suppose so, Etheridge."

I'd meant my words as a period and not a comma, and thought our powwow done. But he didn't remount his bay, continuing to amble along. So I didn't quit his side.

Finally, he said, "There was another thing I wanted to talk with you about."

"Sir?"

He looked to be searching for how to say it. When he found it, I wasn't sure he hadn't misaimed.

"It seems to me that what makes you and your lot good soldiers has to do with what was beaten into you to make you learn to submit. Soldiers and slaves, their daily surrender to authority is similar. The thievery earlier, well—soldiers will be tempted to take spoils, regardless their race. I encountered it in my previous unit and punished the guilty in the manner I was prepared to employ with those men today, had it not been for your intervention. You were right to call my attention to the difference. But there are other things . . ."

His meaning remained woolly, so I couldn't interject to help get him there.

"Some of what I encounter with the men . . ." he said. "It surprises."

"Sir?"

"More than that, it discomfits."

I was at a complete loss now, and he must have recognized it, for he finally arrived at his point head-on. "Privates Prentiss and Dozier in your company, others in the Brigade. They insist on calling me 'master,' and it causes me great embarrassment."

This made me smile. I felt a kind of relief, too, that this was his reaction to it.

I explained, "It's the older men, most often as not. I've reiterated to Prentiss the proper way of addressing you, as 'sir' or 'colonel.' Prentiss, Dozier, the others, they know better. But maybe 'sir' and 'master' is all of a thing to them—as you said, soldiers and slaves sharing a similar training and all."

He took this in without response, and I took his silence as inducement to say more.

"And maybe what causes you discomfort is a comfort to them, sir. You see, Prentiss has been a slave his whole life. Now you say he is a man but call him a private and have him do slavely chores, cleaning latrines and digging entrenchments and the other things we been doing back at the fort. Because, truth be told, this raid excepted, our soldierly lives have much resembled the previous ones."

"Me, my interest has *only* been in the instruction of you men at becoming a good fighting troop," said he, defensive, "never in the upkeep, much less the betterment, of the base. Those directives come from above."

"I know it, we all do. But yours is the face relaying the message."

He took this in, again in silence.

I said, "Being driven to do things we might not choose to otherwise, were the choice truly ours—well, sir, maybe in those circumstances, 'master' might to some men seem as appropriate a term of address as 'colonel.' You might not deserve it, but neither did we deserve the lot we were born to."

He again smiled. "To each his cross to bear, I suppose."

He began to remount but stopped and turned back to me. "If I'm the slave master in the framework as you lay it out, then what does that make you and the other sergeants?"

"Drivers," said I. "Drivers and overseers. My cross to bear."

And I smiled—though rather than jestful, it felt like an observation true.

He climbed atop his big bay. "Well, anyway, Etheridge, all this is to say, thank you for your intervention on behalf of Sergeant Artis and his men. Your advice was sound—no, it was wise and just."

A commotion caught our attention just then, fevered hoofbeats approaching. Revere rounded the bend ahead, riding with some dispatch. Draper rushed forward. Me, I called over toward the battalion, "Relief, halt!" and heard the order repeated down the length of the line. I watched Draper and Revere conferring, their horses wheeling about one another, still riled.

When Draper returned, his countenance was stern and grave. "Double-time the men forward," said he. Then he turned his horse and galloped up around the bend.

I bellowed, "Forward! At the double-time!" and the column jumped to.

With F at the top of the battalion and me at the top of F, I arrived before the rest, and what I met with stopped me dead. Men pushed up behind me, my company and then the others, bending a bunched semi-circle around the patch of field where Draper and Revere and the swamp men sat atop their horses, staring upwards. All were silent but for two of the swamp men, one sobbing audible, slumped in the saddle, his shoulders jerking, the other field-hollering over the wails of the first:

"I stood at the River of Jor-dan

To see that ship sailing o-over"

Three lengths of planking had been twined together to make one stout crossbeam, and it had been posed between the upper reaches of two thick-trunked oaks. From there hung four bodies, two men and a woman—their tongues grossly bulging the *o*'s of their lips, their necks hideously kinked—and a baby, him by his right foot. He was naked and upside down, the free leg dangling loose and misbent at the hip. It was clear that this had been recently done, as their clothes were rumpled but not overly thus and there was no evidence of scavengers about—little pecks of blood and their eyes gouged out.

"I stood at the River of Jor-dan

To see that ship sailing o-over"

A placard was strung over the head of one of the men. It read: THESE NIGGERS HANGED BY ORDER OF CAPTAIN CYRUS W. GRANDY.

A rejoinder to what Wild had posted on the boy Bright, back at River Bridge.

Colonel Draper commanded, "Cut them down, cut them down from there," and Revere and Golar set to it, and praise Jesus for this. For the idea of being tasked with this, of ordering my men to do it, repulsed me to the core.

"Oh Mama, don't ya weep
When you see that ship sail over
Shout, Glory, hallelu-jah!
When you see the ship sail by."

CHAPTER TWENTY

Draper dispatched Revere's detachment to relay to the general word of this grim reply to our River Bridge escalation. I ordered Aaron Mitchell to form a detail to bury the dead, appropriately but hurriedly, for we were in a vulnerable position, surrounded on two sides by thick woods and the pocosin not one hundred yards distant. And before four holes could be dug ankle-deep, my suspicions were proved right. Firing commenced—and in earnest—from the line of trees and brush bordering the swamp.

The force out there was big enough to overwhelm our skirmishers before warning of its presence could be brought in—a *big* force. Blooms of musket-fire burst from the foliage, here and there and there, unceasing. They were two hundred bushwhackers if they were two, and their muskets were belting out a riotous, rough chorus.

I called toward F. "On me! Form up on me!"

Likewise, other commanders regrouped their troopers into rifle lines, two deep and elbow to elbow. As my men fell into place, I heard bellowed "Fire!" and "Fire, men!"

I heard, "Give it to them!"

I heard, "Faster, now! Lay it on!"

I heard, "At will, men! Aim, fire, load! Aim, fire, load!" and it was me yelling it. I was feeling all-over alike and touching at nowhere, swirling that sword in a circle above my head, then pointing it at the trees and yelling: "Low, men—aim low! The kick will land your ball nearer to home!"

Just like we'd been instructed back at Freedom, with broomsticks and whatever shrubbery might simulate a weapon, before General Wild had procured us proper musketry two weeks prior.

"Aim, fire, load!"

Smoke had risen up all over the field like a fog, and the tart smell of black powder burned my nostrils. I felt hot, as though a wind had somehow blown in from summer.

The colonel rode among us, barking, "Command staff, on me!"

I dashed over to Draper. He was directing: "We will form skirmish lines here and here"—he pointed to the places on the field—"and get men to their left and to their right. Smith, you work Company I around the left flank. Keep your men moving." And to Backuss: "Lieutenant, push F around the right and when within charging distance, regroup and overrun their position!" He then shouted, "Etheridge, on me," and he went headlong toward the middle of the field, toward G's rifle line, where the enemy fire was most heated.

I followed while the companies executed the maneuvers.

Lieutenant Conant and one of his sergeants kept G a-going, volley for volley. Smith, on the left, had Company I moving gamely. Out on the right, though, I saw that Backuss had the men fix their bayonets too damned early. It slowed their run, an arcing loop across the field. The men were scattered, awkward, and the bushwhackers, noting the long pikes, gleaned the point of F's movement—their aim to charge and take the position. The Rebels now focused all of it on my company, on my men.

The thunder of their concentrated musket-fire caused me to start.

I paced up and back behind the rifle line where Draper had situated us, screaming, "Faster, men, faster, faster!"

The men of G did as I bid them. It was deafening but in no way lessened the force of the Rebel fire tearing through the ranks of F.

Captain Smith, out on the left, wasn't faring much better. Company I was likewise disorganized and bogging down, even with the enemy muskets focused elsewhere.

Then Backuss broke F's charge, though they were only part-ways across the field. Waving his sword, he directed the men toward a battered outbuilding just farther along, the only upright thing and possible shelter in proximity.

Draper, his horse skipping in place and yipping, hollered out at them: "No, no! Advance, advance!"

F was huddling at the shack.

Draper turned toward Smith and his company's leftward slog, then back at Backuss. He screamed, "For Christ's sake, advance, advance, advance!"

"I will get them on it again," shouted I up at him. "F, sir."

He looked down over his bay's thick neck, pausing.

Then, "Yes, Etheridge. Go!"

It was as hairy a run as I had yet known—up to that point in my life and since still—loping with what felt like lazy-legs across that empty one-hundred-yard stretch, all of Cy Grandy's rough fiends watching a-goggle. Well, watching at first—surprised, I supposed, to see anyone embark upon such a foolhardy undertaking. Then they recovered themselves and opened up on me. Opened up full-on.

I had wanted in it, and mister, I was in it.

I saw Fields rally up a bunch of men and come around the side of the windowless shack toward me. They returned the Rebel fire—there was Hews and Phillips and Land, others too. I ran and ran, expecting to get hit and fall, and yet I did not, and I reached Fields. I patted him as warm a thank-you against his shoulder as I knew how, and he returned it in kind. It felt a joyous reunion.

Bullets pounded the batten-boarding on the side opposite my company; the wall drummed a rataplan better than Little Charley Brown ever could on his instrument. Yet the all-overish feeling had quit me. Without consulting Backuss, I had F gather up in a thick bunch.

I'd known enough successes in my life, regardless how minor, to know that failure was not my given lot. I'd not lost toes to a merciless master; when I cast my seine net, I pulled in fish. And my men! I eyed Josh Land and Miles Hews and Jessie Brooks—just a glancing look and a smile. If anyone's heart was sick with fear, I could not see it.

"This is what we joined up for," said I. "This right here! The field is ours. We shall tip Paps Prentiss's jug to our victory once we have reached the trees and are standing with a foot atop a dead Rebby-boy's neck."

They rousened up a hearty cry at this.

I eyed Fields, who was eyeing me back.

"Squad A!" This was the squad he formerly corporaled, and I addressed them as though he corporaled it yet. "You will double-time it around to the left. The rest on me, and we go to the right. We shall take this patch or rest in it alongside that family back there that got strung up on account of these bushwhacking sons of bitches."

I took to waving my sword back and forth over my head like mad. "Arms, port! Move, men—move!"

And we set off.

Our movements starboard and port around that shack were clearly disorienting, for the Rebel fire came only stutteringly at first.

"Look lively, men!" I called, for I knew the Rebels to be regrouping. "Charge, charge!"

Some men roared as they ran, and this set others to roaring, too, and I heard Thomas Saunders's cackle of a laugh. Me, my throat burned, my limbs trembled—but this in no way impeded my run nor my order-hollering. As I was the one waving the sword, much fire seemed aimed on me. Balls whistled by, and two struck my haversack in quick succession. It felt like fishes nibbling.

I saw Gaylord drop to a knee, raise his rifle, and fire, then commence to reload.

I shouted: "No, no! Get 'em up, move forward!"

Hews of a sudden was there aside him. He'd heard my cry or read my mind, and he was pulling Gaylord up by the arm, and waving up the others who had stopped or slowed too, getting them going. "Let's go, Jones!" I heard him call.

Then he fell, he dropped straight down.

He'd been hit more than once, his head smashed and the right arm a mere red rag. Gaylord bent toward him, then also dropped, collapsed like wet sails off a spar.

"Keep moving!" I yelled to the rest, and I kept us moving, and we left Hews and Gaylord where they lay, their muskets alongside them, Gaylord's ramrod sticking out of the barrel.

In displacing so much of his force to counter us, the Rebel chieftain had left his rear exposed to Smith, who was being reinforced by Revere and the swamp men, galloping out of the woods to the west, guns a-banging. And meanwhile, the colonel continued to pour on volley after volley from the center of the field. Or maybe it was just that courage failed the Rebby-boys when faced with onrushing colored, their bayonets glinting. Whatever it was, the bushwhackers went tail down as we neared the trees, scrambling harum-scarum into the swamp in frenzied retreat.

I called out to F: "Form up and fire after them! Fire gamely!" I heard Fields calling likewise. We had to keep the men grouped together and not haphazardly setting off in pursuit.

Then I saw the orange cloth tied about the neck—stylish-like, with the knot to the side; I recognized the familiar gait. Patrick. I thought for certain it could not be him. These were Grandy's boys, and he was with Elliott. But I watched his flight and I knew.

He was running to the right, where so many of them were going left, leaping over felled limbs and thrashing through the muck. There was a musket and a Colt Navy six-shot on the ground a few yards off. I took up the pistol, assured it held balls, and plunged in after. Even as I knew it wrong to quit my post, punishably wrong, it was bigger than me.

I pushed into the pocosin, rushing as best I could, the water and sludge getting thicker and higher. Soon, the gloom of the trees came to overwhelm the sun. I lost him from view, and before long everything else, too, save the shadows. The sound of firing dimmed, increasingly distant, and I was uncertain how far I'd strayed from my company.

Off to the left, I heard a rustling. The foliage there seemed too well laid and thickly arranged. I burst in, and there was Patrick, on a thin patch of firm ground clearly designed to be a hide-out. I leveled the Colt at his head, advancing, full of a rage like none I had yet felt in my life—a screaming-to-the-heavens rage! Yet I did not scream, to Heaven nor elsewhere, and I did not fire.

Patrick looked resigned to it, to whatever was coming, with not a bit of fear and neither of protest. He wore butternut gray, forage cap to gaiters, and leaned back against a tree on the tiny rise of land surrounded by mire. He slipped down its trunk and sat there.

I sighted down the Colt's long barrel. "You were party with them that hung that family?"

"I had nothing to do with it."

"Nothing, Patrick?"

"No way, I could not do it."

"But you did not stop it?" said I.

"How was I to?" He stared up the length of that Colt back at me. "And find myself strung up there alongside them?"

His knees pulled to his chest, he looked a child, lost in the bulk of that butternut coat.

"Even the baby?" said I. "And the woman, Patrick? What if it had been Fanny?"

"That heifer," he'd called her. He'd tried to ravage her in the woods.

Patrick dropped his face onto his knees, and I wanted to explode a Minié ball into the melon of his head.

I did not fire.

I only then noticed that I had at some point abandoned my own greatcoat. I was cold, cold to the bone in the over-all wet of the swamp, and felt unmoored, my head airy and rolling, and I lost my breakfast into the wretchedness engulfing my feet. It all surged up and out of me and fouled the foul water.

There was a stump of tree on Paddy's tiny piece of land. I went over and sat on it, setting the long, heavy pistol on what little ground was available aside me. It was an easy, snap-of-the-wrist distance from him, and I saw that he recognized this. I knew he would not do it.

"What are you doing out here, Paddy?"

He didn't respond, just kept looking at me.

"Did you fire at me as I ran across the field? Did you want to kill me?"

"No, Dick," said he. "Hellfire, no."

He looked away then, and so did I.

"I thought you Elliott boys had fled west, into Perquimans." This was what Holman had told Wild.

"We doubled back. Joined up with Grandy's band and some others."

Though I should have, I didn't care about this intelligence. I wouldn't be able to relay it to Draper anyway, for how would I explain its provenance?

He said, "I lowered my rifle when I saw it was you, Dick. You know I did."

It was impossible to tell if he spoke truthfully.

There was a long pause before either of us said more. He did first.

"I just want back what's mine. Wasn't no possibility of regaining it on Roanoke, so I thought maybe out here."

I turned toward him. "What's yours? Like, me?"

He wouldn't return my gaze and did not attempt a reply. Instead, he said, "Strange times, these. Damned strange times. The old folks will die off and those of us that survive this will replace them. And what for? Uncle John will pass on and I will become him, but what will be left?"

As much as regretful, he seemed truly a-wonder at the puzzlement of it—that our freedom, my freedom, though previously implausible to him, had come to pass nonetheless; that I was a man, my own man, and would do my all to usher in Jubilee's arrival. But I marveled then and marvel yet at how he could not have recognized its dawning approach. If you look upon a man and see only a mule, is the fault his or your own? Patrick had known me since we were boys. We'd been game at whatever we undertook, and I gave as good as I got and bettered him more often than not. Yet where my knowledge of him had grown as we'd aged, his of me had only narrowed. When was it exactly that he came to see only a nigger?

"Why is it I always have to teach you a thing that you ought to have known of your own accord, Paddy? Why is it that, when it comes to colored, white folks need teaching every blessed time, and you have known me your whole blessed life and yet do not know it?"

We just sat there. Here and again was gunfire in the distance.

There was movement nearby, and Fields burst into our patch. He looked relieved to find me there, then distressed at my butternut counterpart. He leveled his rifle before recognizing the enemy as Patrick.

I didn't stop Fields nor intercede, whatever he might do—though I was not indifferent either. Who knew who it was that he sighted down the barrel of his rifle? Llewelyn Midgett? So much history, finally come to account?

Paddy just looked up at him as he had at me, as though he had yet to give one shit about the outcome of it all.

"Goddammit!" Fields lowered the rifle and sat.

Paddy said, "Why, this is kind of like the days gone by of our youth, ain't it?"

It was a poor joke.

And familiar all the same, for such had always been Paddy's jestful nature—mostly inappropriate, often poorly timed.

Fields said, "What are you doing, Richard?"

"For the time being, just sitting." I wasn't aiming to crack wise, just stating my condition of indecision.

Fields said, "We got to take him in. Got to." The cold smoked his breath as he spoke. "He done done what he done, and now we got to do what we must. Ain't two ways about it."

He was right, there weren't two ways. Paddy rode under the Black Flag, a land pirate, and Sand Bankers knew all about pirates and buccaneering, as we were known to harbor, and maybe even foster, too, some of them out there among us. And so the path Paddy had taken was not chosen from a place of ignorance.

Neither was I ignorant of the consequences of his choice: so many bodies slow spinning below improvised crossbeams, crab-apple-cheeked boys and broke-hipped babies and women.

Fields fiddled with the stock of his rifle. "I tell you what, when this is all done, me and mine, whatever's left of us, we're setting off for Africa, for certain sure." He didn't look up, yet spoke with a conviction I hadn't in a long while heard from him.

"Africa?" said I. "Truly, Fields?"

"Liberia," he said, "like is talked about among some of the men."

He had not before uttered word the first of this, not to me, anyway. I didn't even know he knew of that country's existence. "What about home?" I asked.

"Home! What is home?" He sniggered, sardonic. "Over there is freedom for colored. Even the name shouts this out. No matter the result of the fighting here, it ain't about our freedom. It's about union and who gets to say who tells us what to do."

"But Africa?" said Paddy. "And why not the moon?"

Both Fields and I gave him a look of *Shut it*.

In so doing, though, I realized that Paddy hadn't been completely wrong before. This indeed recalled of days gone by—the roles reversed, but familiar.

I told Fields, "Adkins studied on this, intending to go himself, and it was not for him."

"I'm not Adkins, Richard, just as I am not you. Your Sand Banks weren't ever what they was for me. So, how will what they hereon become be any different?"

He laid his rifle down and faced me directly.

"Some time back," he continued, "I come upon Revere, talking to Robinson Tynes and a few others about his plantation days. He was saying how, when his Mass would whoop him, which he said was often, he'd secretly revel in it. Sure, it hurt, he said—but with every lick that man gave, he was removing legal tender from his own damned wallet and couldn't even see it. This encouraged Revere to act out, despite the cost of it to himself."

There was gunfire again in the distance, and this caused him to pause. All three of us turned toward the sound.

When next there was only the whistling of crickets and rustling of leaves, Fields went on: "Revere said that, if he didn't even own his own self, what did he really have to lose? That's how that man thinks, and he's right, Richard. You ain't of this mind. You think some part of the Etheridge House reflects upon you, like its grandness says something about *you*. But Revere is right. Ain't nothing here in this country says anything good to my ear."

Paddy jumped in. "We are Bankers, Fields, born to it and made of it. Uncle John once told me that we was all of a piece out there, that living on an island makes it so."

"Do you not even hear what your own mouth says, Paddy?" said I. "Of course we're intertwined, and by blood at that. This isn't what Fields is saying."

Paddy looked at me, uncomprehending.

"How is it you don't know any better than you know?"

I felt exasperated, but not only by Paddy and his studied obliviousness. I'd likewise been blind my own damned self. Fields's words were a revelation to me, of the shameful kind. The damnable thing for which I condemned John B. was, it turned out, akin to damnable things that I refused to recognize in myself. At heart was this: the great gift of my privilege. I'd latched onto my name and my blood and assumed I deserved what I got and had come by it hard-earned. But it was all bequeathed, a gift few others got. Lesser than that given to Paddy, sure, but greater by far than what was ever offered to Fields.

If I'd been born white, would I have forced myself on Fanny like my gut told me that Patrick had? Like John B. had done my ma'am?

Revere had been right. How much did I hate my own skin?

And like a demon summoned by the mere thought of his name, there stood the man. In the shadowed dark, Revere seemed just another of the trees, and he held a pistol on Paddy but stared in puzzled disbelief at me. "What is this?" he said.

Of no use protest or vain attempts at explication. I rose, deliberate and slow, forming up my aspects as lethal as I knew how, the Colt Navy anew in hand. Revere, not unnoticing, shifted his aim from Paddy onto me, so easy a movement it hardly seemed movement at all. But now I stared into the mouth of his barrel.

"What is your side, Etheridge?"

I wasn't sure when I'd made the decision about Paddy, but it had been made. "I have things in hand here," said I. "Move on."

This echoed the claims I'd made out at Leonidas Midgett's farm, only now more meaningful, as I, like Revere, outstretched a pistol, just as easy, just as intentful.

I'd never truly taken in his face, full-on. Yet it was a fine one, his skin smooth, his features sharp. A face much like my ma'am's, in fact; a finely wrought mask that refused to reveal what lay behind. But for the eyes! He glared at me steady, each push of frosted breath fanning the embers behind them.

"It don't end like this," I heard Fields say. He was aiming his rifle from where he sat, and thus broke the tie. "Move on, Sergeant. We have things in hand here."

Revere only glanced his way, then back at me. "You have spoiled this man for fighting," said he, and he spat at my feet. "We need warriors, and your troopers comport themselves like you do, bowing and scraping."

"Your insults have gone stale. *Spoiled*? Tell me, Revere. Would me spoiling the disposition of your face convince you of my capacity at proper leading?"

The mask loosed then, with a gun put to it. He smiled a smile true. "Okay, Etheridge. Okay, then." And he backed out the way he had come in.

When he'd disappeared into the trees, I slipped myself behind my stump, crouching there, my pistol aimed at the dark. Fields scuttled for cover, too. Only Paddy did not move.

The ball did not come, and slowly, Fields and I rose up.

We both continued to study the tangle of trees that Revere had withdrawn into. "Twice now you've confronted that man, each time notched up over the previous one," Fields said. "He will not allow a third."

He didn't know about the harsh words we'd exchanged at the celebratory rally in Elizabeth City. "I expect not," I said.

The dark remained still.

"I will do all I can to watch out for you," said Fields, "always. But the danger from here on is no longer just the Rebby-boys."

Here I was with two "nigh on" brothers. Only one had ever proved a brother true.

I turned. "Go, Paddy. Go on home."

He sat there yet. I'd have sworn he looked sad to hear my words.

"Take off that damned butternut coat and go home," said I.

This he did, rising. He removed the coat and cap and let them drop into the muck. "When we meet again, Dick, we will be equals, you and me." A smile played on his face. "Just think on that!"

"We always were, Paddy."

He didn't reply but turned to Fields. "I always knew you for a good one. If I hear rumors that you've made it to the land of Africa, I will know it for true. I hope to hear it."

"Go, Paddy," said I, "there's no time for this. Go now, run!"

His mirthful eyes took me all in. "What a world we live in," said he. In his voice was utter wonderment.

Then he made off, bolting into the swamp.

CHAPTER TWENTY-ONE

The battalion was hangdog about our losses, about our eight lost friends. It was clear that we'd done considerable damage to the bushwhackers—this beyond the thirteen dead they'd been obliged to leave behind during their hasty flight. Yet and still, we all felt as though we hadn't won the day, as though we'd failed at soldiering or at properly being men. We stacked their dead any old way beneath their impromptu crossbeam at the two thick-trunked oaks; this was as good as they deserved, maybe better. Ours we laid out side by side next to the ball-battered shack, each one's long musket on his right, nearly as long as the man, equally unmoving.

Each was a mess of shredded flesh, with a ragged or dissevered limb, hardly recognizable as the man we'd known, save for some bit that distinguished him. John Preston had sewn his socks to the bottom of his pant legs and wore them tucked into his brogans, swearing that this better kept dry his feet. Isaac Brimley wore like a locket a small leather satchel that he called a "gree-gree." The token had survived our charge, though his neck had not. His head was connected by a mere strip of sinew. I recognized Miles Hews only because I'd seen his body drop and the image would not leave me. The green tassel attached to his haversack, the mess of red that had been his face. Paps Prentiss knelt over him, cap in hand, repeating over and again: "A fine boy. What a fine boy, he." Pap's aspect, unsmiling and tight, showed every bit of pain that his coon-act grin always worked so hard to mask.

Me, I thought on Hews's upright bearing, on his seriousness and reliability. Though not old enough for it, I felt like a father who'd lost his son. It was me, after all, who had named him—in the enlistment line at Fortress Freedom, as he bent over the table, wearing a cotton shirt so thin you could see right through and trousers that had frayed at the cuffs. I'd watched his pause, which was holding up the queue.

Lieutenant Longley had barked at him, not even attempting to disguise his disgust: "Just scratch an *X*, boy, and move on!"

Miles had just stood there, pondering.

"I was called Hughes," he'd explained when I scooted over to offer help. "H-U-G-H-E-S. But that was Mass's name, and now it don't seem fitting."

"Well, how about *Hews*, then?" I'd said. "H-E-W-S?"

He'd smiled broad. "Right! My name like I've known it all my life, only *mine* truly now."

He had looked so happy, which was his way generally to look upon things. How could his Barbery have betrayed such as him, why would she ever?

I would make it my mission to locate Miss Anna Lipscomb, his newly betrothed, upon our return to Freedom, to notify her of his bravery, even unto death.

A group of us met over beyond the shack, all the sergeants and corporals and several of the more leaderful privates. I took the outcome of our council to Draper, who was over in the shade of an oak tree, far enough from the battalion for solitude.

"The men want to take them back to Shiloh," said I, "to the church we occupied, and bury them there and bury them proper."

"Our dead?" asked Draper.

"Yes, sir."

"But it's a white cemetery."

"Precisely, sir. The mother church of the state entire, and so the only place befitting their sacrifice."

I hit the last word a touch harder than intended.

He didn't hold it against me. He stood a long pause, in reflection.

"It's not wise," said he. "As soon as we've gone, they'll unearth and desecrate the corpses." Even in the semi-light beneath the oak, I could read the great sympathy tormenting his face. "No, let us bury them on the field where they fell as heroes. And when the name *Indiantown* is one day on the lips of every schoolchild studying this great revolutionary action undertaken by the African Brigade, so too will ring out the names of those men."

Even could I have overruled his decision, I would not have, for he spoke sense and right. He repeated these same words to the battalion, assembled in a mass afore him, and all the men received them as I had. Yet, I vowed to myself that, if I survived our "great revolutionary action"—words which stuck in my head and raised up my pride—and emerged the other side of it alive and free, I'd one day return to this field and place a stone of some sort, a proper commemoration, in memory of Miles Hews, John Preston, and Isaac Brimley, of Joseph Mullen and Caesar McCawsey, and of the three whose names I did not know in that moment but which I sought out shortly thereon and have never forgotten since: Charles Small, Valentine Dozier, and David Scott.

Revere and the swamp men had quit camp before Fields and I emerged from the pocosin. This was a relief, for I wasn't sure how I would have explained to Draper my actions therein, from letting a bushwhacker go free to leveling a weapon on a companion-in-arms in order to accomplish it.

As the afternoon aged, it became increasingly apparent that the colonel was wholly unaware of my detour after Patrick. Why Revere hadn't reported my treason was a mystery to me, and not one I trusted. Did he intend to go to General Wild directly, the higher authority and one with whom I had no truck, and in this way ensure to see me court-martialed and hanged? I could not know, but a messenger came to us from the general with orders for our battalion to meet up with his at the MacIntosh plantation, just up the road between Indiantown and Sligo.

This worked well for us—if not necessarily for me—given our wounded. We had several, Simon Gaylord among them. He'd been hit in the rib cage, a glancing shot that broke two of them. He bore it bravely. He and the rest—seven all told—filled our hospital wagon at the rear, as well as two other carts seized especially for their transport. Reuniting with Wild would allow us to get them proper doctoring and see them evacuated back to Freedom in sooner fashion. As for me, I could only hope I wouldn't meet with arrest and imprisonment.

A rain had set in, making our slog up the road slow and our morale even lower. The jostling of the hospital litters would periodically cause one or another of the wounded to cry out in pain. It was a shrill and agonized sound, and many of the battalion became tetchy. Was this what victory in battle felt like—like paying over-dear dues to the devil for chits as yet unused and perhaps never redeemable?

We made the MacIntosh farm by dark. It was big like Hollybrook Manor, with a two-story main house, alit from inside by lamps. Huge campfires in the fields surrounding the mansion made a daytime of night. Word of the fight at Indiantown had preceded us—owing to Revere, I imagined. And as Draper had foretold, we were heroes, greeted with back claps and huzzahs. It was raucous and festive, as troopers clamored to hear tell of the battle firsthand.

Me, I fretted about what other information Revere might have
purveyed of the events of the day, and to whom. I slipped off as soon
as I could and began ranging the grounds, looking for the hired-on
helper women, looking for Fanny. The general's column had come
away with many more contrabands than were figured to still be out
here, much as had our own, and also numerous horses and mules
and several yoke of oxen. In the distance in several directions, the
shimmer of flames gave a red tint to the darkness. I learned from
Orange Redmon, whom I stumbled upon, that squads had been
dispatched to put a match to the homes of local guerrilla sympa-
thizers. Clearly, there were many. Redmon couldn't tell me where
to find the helper women's wagons, though.

Word circulated that all command staff was required at headquarters, inside the MacIntosh house. I cut short my search and
headed over there. Although it had been only a few days, it felt
a joyous reunion to find Henry Adkins and Cornelius Crowley
and all the others milling about inside the entrance hall. If I was
to be arrested, none here yet knew it, for men congratulated me
heartily on a job well done. The general's brother called us into
the library. Sensing that I'd be tied up here for a long while, I had
a private from Company A, whom I'd spotted tarrying nearby the
kitchen, carry a message to Fanny, telling her I'd come find her
as soon as I could.

I didn't know why, but I expected General Wild to look different. Perhaps it was that, after Shiloh Church and Indiantown,
after the strung-up family and capturing Paddy, *I* felt different.
The meeting went much as had so many before, with reports on the
numbers of contraband taken in, and on the loyalty and disloyalty of
the local citizenry. Colonel Draper gave an official summary on the
resistance we'd encountered, informing the general that it had been
a mixed group of guerrillas under a man named Grandy, with maybe
even elements come down from Virginia. I knew Elliott's band to

also be with them, news that would have elated Wild. I didn't offer it up, as to do so would mean having to reveal how I'd come by it.

Draper wrapped up: "The men conducted themselves well in the field, with swift compliance and great propriety." He said this as though he esteemed it the highest compliment possible, and General Wild seemed pleased, if unsurprised.

He told Draper, "Your men shall have a chance at them again. We got intelligence that the land pirates are in the swamp, on a patch of land called Crab's Island, where they make their camp. Take your battalion there in the morning and have at them."

"Yes, sir," said Draper, seeming neither pleased nor displeased.

The meeting broke up with no mention of dereliction of duty or treason. I should have felt great relief, but like Draper, I was neither pleased nor displeased, just exhausted, more exhausted than I could ever remember feeling. As I was leaving the room, Captain Wild waved me over. Before alarm could take hold, he set in to explaining the reason. Apparently, a mail pouch, bound for Fortress Freedom from Roanoke, had made its way into camp, the huge column a safer means of conveyance than the unaccompanied sloop upon which it was being transported. In it was a letter for me from Sarah Etheridge, dated late November—from about the time of our foray out to the Clapson farm.

Captain Wild handed it to me but looked inquisitive. By his expression, he clearly wondered at the nature of my relationship with this woman who bore my name and, in a graceful script, had written as return address, "The Etheridge House"—this only, as though all would know it.

I ignored his unuttered question, took the envelope, and excused myself.

I'd gone not two paces when the private from A whom I'd sent after Fanny hailed me also. He had a return message. She relayed that she was busy, helping to tend to the wounded, and said it would be best if I came by in the morning. I dismissed the private. Fanny's response struck me as cold, maybe even deliberately so, and I imagined that she might yet harbor lingering anger after our last time together.

I was too tired to overmuch trouble it—bone-tired. I bunked in a pantry off the kitchen, within easy call of the colonel should he need me during the night. At least, this was the excuse I made to myself to justify not sleeping out in the wet cold with my men. The space was tight and the floor hard, but the air blanketing me smelled of fresh bread, on account of the nearby hearth.

Before shoving off for the Land of Nod, I rousened up sufficient enthusiasm to read Sarah's letter, for I feared the voyage through sleep might be restless if I did not. "Dearest Dick," her usual greeting, and after:

> It has been some time since we received news from you. I am sure that military duties take up your every waking minute, being a non-commissioned officer in your regiment. Still, just a word or two, a simple postcard to let us know that life among the Yankees is all that you had hoped it would be.
>
> Out here on the Banks, isolated as we are under the watchful eye of an Occupying Army, we find ourselves fairly bereft of news from abroad. The only account of current affairs we receive anymore is by way of the cast-off refuse of the Malmsey-nosed Zouaves, who ball up their broadsheets and toss them off all over the Island. Oh, those Zouaves! After your President Lincoln recently declared Evacuation Day to henceforth be a time of giving thanks, the foul Occupiers imposed the decree in full force. A group of ten or so trod into our yard, crapulent and rough, and deprived us of each and every one of our last barn fowl, and did likewise in the yards of our neighbors.

If I had the chance, I would tell Dishonest Abe to keep his Thanksgiving and Evacuate these beastly men from our midst!

Our way of life is in such a great dis-order. Conditions on the Island are in a terrible state, Dick—oh, just terrible! Neighbor no longer trusts neighbor. Where once were offered friendly "Halloos," now stern looks and turned backs are the sole reply. For some, like Ike Meekins, it is rebuke for imputed leniency with servants, for the indulgences that Meekins believes have resulted in acts such as you undertook. For others, William Bosworth and Wilson Tillett and their ilk—Candidian dolts incapable of recognizing reality, even as it struts about the Island in red breeches and fezzes—the future has arrived and it augurs a New Jerusalem on our sad Sand Banks. To them, the actions of boys like Patrick—which I will not openly pronounce here but which, I am sure, you might divine—cast even greater shame over the Etheridge House than did your flight.

(Though my head cries "No!" and fears for what it may cost to his welfare—to say aught of the cost to his and the family honor—my heart swells that Patrick should have followed his passion and broken free of Father's hold over him. He has become a man—finally!—expressing bravely his innermost conviction, however irregularly.)

I must tell you, though: the greatest upset to our lives out here has been at the hands of you colored. More and more wash ashore from inland plantations across the Sound—some quite literally washing ashore—and thereafter more and more of our own abscond from their homes to join the new arrivals at the Runaway Colony. You and the rest who were first to run off must have known that such would be the case.

Let me speak candidly. Where once I felt a small measure of pride at your nerve, I now only feel disappointment. Our choices result in consequences, Dick!—this is the first lesson

a child learns when passing into manhood. I'd have thought
you well enough reared to understand this.

So be it.

Among the latest news gleaned from the Yankee rags, I have
read that Old Abe is countenancing arming you smoked Yanks,
they say it is inevitable. More choices made without heed of
consequence. I am not surprised and so cannot say that I feel the
strong upset that others do, though I will confess that I worry.
We have not heard from you in so long. You have habituated
us to your absorbing anecdotes and clever asides, and cannot
now so brutally cut us off from their source. Do please write.

Yours truly,

Sarah

Ah, my dearest Sarah . . . Patronizing unto the end! The world
for you cannot hold one drop more than your small understanding
of it. Would that you knew that I had spared Patrick! He is surely
home by now, and equally surely has not admitted the truth: his
brave conviction, your pride at his passion—that I beheld them at
the end of the barrel of a pistol and did not fire!

Her haughty scorn enraged but could provoke no more response
than merely that spark of fury, felt in a rush and just as quickly
faded—such was the depth of my exhaustion. I surrendered to it,
surrendered fully. Pulled down the brim of my forage cap so that it
covered my eyes, making even darker this plenty-dark cubby, making
more bedful the hard floor and these cramped walls.

I thought the Land of Nod attained. I thought myself far away—far,
far away—but for a sound rising in my ear. A faint clanking, coming
from somewhere in the house, droning persistent and pulling me
back from the deep sleep into which I'd fallen and felt I deserved.

It was musical in a way, though off-key; not suspicious in the way of threatened security, just odd and thereby curious. I rolled over and curled into a ball, as though this might somehow muffle it. When it did not, I quit my cubbyhole to find out the source of the disturbance.

Where the house was dark, I saw through the uncurtained windows that the camp remained glowing from the bonfires, though largely still. At the far end of the library, a line of light emanated from beneath a door, and along with it, the insistent "music." I knocked but didn't await reply and just entered.

Across the way was an upright piano, and on the bench afore it sat General Wild, his one good arm tapping at the keys. He stopped upon my entry.

"Oh, pardon, sir," said I and began to retreat from the room.

"No, no. Come in, Sergeant . . . ?"

It was the third time I'd told him. "Etheridge, sir."

He nodded as though he'd remembered, though clearly he had not. And why would he? He commanded a thousand of us, nearly two-score of whom were sergeants and, beyond this, even more corporals—more men than I myself could even keep track of. Yet, given our previous interactions, given my role with Draper, a part of me expected him to.

"Are you musically inclined?" he asked.

It was a common belief that we all were, so I appreciated his asking and not just assuming. "It's been said I can carry a tune. As to instruments, no, sir—and no discernable talent for them either."

"I would teach you, but . . ." He raised the spoiled arm.

I smiled, sincere.

He said, "Music has been in my family for generations. I was raised on it and was quite accomplished—a prodigy in my youth. I could play just about anything, stringed or wind, and improvise with ability. It's the one great regret of my injuries."

There were a bugle and a fife on the floor at his feet, and he lifted the bugle to his lips and honked out a few notes.

I said, "No need of two arms for playing that. But not much range or possibility with it either, I expect."

"No," said he, lowering the instrument and chuckling. "It doesn't lend itself to Haydn."

I didn't know who this was and used silence to conceal my ignorance.

He faced the ivories anew, his back to me. "I knew you knew the difference, you know, back at Pool's."

"Sir?"

He glanced at me over his shoulder. "Between the guerrillas we're hunting and the African beasts." Recalling the incident seemed to embarrass him. "I had no doubt."

He didn't apologize, though. As he was a general and I just one of his troopers, he an Abolitionist hero and I just another of his freed Negroes, I supposed that he had every right not to. I accepted his mention of the incident as apology enough.

He haphazardly fingered the keys, continuing. "I've seen the other, the wild beast, years ago in Constantinople, caged in the royal menagerie of Abdul Medjid, the sultan there. It had such sad eyes, deep and sad—at its captivity, I expect." He looked up, though not back at me. "The way we've treated you here is no better. No better."

It was meant as an offer of sympathy, but the "we" and "you" stung, for they made of me nothing more than a victim.

Me, just a victim? Perhaps not equal to him in adventuring and experience, but this, due to our individual circumstances and the chances tendered by fate. I'd survived the trials of slavery; I'd taken full advantage of the opportunities availed to me—my determination to join up, my sergeanting of F.

No. No mere victim, I.

"May I, sir?"

"Speak freely, please."

"What will become of *us* colored when this war is done?" The added emphasis was intentional.

Wild seemed not to have noticed. "Why, you will be free!" he said, as though I'd posed the most ridiculous question, guerrilla and gorilla.

"We will come and go as we please," said I, "but where shall we go to? Up to your home in Massachusetts? And will there be work for us there? For a fair wage? Or will the workers already possessing the jobs want to fight us for them?"

His long, probing look told me that he was as pleased by my cheek as he was irked by this interrogation. "Good questions, Sergeant. Good questions all."

I had more to say. "Permission, sir?"

"Go ahead, speak."

"And when white and colored make babies, when Anglo-Saxon blood mixes with the African—which seems inevitable, as it is already so common here in the South—what then? Will our victory seem so glorious after all?"

He sat still a long pause, then said finally: "I want to tell you that I wouldn't give a good goddamn about Anglo-Saxon and African mixing. But I don't have children, much less daughters. So if I told you this, I could not be sure that I wouldn't be lying."

Aside from his lament on the cost in musicianship of the loss of his arm, this was maybe the most honest thing I had yet heard him say, rousening speeches and all.

He crossed one leg over the other, resting his hand upon his knee. "When I began in medicine, well before the war, I attended lectures in Paris. I was a young general practitioner, not yet married, and I aimed to improve my skills with plants and the like. Generations of Wild men have been doctors, but my father never had the chance to further his particular passion, which was for homeopathy.

His disappointment presented me the opening by which to make my own place in the family business. The usual rivalry between fathers and sons, you see."

I *did* see, little did he know.

"I was there several months," he continued. "The Parisians, they don't care one whit whether a black couples with a white, or a man with another man. For them, freedom is freedom." He set to gently tapping the keys again, with just one finger this time. "They're wrong to interpret freedom in this way. They think that imbibing in the extremes of theoretical liberty is the purer, more genuine form. But it isn't libertinism that is the measure of liberty, but rather, responsibility and accountability."

"Responsibility?" asked I, not fully following his meanderings, but suspicious of the tone that they'd assumed. "Accountability? To whom?"

"To God!" He threw the one good hand into the air, proclaiming this with such great fervor that I feared he'd awakened the house.

Yet, his ardor didn't make the answer any more satisfying. For had I not until then been a slave under God's regime? What random factors pushed Him to make white men feel accountable for us now, but under other circumstances not at all?

Wild sunk into the bench, slumping over the keys. He appeared to have offered this zeal as much to convince himself of his words as to convince me, and he now looked glum, defeated even. I figured it was time for me to quit this scene and started to, but he set in again.

"I became quite friendly with another young doctor, a man of noble birth from Upper Silesia who was an expert homeopath but was seeking greater practice with surgery. Paris was the most fertile ground for expanding one's education—intellectual as much as sentimental, you understand"—he sought my eyes—"for life just thrives there. But this young doctor was quite blocked, on both fronts. Improving at medicine, like undertaking sentimental journeys, is a game of change, sometimes radical change, and sometimes uneasy, too. His failure was a failure at reconciling his intellect with what his feelings and instinct told him to be true."

I had returned to the role that colored always play for whites in their quiet moments of introspection, as confessor. Now "free" and my own man, I should have resisted it. Instead, I asked, "And you, sir?"—unsure of what exactly I was asking, for his story was winding, a puzzle.

"It was knowing him that taught me to reconcile the two. His difficulties reflected my own." Wild ran his hand through his beard. "Our interchange was how I came to understand the differences in what is meant by freedom. We were in Italy by then, he and I, and our discussions, which were sometimes not so easy, made me realize that the good fight that I was meant—am meant—to fight is here. Abolition and all that. Not Garibaldi's war, not Omar Pasha's, not even my own, within myself. And this I am doing despite the great price exacted."

I continued to struggle to follow him. He recommenced his awkward tapping at the keys, and it seemed an apt accompaniment to this scene and the strange mood.

"They say I'm reckless," he said, "that my behavior in the field is criminal."

"'They,' sir?"

"Our side just as much as theirs."

"And what say you? Do you accept this judgment?"

He stopped tapping, and straightened and faced me then. "I'll tell you this. I enjoyed kicking loose the wedge that triggered the gallows of that whoreson Bright. Enjoyed it with relish."

By his flinty look, I did not doubt this one bit.

He said, "Having bought truth dear, we must not sell it cheap, not one grain of it for the whole world." A knowing smile crossed his face. "An esteemed settler of New England wrote this."

"And you agree, sir?"

"I apply it as I would Holy writ."

He returned to tapping upon the ivories. He didn't bid me to leave, but it was as though he had nothing more to say, as though, in fact, I was no longer even in the room.

"May I get you anything, sir?" said I in advance of making my exit.

"Go on, Sergeant. Get some rest. I'll retire in a bit."

"Good night, General."

With this, I left him and returned to my cubby.

John B. came to me in a dream. His slouch hat shaded his eyes, his smoking pipe pinched a-tween his lips, and he addressed me earnestly, fondly. He thanked me for sparing Patrick, for letting him return home, and I will confess, it made me wish that I hadn't. I couldn't say why I regretted my forbearance, but in that moment, put to me like that by him—by John B., or my dream-made imagining of him—I wished my actions of the afternoon had been bolder, more final. Like Wild, relishing the boot he'd put to Daniel Bright's hangman's barrel.

Having bought truth dear, the general had quoted, we must not sell it cheap, not one grain of it. How cheaply had I sold my truths? Maybe I had no more truly loved Patrick than this: I'd wanted the father's approval, much as did he, and I'd thought that showing myself to be Patrick's better would get me one step closer to it.

Yet John B., just like Patrick, just like Sarah, was incapable of seeing me other than how he did. I knew this now. In John B.'s eyes, I'd always be more akin to Syntax or his prized schooner than a man. So how, then, could I ever be a son? For him, I was an object of praise that other white folks might take note of on account of my fine upbringing and usage, but though flesh of his flesh, not worth anything more than my unbroke back, despite my "pedigree." His use of the word was not admitting me as kin, but granting me exception. Those watchful glances on the verandah while Sarah drilled me in grammar balloons—he was merely a-wonder at the oddity of a dark hue reflecting so many similarities. But seeing me, truly me? No. Clearly not.

Ma'am had known this all along and striven to give me the knowledge. I'd refused it, and maybe even cast an angry word her way for wanting to teach the lesson. In striving to be a notable son, I'd failed utterly at being a son to the only true parent I'd ever had.

The cookfires were going well before first light. I sought out Fanny in the wagon train where the hired-on help was preparing soft bread and fried ham for breakfast. She didn't jump into my arms as she had upon our chance meeting on the docks at Elizabeth City. She stood afore me, wrapped in shawls and blankets from her head down to the outsized brogans she had procured for her feet. She said, "I have heard men were killed. I heard youall were in it."

"Full in it, girl," said I. "We were full in."

"I'm glad it's not you left back out there, or among those wailing and dying in the hospital tents."

I bid her to follow, and we stepped away, out into a nearby patch of trees. I confessed the thing that had pulled me from sleep. "I'm tortured, Fanny. For from the start, I've only betrayed my ma'am and let her down." I didn't know how to say more nor how to say it otherwise, so I just added: "John B., all that."

What John B. did to her!

All I'd ever concerned myself with was what the man might do for me.

The frosty wall of displeasure that had been keeping Fanny from me melted away then. "Ah, no, Richard." She took my hands in hers. "No, no. You're missing the forest from too close focusing on the single trees. You are Ma'am Rachel's joy, the pride of her life. What that man took from her, she wanted you to take from him— everything you deserve of the world. And you have. You haven't cowered like the bent slave they expect us to be. All along, always, you've stood tall, your own man. This is Ma'am Rachel's doing."

What she said was pretty, but I wasn't much-all convinced by it.

She must have felt this, for she went on: "She knew she'd lose you, on down the way. This is the sacrifice mothers make to raise good men. They teach you to leave, despite their own need of you to stay, to stand up and face all those odds set agin you—but off from behind their skirts."

My Fanny, her angel's face unshadowing in the dawning light. This was the girl who would become my wife.

"And you?" said I. "Don't ma'ams raise girls the same?"

"They teach us to be mothers. But as to our boys, yours and mine, I will raise them just like Ma'am Rachel raised you."

We held each other then, alive and close, until, with the sun's slow rise, we were more readily visible to anyone who might chance upon our loving reunion.

Quitting the trees, I noticed Colonel Draper off by one of the wagons, staring. His gaze appeared to shift between me, putting myself back together, and Fanny, bundling herself up anew in those swaths of blankets. I knew not what he'd seen of us in the woods or what he thought he was presently witnessing, but I helped Fanny adjust a shawl over her shoulders in such a way that Draper might take note of who she was to me. Thereon, I returned his intentful watching.

It was still too dark for our eyes to meet, yet I felt as though they did and felt in that moment more revealed than I had the entire night previous, sitting with General Wild, attending to his confessions. I was *seen* somehow, though Draper couldn't rightly see me.

Not Sergeant Etheridge, his boy Friday, but me, a man, and fully so—as big and broad and rich of substance as he understood himself to be. It was like being naked, though, of all things, completely uncovered. Draper, looking on at me emerging from the woods with my girl on my arm, was eyeing something true, and it raised a sense of alarm in me, even as it felt freeing. For I understood that this was what equality would look like, should we actually one day attain it: each of us would, without forethought, understand the other to be as simple and as inscrutable, as vexing and as compelling, as we were ourselves.

Draper didn't nod or otherwise offer any sort of salutation. His shadowed form appeared at ease, though, not at all surprised by this genuine moment shared between us. I wondered if, even only the week before, he would have been capable of it. Would I have been? Now, here we were.

Fanny, heading toward the cook wagons, still did not notice him, and I walked alongside her, my arm through hers. Draper turned and disappeared into the mess of movement that was the camp coming to life.

CHAPTER TWENTY-TWO

It wasn't long before our battalion was mustered in and ready. We numbered fewer, just two hundred. The general and the colonel thought this sufficient to take on what remnant of the guerrilla force we might find. We were shed of Backuss, whom Draper arranged to have join the general's staff, but acquired the newspaperman Tewksbury, who boasted, puffed-up like, that he wanted to be where the fighting was. Our column set off, four abreast as before, down a road adjoining the one we'd come in on, with a lively chaos behind us as Wild's men struck camp.

The morning was exceedingly cold. The newspaperman rode aside the colonel, and as a result, he was nearby to me as well. The first fire we received, maybe an hour into the march, had him scrambling off that horse for cover, ducking behind the wall of men who rushed forward, barrels raised. The potshot had gone way wide, and Tewskbury's rabbit response caused some of the troopers to snigger.

Paps Prentiss said, "Why, that ain't but a hoot owl's fart, Mass. You ain't afraid of a tiny bird, is you?"

I ordered Fields and my corporals to have their men remain ever more vigilant for movement in the trees, and Draper sent out an additional squad to join the skirmishers already on our flanks and rear. I'd taken to treating Fields as a corporal again, though he was not one, and he responded gamely. Draper either trusted my judgment or did not notice. I preferred to think the former.

We arrived at a farm on the Sligo road that Wild had identified as belonging to a family that knew the location of the guerrillas' base in the pocosin. Draper forced the master of the house into our service, at the point of his pistol. This man, Burgess, was none too pleased to have to join our ranks.

"You done took my niggers," groused he. "And now me, too?"

His wife, two sons who were on about fighting-aged though not quite there, and a daughter just topping the ma'am's waist stood by, equally displeased.

"In exchange for your service to the Union," said Draper, "we'll leave your home and outbuildings standing."

Burgess harrumphed at this but led us along. The lane we passed down was obscure and not well tended, and I feared he might be leading us into a trap. Draper seemed not to share my fear. He rode tall in the saddle just behind Burgess, sometimes speaking at him. About two miles along, a-border the pocosin, Burgess sat his horse and pointed into the swamp, considering his duty done. Draper tied his own horse to a tree and, with pointed pistol, inspired the farmer to follow suit.

Burgess guided us in on foot. We proceeded single-file by squads, extra vigilant, muskets at the ready. The pocosin was more spotted dark than light, and the cold became wet and heavy. Tewksbury narrated in whispers his future reporting. "A Sabbath silence brooded over the mire," he mumbled—more to himself, really, than to us others, as though the sound of his voice might distance him sufficient from here and now and thereby allay his visible quaking. It was as good a turn of phrase as I had yet heard from him.

The way in seemed a bit haphazard until, in due course, I noticed that our zigzag route through the slough had been fairly easy, the footing firm beneath me—not like slogging through muck and underbrush. And then I saw why. We were moving over felled trees that touched end-to-end, just below the surface of the water:

a deliberately laid footpath. Similar such paths, I noted, looking around, were all over out here, all leading in one direction.

Maybe a half mile on, a hummock rose out of the bog. Crab's Island wasn't an island, properly speaking, but it was island enough. The general had called it a "swamp city," maintained out here by the guerrillas. He turned out to be damned near right. Tewksbury described it thusly, in a bolder voice this time, as the site was abandoned: "The camp, finally found in the interior of this dense swamp, consisted of nine log-huts, containing bunks enough for seventy-five men, and a number of tents. Fires were found burning. Everything indicated a hasty retreat from the place." The houses and sheds stood atop short, stout stilts, raising them out of the muck, with peat moss overgrowing every surface such that they blended in with the surrounding trees. I wondered if the hamlet where the swamp men lived in the Great Dismal looked similar.

As Tewksbury had observed, many men had been here just recently. So speedy was their withdrawal that they'd left behind their stores: some sixty-odd muskets, most of them new Enfields; a larger number of bayonets and cartridge-boxes; much Rebel army clothing; and the prize of prizes, their muster rolls. Here were the names of every bushwhacker of the various bands of the neighborhood. Included among them was Patrick's.

Fields found me and led me to a discovery made by his squad behind the farthest of the log-huts: two distilleries. One still dripped liquid fire into a wooden keg. "To help keep themselves warm, I expect," said he, smiling jokey.

Paps Prentiss asked, "Should we provision up before alerting Mass Colonel?"

Those around him laughed, but it was clear the old man was serious.

"Run over and alert him of our find," I ordered Paps, choosing him to create a distance from all this temptation.

When Draper arrived, along with the bulk of the battalion and the farmer Burgess, he praised me for my good work, which I passed along to Fields. A huzzah was rousened, the men raising their rifles and cheering. Draper ordered that we use the contents of the kegs as fuel and splash it overall the camp, seized weapons excepted, which we would take away with us. Once this was accomplished, he went from log-hut to log-hut, tossing bits of kindling into each. A roaring blaze erupted throughout the swamp citadel, producing a pungent black smoke that climbed toward the sky. We knew the general would see it. Hell, Creecy himself back at Elizabeth City would likely see it, such was the density and breadth of each rising black finger.

"It is an instructive turn of the tables," narrated Tewksbury, "that the men who have been accustomed to hunt runaway slaves hiding in the swamps of the South should now, hiding there themselves, be hunted by the former slaves."

Indeed, thought I. And nicely expressed.

We wended our way out the way we'd come in. Draper released Burgess from service, even though we followed his horse's unhurried saunter down the lane, toward the main road. We'd not traveled a mile before we heard bits of rifle fire in the woods on our left flank. Our skirmishers rushed in, and behind them we saw amassed at the edge of the trees a fairly sizable number of the bushwhackers—ninety, maybe a hundred.

Draper began shouting, as likewise did we sergeants and corporals:

"Form up! Arms at the ready!"

"First platoon, extend to the flank, twenty paces!"

"Close up, second platoon! Close up!"

This got the Rebby-boys excited, and they commenced their yipping and yelling. Burgess, caught in between, spurred his horse and circled around behind us, where he found Tewksbury already there, a-crouch behind the highest stump on the field.

Then it became apparent that only some of the bushwhackers had rifles—very few, in fact. Many were without coats, just in their shirtsleeves, and a few without pants, only in long drawers. They were the boys from the swamp citadel, for certain, confirming the extent to which our approach had caught them unawares.

"I think we've deprived them of some required fittings," I said to the colonel.

"They seem distressed by it," replied he.

Others along our line were likewise apprising the situation, and laughter broke out general, even from the farmer Burgess.

Draper wheeled on his horse. "Fix bayonets!" he called.

"Fix bayonets!" we sergeants repeated. "Fix bayonets!"

"Charge bayonets!" called Draper, and the buglers sounded the order over the din of all the rest—over the shouts conveying directions and the troopers returning the Rebel yells, yip for yip, and some laughter also, yet ongoing. With our charge, the bushwhackers turned tail quicker than quick, scrambling off into the woods.

At the tree line, we ordered the men to halt and spread out.

"Fire at will!" we hollered.

I heard a ball sail by—though none of the bushwhackers seemed to be shooting back—and damned close to my ear, too, and from the rear. I turned, and a hundred yards distant sat Revere and Golar, a-mount, Revere lowering his rifle. Troopers were forming up around me to bang out their fare-thee-wells at the running Rebby-boys; it was this that saved me another, maybe better-aimed, attempt. Golar lowered his gun, and the two of them turned and disappeared into the trees.

Then Fields was there aside me, speaking the self-same words that were clenching up my mind. "Did my eyes see true?"

I didn't know how to answer him.

"We got to report this to the colonel!" said Fields.

Our men surrounded us now, a few still firing at the bush-whackers, but most just whistling and hooting.

"Keep calm," I told him, "keep calm. We can't do that. He would tell of our encounter with Paddy, and it'd be hell for you and me. Maybe even worse."

"So you just going to let the man snipe at you at his leisure?"

"For the time being," said I, scanning the trees that they'd disappeared into, not so much for sign of the swamp men as to avoid having to full-on face Fields. I didn't want him to see the dread that I was feeling and that must have been rising into my face. I needed to think this through, but just that moment wasn't the right one for it. My immediate duty was to sergeant my company and aide-de-camp the colonel without allowing that either the former or the latter became suspicious of my present peril.

Back up the road, at the Burgess place, we came upon a gruesome-ness, pure and plain. The farmer's two boys, bloodied and leaking, had been hanged from the crossbeam above the entry gate to the premises. One flopped limp over the shoulder of his father, who'd cut the line and was struggling to free the body from the girder. The other was still affixed by a length of rope about his neck. Beyond, the main house blazed, a thick black smoke accumulating and beginning to rise.

Burgess could have preceded us by only mere minutes.

He'd armed himself with a fowling piece and presently let the boy drop to the ground so that he might raise up the gun. He aimed it wild and all around in our general direction.

"What did you do? I helped you and what did you do?"

Draper didn't unholster his pistol, which I would have coun-seled, but approached, his hand held out, to calm the man's wild aiming, I supposed. "It wasn't us," he said. "We were engaged with the bushwhackers. You know. You saw us."

"God damn you, God damn you!" Burgess wheeled the scattergun about, but with so many targets at hand, he did not fire at any.

And where were the wife and the daughter?

Draper gestured me forward, to help cut down the second boy. As I moved to do so, Burgess set the barrel on me and kept it there.

"You leave him be. Get! Get out of here! You have brought ruin on me."

Draper complied with his wishes, waving me back to the column, and the column forward. He remained behind as the men double-quicked past, and I stayed back, too, to second him as best I might should Burgess reconsider and decide that shooting the man who'd taken him away from his family at gunpoint might, after all, suffice to avenge his sons.

When the last of the battalion was by, we then set off, and not so slowly either. Draper, distressed, asked, "The bushwhackers, do you think?"

I didn't reply, but I had difficulty seeing it. They'd been tail down, with no time for murderous mischief.

I rejoined my company. Fields, once we were down the road a ways, confirmed his suspicions to mine. "Them boys' bodies, peppered of gunfire when the bushwhackers were short on arms? Plus hung, to boot, and the house in flames? It was Revere."

I couldn't bring myself to fully believe it. "And the woman and the girl?"

He didn't immediately respond. When finally he did, he said, "That nigger on a rampage, and you the spark that tindered his blazing."

*   *   *

We made it to the village Currituck Courthouse by mid-afternoon, still finding slaves to free along our route, though far fewer. The men kept a sharp eye out for the bushwhackers. Me, I stayed nearby my company or Draper, close enough to discourage any potential sniping by adding the risk of hitting someone other. I hoped—nay, I prayed to the Lord Almighty—that this would be a deterrent to Revere and Golar.

Currituck Courthouse, on the Currituck Sound, was no larger than Indiantown and completely overrun with colored troops and contrabands. Soldiers and former slaves alike loaded captured goods and matériel onto one or the other of the two transport steamers at anchor off the docks. From various quarters could be heard "Kingdom Coming," either played on fife and drum or sung. The most common thing repeated throughout the crowd, announced with both relief and pride, too, was "We headed back!" We'd accomplished something out here, and everyone knew it.

My own feelings ran toward wariness. This and great, great fatigue.

I learned that the hired-on helper women were already aboard the transports, and this was a comfort, as I didn't want Fanny anywhere near me when Revere might pop off a shot given the least opportunity. Fields made a point to stay aside me, intently scanning around us.

"What we done out there in the pocosin," said he, "I fear it was the wrong decision."

I didn't disagree, nor did I truly agree either. All I knew for certain was that I couldn't kill Patrick or see him killed, unarmed and in flight, without an attempted intervention.

Fields said, "It's like we've jammed a stick into a hive, hoping it would break our way and the bees not rousen up. With Revere, that was damn fool hoping."

Josh Land approached and told me that the colonel was looking for me.

"Where is he?"

"At the docks, with the general."

Fields accompanied me there, ever watchful. The general spoke
at his brother and, though clearly seeing me, didn't acknowledge
my presence. It was as though our late-night exchange had not
happened—or that it had and he regretted the intimacy.

Upon noting my arrival, Draper broke away from him. "Etheridge, form up the men we took into the swamp. We will board the
gunboat *Flora Temple* before first light and ferry over to Knotts
Island. The roster we uncovered shows that a few of the Pungo Raiders from north of the border are based on Knotts, including Edgar
Clapson's second, a man named Henry White, and his brother,
Caleb, who is likewise a prominent guerrilla. We're to arrest them,
after which we'll march into Virginia and back to base."

I could feel Fields tensing up at this news. "Begging pardon,
sir," said I, "but isn't there a federal garrison nearby to Pungo Point?
Couldn't we leave it to them to gather up these men?" It wasn't
concern for myself in this feud with Revere that prompted the
suggestion—truly—but regard for the men. I added: "The troops
are pretty worn out right about now."

"I know it," said Draper, showing genuine fellow feeling. "The
strain of being out front is tremendous. But General Wild wants it
so. He wants the affair with Clapson and his raiders concluded by
Company F. It began with us, and this final action would signal
complete success."

CHAPTER TWENTY-THREE

Given our number, the *Flora Temple* had to make two trips to convey the battalion across the Currituck Sound. Before the first group boarded the steamer, Draper addressed the assembled lot of us. "That was some bad business back at the Burgess farm," said he. "We are gallant soldiers, not marauders and murderers, and so I will assume it was those land pirates in their flight who laid desolate that man's family."

He paused then and scanned the faces around him—a searingly long pause, as though he aimed to meet each man's eyes, trooper after trooper, before proceeding on. I set my own upon Revere, to the right rear, with Golar, as always, not far from him. Revere hawked me back, steady and unceasing, indifferent to the colonel and his admonitions.

"We've been at it three weeks," continued Draper. "We've endured much and met the highest standards of soldiership, and this with only very little proper training beforehand. Keep your heads, men. Don't let ungoverned passions spoil what has been, to now, a glorious victory."

Revere's detachment was transported over with the first group. I was spared having to watch out for ambush for a few hours. Draper, who had matters to conclude with General Wild, dispatched across the Sound with us in F, in group two. He found his way to me, standing at the forerail of the *Flora Temple*. Fields used his arrival as cause to excuse himself and went below with the men.

Draper and I leaned over the handrail, watching the water lap up against the ship's prow. "Who do you think did it," said he, "back there at Burgess's?"

I resisted telling him what I thought—what in my gut I knew. "The bushwhackers are playing a rough game," said I and left it there.

He didn't say more either, but looked about at the surrounding scenery, dawning in the twilight. I wondered did the coast up in Massachusetts look like this. Was he imagining his home?

The *Flora Temple* dipped forward in the chop, bounded up, then down—very hard. He gripped the bar tightly. When the steamer ride evened, he said, "You did well back there to call my attention to the condition of the men."

"Thank you, sir."

"It was good leadership, as before. Just what is needed."

I appreciated the compliment, though I recognized this time to be different from the other, with Thomas Artis and the three thieves. This had been just typical sergeanting.

"The men . . ." he said but did not finish.

"Sir?"

He stared over at Knotts Island, a small rise of land growing taller with our approach. "Some of the men," said he. "I've heard them refer to the general as a 'nigger.'" He winced at the word.

Indeed, we did. But how to explain it to a man whose first encounter with colored, up close, had only been a few months before?

"It's just them being playful is all."

He looked pained yet.

"You see, sir, when alone among ourselves, we use the word sometimes. But not in a way to mean disrespect. Quite the contrary."

"Precisely!" said he. "When I've heard it, it's said in a glowing light."

"Right, sir. Like he is one of us."

"And why not me?" said Draper.

Ha! thought I. I did not know him for a jokesmith.

But he was serious. "Don't the men hold me in high regard?"

I told him, "It would be an honor to call you my nigger, sir."

He smiled, pleased, not recognizing my attempt to smithy a joke myself.

Revere and the swamp men were nowhere about when we landed. Though our task was to hunt for irregulars, I couldn't help but feel like it was me being hunted. I could not know when Revere or some swamp men might appear at a scene. And if they did, would it be me in their gunsights?

The battalion formed up just beyond the landing. Draper had Captain Smith and Company I and Lieutenant Conant and Company G fan out over Knotts to the homes of the bushwhackers from the muster roll. Draper himself led F north toward the White house. It was maybe a mile to our destination. Knotts Island was mostly tidal plain, with plenty of marsh, and here and there a copse of trees, but only few residences. Most looked mean and still. Likewise, there were hardly any colored out here.

The White place was very much like the others we'd passed along our route. Its inhabitants were clearly watermen, as the outbuildings were festooned with hawsers and lines and tackle, and nets of sundry length and heft hung from every wall in sight. Draper had Robinson Tynes take a squad out into the surrounding country, as pickets. Then he and I approached the door.

Before we arrived, it opened and out stepped a woman who was great with child. *Very* great with child. It seemed like her belly preceded her onto the porch by a full beat. Behind her came a girl of nearly briding age—fifteen, maybe sixteen. She wore the same style of homespun dress as the older one—her mother, I supposed—with sleeves to the wrists and hem to the floor and an apron overtop, and she had the same air of sass and spit.

"What is it you want?" said the woman.

Draper removed his hat, a gesture of politesse, though his voice rang of steel. "Is this the home of Henry White?"

"I'm Susan Fentress White and it is my home," said the woman. "Henry's, too."

"Please call him out here," said Draper. "I'm charged with his arrest, and that of Caleb White."

"Caleb is his brother and stays here as well."

"Call them out, then, madam, or my men will have to go in and get them."

She did not blink nor did she budge. The girl looked on curiously, as though intrigued by what might happen yet.

Draper turned to me, ready to pass on the order, as Susan Fentress White next spoke. "If those niggers breach my doorstep, my husband's men will manure the fields with their black carcasses."

It was a hearty threat and appeared to impress the daughter.

Draper, much less so. He hatted his head and called out: "Henry and Caleb White! Come out now!"

"Holler all you want," said Susan Fentress White, resting her hands on her bulge of midriff. "We knew of your coming and they are not here."

"Where have they gone to?"

"They are not here" was all Susan Fentress White would say to this.

The girl looked no more inclined to answer Draper's query than her mother.

"This must be verified," said he. He was losing patience. "We'll have to go in."

"Not the niggers," said the woman. "You."

Draper stared at her a long stretch.

She stared right back.

Tewksbury had quit our column to return to Virginia with the general. It was the first I truly missed his presence, for I wished him here to record the scene.

Off in the distance, curling black smoke rose against the morning light. Smith and Conant were burning liberally, as Wild had ordered.

Draper whispered to me, "I'm tempted to send you in, to make a point."

"It might cause the baby to come precociously," whispered I back. "That lady would do it just to spite you."

Draper went through the doorway, pistol drawn, and the girl followed after. Susan Fentress White remained outside, hands a-rest atop her bulging middle. Me, I kept at a safe remove, far enough to avoid rousening the woman's ire.

And I wondered where was Revere. Was he out in the trees, sighting me in this woman's yard? His shot would be readily mistaken for Henry or Caleb White's, or that of some other bushwhacker, and my life would thus be ended with no consequences to him.

I heard, behind me, troopers shuffling from foot to foot.

Draper returned, his expression confirming what the woman had claimed. The girl emerged, too, returning to the side of her mother. Draper holstered his pistol and descended off the porch, telling the woman, "You'll have to pack up what you urgently need and vacate the premises. As this is the home of known guerrillas, the penalty for their disloyalty is dispossession."

"If you attempt to dispossess me of my house," shot back the other, "there will be no houses left standing on this island."

"Pardon, madam, are you threatening——"

"If you burn this house," said she, hands now on her hips, "then them out here that have remained loyal shall find themselves without houses, too!"

Draper took a step back as though surprised by this last bit of bile. He crossed his arms over his chest, considering, then whispered to me, "What do you think, Etheridge?"

I didn't think much about it at all, to be honest. My mind troubled my more pressing concern: Revere.

"First she threatens the men," said he, "and now the loyal citizens of the neighborhood."

"Indeed she has," I said.

This appeared to have decided him on the necessary course of action. "That's it!" said he, striding away. "She's under arrest. She comes with us."

Susan Fentress White's face fell then, and her sass did, too. "But I am expecting . . ."

Draper was anew atop his horse. "Etheridge, get a squad to find appropriate transport, whatever wagon or cart they have, and let's get on with it."

Susan Fentress White dropped in a heap, her face blanching, her hands thrown up to the skies. "I am expecting! I am a lady, and I'm with child!"

The woman sobbed loudly, with face in hands and shoulders jerking. It was an impressive display, and quite unexpected from someone who until then had demonstrated so much pluck.

"Oh, Mama! Hush that now, you are embarrassing me," said the girl.

It was the first she had spoken.

"I will go with them and return in a jiffy," she continued, as much to Draper as to her mother, and she looked pleased by the prospect.

Draper stared on, no less baffled than I at the sudden and theatrical turn.

"But my, what shall I wear?" said the girl, and she disappeared into the house.

Draper watched her go, then said to the mother, "Henry and Caleb can turn themselves in at Portsmouth, in exchange for the girl's release."

She didn't reply. Her head hung and shoulders shook.

He continued: "We'll leave the house be, given your condition." Then he turned to me. "Which is it today, Etheridge? Are we fiendish angels or lupine lambs?"

I struggled mightily to keep a guffaw from undermining my sergeantly posture.

Before long, the girl re-emerged. The dress had not changed, but she'd removed the apron and added a floral-print bonnet, white gloves, and lace-up boots that looked impractical for rough travel. She dragged a trunk—of yet more clothing and sundry affairs, I expected.

Draper didn't protest, though he showed clear fluster.

"I shall return presently," the girl told her mother. "You'll be fine."

I had Fields fit her up in a buggy we seized from one of the outbuildings, and we proceeded up the road, away from there. Susan Fentress White cried after us, "Oh, my daughter, my daughter! My only helpmeet!"

We regrouped with Smith and Conant, and the battalion traveled up the east bank of the North River, finally headed back to Portsmouth. Behind us, black smoke puffed skyward where bushwhacker residences had been set aflame.

The day gloomed cloudy, and it mirrored our mood, solemn. Our feet were swollen and sore, our backs ached from too many nights' sleep on hard, cold ground, and freedom awaited us at Freedom—as did, for me, my Fanny, too—where only death remained out here. This caused the last stretch of our march to feel even longer.

Draper and I headed the column, and just behind us, Fields, driving the girl in the buggy. She told us her name was Miss Nancy White and did not stop there. "Papa and Uncle Caleb took to the tall timber when word come that youall was sailing over after them, and I do not blame them. Mama was sore and let him know it—but how could I be? What man would sit around, waiting to face jail and maybe the hangman's noose? Not me, if I was a man, that is for certain sure."

It wasn't clear whether she intended her words for Draper or Fields or me, as she faced the open air out front of the buggy, addressing whoever was in proximity. Neither Draper nor Fields nor I responded, didn't even acknowledge that she'd spoken. This did not slow her.

"Papa says that Knotts is its own sovereign patch, or should be, and deserves recognition as such. He taught me this term, *sovereign*. Do you know it? It means free and self-determining. It is why he's taken up his musket, to defend our sovereignty."

The North River straightened considerably as we crossed into Virginia. The bank opposite, where we had no pickets, neared within sharpshooter's distance. No sharpshooting came. It was maybe the girl's presence that protected us, or maybe no one was out there. My feeling was that we'd exhausted the bushwhackers. Like the White men, they were scattered and running. We'd tamed this corner of Carolina—around Elizabeth City, out in Camden, now on Knotts.

"You don't hardly see niggers out here on the island." Catching herself, she corrected: "Is that rude? I'm sorry. Is *Negro* better?

African maybe? Well, you don't hardly see *Africans*"—she smiled broad, first at Fields, then at me—"out here on the island, 'cause most cannot afford to keep them. So says Papa, anyway. Otherwise, he says he would have bought himself a passel."

As foreday became noon, it became calming—this incessant jabbering. A body could get lost in it.

"I wouldn't own one of you myself, for I find it improper and un-Christian. I have read the story of old Uncle Tom and the beautiful mulatto Eliza Harris. Papa brought it back from Norfolk once when he was selling his catch of terrapin up there. This was a few years back. He said the book was proscribed—that means forbidden by the law. But he said he was curious to know what all the hullabaloo was about, and that he wouldn't have another man tell him what he could read and not. Though he cannot read proper himself, of course, and expected Mama to read it at him."

Miss Nancy White leaned toward Fields and smiled slyly. "I snuck it and read it myself, by candlelight, when he and Mama were sleeping." Then she returned to her proper seating. "I can see why Papa didn't want me in it. I find the treatment of the niggers—I *am* sorry. I mean, the treatment of the Africans in it un-Christian and disgraceful. This is what he must have feared, I expect—the broadening of my mind beyond our sovereign shores."

She smiled slyly again, more general this time. "It is not all that I have read by candlelight."

By the overlong pause, it was clear she awaited someone to inquire what this other reading matter might have been.

Before any of us could venture a guess, though, she continued: "I have also indulged in the romance of the foundling Tom Jones, which I discovered secreted in the clothes trunk of my Auntie Charlotte. It's said that God cast an earthquake over all of Old England as retribution when the book was put out over there. I believe this after reading it." She held herself taller and straighter on the bench of the buggy. "I envision myself as Miss Sophia, finding a way to be with my true love, despite all the hardships and rebukes." And she smiled coyly, seeming to imagine Draper—or perhaps even Fields or me—as the Tom Jones of her spirited fancy.

Miss Nancy White had won her way into my esteem. But the federal outpost at Pungo Point came into view, recalling me to my duties. It turned out not to be a redoubt as I'd expected, but a tall and stately manor, surrounded by fields and fields of crops. Draper called for the column to halt.

Miss Nancy White stood up in the buggy. "Why, that isn't a federal fort, it's the estate of Mr. Harper Ackiss." She looked pleased. "He is *very* highly regarded hereabouts. His people figured importantly in the Revolutionary War. Papa says that if he were cursed to be an African, he would want to gin cotton and dance and sing for Mr. Harper Ackiss." She leaned toward Fields. "Of course, that isn't precisely how he put it."

Fields ignored her, as did Draper and I. Peering more carefully, I observed that there was a boat landing aside the bridge, and docked there was a river steamer flying the Stars and Stripes. Likewise, men in blue coats came and went from the various outbuildings.

We were near to Fortress Freedom, this mission nigh on done.

Draper turned to me. "The Ninety-Eighth New York is posted here. Gather the men in that field there while I salute the commander."

He rode off.

The girl sat back down on the buggy's bench. She looked angry. "I would've enjoyed accompanying him to see Mr. Harper Ackiss. I find it rather rude that he did not ask."

Fields scanned the trees on all sides. "Do you suppose Revere and them to already be hereabouts?"

As they were our scouts and advanced guard, it seemed impossible that they weren't. "Unless he is derelicting duty, yes," said I. "Somewhere."

I passed along Draper's orders to the officers of G and I, and we moved the battalion into position. We came across pickets from the Ninety-Eighth, but they largely ignored our halloos. Some gawked, others glared. The column hadn't fully fallen out before a messenger came from the outpost, searching for me. He carried a note from Draper, directing me to bring the girl forward. She overheard as I told Fields and looked vindicated.

It was a short ride, with Fields and the girl side by side on the bench and me seated on the back boot, atop her trunk. A large number of the Ninety-Eighth, what appeared to be a few companies at least, were concentrated around the main house. Many looked to have no real military task, and after all the time in the field, I envied them their leisure.

And oh, the stares shot at us from the white troopers that we passed! They were especially vicious. I supposed that seeing two colored in charge of a white girl unsettled them. Well, so be it.

Fields reined to a stop the horse leading the buggy. We were afore a broad verandah. A mustachioed sergeant, waiting there, led us through the front doors. The girl was awed by the swank surroundings, strolling about, mouth agape, and running her fingers along the surfaces of things, pieces of furniture and such. We found Draper in the library. Fields had to whisk the girl in, interrupting her ogling of a finely wrought vase.

We caught the Ninety-Eighth's colonel mid-phrase as we entered: ". . . and my jurisdiction extends from the lower end of Princess Anne County, here in Virginia, and includes Knotts Island, down below the border."

"Etheridge, Midgett, good," said Draper. He'd removed his sword in order to sit on the settee in the middle of the room but otherwise looked uncomfortable—perhaps just wearied by the other colonel's apparent speechifying.

The other colonel greeted the girl with a nod and a half-bow, though not Fields and me. Rather than appearing courteous, he came off as overmuch formal, like he might not mean the niceties that he'd proffered.

He then continued, toward Draper: "I think it not improper to inform you that the inhabitants of the region have taken the Oath of Allegiance to the United States, almost without exception."

"Yes, I know," said Draper, "as you've twice already repeated this to me, Wead."

"Many have come to me expressing fear. They believe that depredations will soon be committed on their properties and want protection from your troops."

"If they've sworn loyal, they need not fear."

"I am directed to protect private property," continued the other, this man Wead, as though Draper had not even spoken, "and especially that of persons who've taken the oath, against violence of whatever nature."

And with this, he lunged for Draper's sword!

Draper, though obviously unexpecting, was just as quick, and each man held a two-fisted grip along the shaft of the weapon.

The girl threw a hand over her mouth. Fields and I stared, frozen.

The sergeant who'd led us in had left the room, and this was a relief. I did not relish the thought of attacking another Union man, though I would have, to protect Draper.

"In your excursion to Clapson's farm," said Wead, yanking at the sword, "and now onto Knotts Island, too! You've usurped my command authority."

Draper yanked back. "What are you doing, man?"

"I know what you and your troopers are up to. The insulting language and profanity, committing the grossest outrages—and now this girl! It's a violation of the laws of war and of humanity, and she will remain in my custody."

"The hell she will." Draper dropped one hand from the sword and landed a clean left upon the point of Wead's chin.

Wead staggered backward, releasing his grip.

"Etheridge, Midgett, get the girl back to our men!"

Wead quickly righted himself and drew his revolver from its holster. He leveled it at Draper's chest. But Draper didn't hesitate, he grabbed the pistol by the barrel. The two men crashed into a bookcase.

The door we'd come through was locked, as were the French doors opposite.

"The windows!" said I to Fields. Our buggy stood not far beyond them.

We rushed there, and I flung them open. The girl followed without need of prodding.

She smiled gamely. "They're fighting over me!"

She was living the stories she'd read by candlelight.

Fields climbed out, and the girl scrambled after him.

"Get her out of here, Fields," I cried, "and bring the Brigade forward."

I watched them dash to the buggy and get in. Fields whipped the horse into motion before any of the Ninety-Eighth, who were jumping to, could get at them.

When I turned, Draper had disarmed Wead and stood over him. "Are you mad?" he said.

Wead bled from the mouth.

"Let's go, Etheridge," Draper said to me. "Let's go now."

We exited the library.

But it wasn't over. Wead followed at a few paces, wiping where Draper had bloodied his lips. As we passed through the great doors, he began to holler: "Arrest these men! Arrest them!"

The array of troopers—some on the verandah, even more out in the lane—set upon us. Draper and I were roughly handled, with fists and kicks. There were grunts and curses and swearing. "God-damn nigger," I heard. I was being jostled by the collar.

Draper's sword was awkwardly bent from earlier, no longer effective as a weapon. He didn't notice or did not care, raising it above his head and swinging vigorously.

"Back away, you dogs! Back away!"

The effort was rewarded. A halo of space opened around us, we rushed back into the house, and I closed and latched the doors. He and I plunged into the library, and I again latched the doors. We sat, side by side, our backs against them.

He looked at me, and I at him.

There were elements of the comical in this scene. Draper was hatless now, his shell jacket ripped open at the collar, the bent sword still in his hand. I noted that my forage cap was gone from my head, my clothes rumpled, several buttons missing. I thought that, if he and I survived this encounter and the war thereafter, we might laugh about it one day.

Draper, in fact, smiled. "Well, then," he said.

With his free hand, he combed his fingers through his tousled hair.

"What do they call you, Etheridge? Your family and friends, I mean."

"Dick, sir," said I, and I wondered at having offered this one and not Richard. Regretted it, even. "But them closest to me call me Richard."

He merited this. We'd come a long way, he and I.

"Mine call me Allie. Short from Alonzo." He outstretched a hand, and I took it. "I hope to one day be in a situation where I can call you Richard and you can call me Allie."

I hoped so, too.

There was a jostling at the door, a vigorous shaking of the knob—Wead and his men, trying to enter.

Through the window, though, we saw colored troopers amassing. Draper and I crossed hurriedly there and found the African Brigade arriving afore the house, on the double-quick.

Opposite them, the Ninety-Eighth was drawing up in battle array. They outnumbered us greatly.

Draper dropped out of the window to the ground, as did I, after. We made for our men. He yelled, "Form up on me!" Then, to Smith and Conant: "Get a skirmish line there and there!"

We were battle-hardened soldiers now, through and through. Our companies fell out as ordered.

As did the Ninety-Eighth, not thirty yards distant. Wead, his face still showing blood, stood at the head of his regiment, likewise shouting directions.

Each side leveled its muskets at the line facing it.

I heard the beat of hooves and saw Revere and the swamp men, circling around, behind the Ninety-Eighth's position, even as white troopers continued to surge from various buildings.

Draper stood at the end of our line, bent sword raised. He glared at Wead, who likewise glared back at him. Draper's jaw was set but his mouth seemed to tremble, as during the instant before a command was shouted, and I wondered, What would Wild do in a mess like this?

"Having bought truth dear . . ." I imagined him saying, and I knew. I knew that he would call the order to fire, on the spot and without hesitation, and that he'd see it as a justified response against these whoresons—and maybe even a needed one, too.

Yet Draper sneered, his lips a-tremble, the pause deliberate.

"Stand down!" we all heard. "Stand down, please!"

It was a chaplain, by the looks—all in black, with a gold embroidered crucifix on his collar. He ran over from the main house and placed himself between the two lines, arms outreaching, one each way.

"Please," he said. "Please . . ."

No shot was fired, though neither was a single musket lowered.

The chaplain took in each of the two sides and decided to approach Draper. "Colonel, sir, please. You're outnumbered two-to-one. Let cooler heads prevail."

"Cooler heads?" said Draper. I'd never seen him angrier. "I do not care a damn if they are ten thousand!"

And neither did we, his men. I looked out over our rifle line: not a single trooper seemed to weigh the odds of victory, only the defense of our pride and dignity.

"I am a colonel, goddammit," said Draper, "and that imbecile over there but a lieutenant colonel. Get him to cool down if you want, but my orders make no reference to any such thing. Only to me returning with my prisoner to Portsmouth."

The chaplain recognized that he'd chosen poorly. He crossed over to Wead. The two entered into a lively conversation, though too distant for me to hear. Wead gestured broadly and with over-much animation.

After a bit, he pulled away from the chaplain and hollered over at us. "I merely ask that you release the girl into my custody. Turn her over to me. I'll see that she gets safe passage to Fortress Monroe."

"I am your superior officer—and your superior!" replied Draper. "You will stand down!"

This rousened huzzahs from our line. For we were warriors, mister, and better ones than them, and we were on the side of right.

Wead conferred further with the chaplain, a mite less lively now. The latter placed a hand on his shoulder. Wead joined a collection of his officers, huddled in a bunch. It took a long minute, but then he turned and quit the field. His officers gave orders to lower arms.

We lowered our own.

Our men regrouped into companies, and we marched back down the Princess Anne road toward our camp. There, the girl, a-seat in the buggy aside Fields, encircled by a squad from F, welcomed our arrival with clapping hands and shrieks and cheers. She was as sporting a hostage as I could imagine.

The battalion didn't tarry. Draper had us quick-time it past the Ackiss farm, and we pushed on well into the night without pause for rest. Though we were full in Union territory, we all now knew that the danger had not yet passed. No trooper needed prodding. Each one kept his step at a hearty clip. But for our footfalls, silence prevailed. Draper, hatless, trotted his mount slowly alongside us. His guard remained up, his eyes and ears vigilant, appearing mistrustful of the surrounding dark.

And likewise me. Revere was out there somewhere, this was sure. But it was too dark for him to potshoot me, if he remained desiring to, and by and by, my mind eased into the up-and-down pounding of the troopers' brogans on the frozen road.

The march was toilsome, but I felt joyful yet and still, triumphant, and could sense that the men about me did, too. We passed within shouting distance of the Clapson farm, in the night, to our east, then into and through a sleeping Kempsville on about midnight. Next was Fortress Freedom. We attained her moated walls deep, deep in the late hours. Home, I supposed. All the home I could anymore imagine, though not a home truly. Fanny had certainly arrived by then, Ma'am was yet to come.

It was Christmas's Eve, 1863.

AFTERWORD:
CHRISTMAS 1899

Christmas's Eve, actually. A Sunday. And it is today that the memories have come roaring back, memories of our march through the night to attain Freedom after a three-week sortie granting it. Through the Great Dismal we'd trooped, down to Old Elizabeth, on to the church at Shiloh, then to the hanging tree outside Indiantown, over to Knotts Island, and up to Pungo Point in the company of Miss Nancy White. Hail the African Brigade!

Those were times of overmuch feeling. And the day's earlier encounter with Patrick was the what-for that had rousened them to life anew within me.

Being a holiday today, and as the weather and condition of the surf permit it, I have given my U.S. Life-Saving Service crew leave to sail to their homes on Roanoke, to be with their families. Me, I would keep things operative out here, at our station at Pea Island, tending to the watch. Passing shipping does not drop anchor for reasons of sentiment, neither Godly nor National, and so a watch is required, to ensure that all is well. Fanny never expects less of me. My children have come to understand it. Such is the stuff of good leading.

Should some ship meet with trouble, either out on the Atlantic or on the Pamlico Sound behind, our modernistic telephone would

connect me to the neighboring stations at Chicamacomico or at
Oregon Inlet in the time it would take to turn the hand-crank. The
next century, nigh upon us, and all is so new.

And not so much new, too. These telephones, for instance. The
Island's Board of Commissioners contracted business outfits from
across the Sound to survey all of Roanoke and build lines so that
the house of every single Sand Banker might have one. Yet Fanny
remarked that she had yet to see a single contractor on the north
end, where most colored live. No lines and no telephones for our
quarter, apparently, nor notice of the discrepancy.

New and not so new. Such is the way of things.

I have been helming this crew some twenty-odd years, and
I'd be lying if I did not admit that a day on my own is rather welcomed. During the bright and prosperous years of the seventies,
when the federal government built these houses along the Nation's
many beaches to safeguard our coasts, Fields and I sought in it.
A number of colored veterans did. Many a Sand Banker resented
those few of us hired, though, and before long, the Northern pols
tired of attempting to Reconstruct long-held views and decided
to organize the scattered lot of us into one single crew. No colored
would have gotten to stay on in the Service otherwise. They placed
me at its head, and its captain I remain.

While watching out to sea from the observation deck atop the
station house on this Christmas's Eve, I heard called, "Halloo!"
and recognized the voice before seeing its source: Patrick. He was
descending the dune behind my station, in a blue USLSS long coat
overtop his uniform, captain's insignia prominent on the sleeve.
He'd taken to sporting a dangling scruff of beard that made him
look not so much of age as just increasingly unshaven.

"Hello, yourself," I called back, rushing over the widow's walk,
down the ladder, then the stairs, and out to meet him.

My brusque arrival onto the porch blunted his approach to within a few feet of my station's front steps, and this was as I wished it. He stood below me, gazing up—and smiling all the same.

"I saw your skiff hitched on the Sound as I was boating by," he said. "How is it you come to be out here when a Holy Day would give us leave to go home? Me, I've got Judson Demps overseeing my station till tomorrow evening, when the others will return. Demps owes me."

"We guard the coast," I told him, "we save lives. This is our duty."

He guffawed. "Like I don't know it!"

Patrick has been in the Service nigh on as long as I have and is considered a hero, not just along the Banks but throughout the Nation. Newspapers and magazines from Raleigh to Washington, D.C., have written on his famous exploits the day in 1884 when the barkentine *Ephraim William* ran aground atop a shoal five miles off our coast. The nearby station crew thought the rough conditions made succor impossible, but Patrick rallied the crowd of standers-by who had gathered on the beach and, in a six-oared longboat, guided a group of them out through the breakers and abreast of the ship. All nine souls aboard were saved. It earned Patrick a Gold Life-Saving Medal, and he rightly deserved it.

Still, he remains forever the Patrick of our youth. "Annie expects me home for the holidays, and I *always* abide by the missus's wishes," said he. "But ain't it just like you, Dick? Over-exacting of yourself and over-indulgent of your crew."

He'd meant this for jestful, but I took it otherwise, as a reflection on our lives and the choices we had made, some for better, others for worse.

He approached closer, placing a foot upon the bottom step, breaching the threshold of my porch. He leaned over a bent knee, and I supposed the gesture to foretell something serious. But as always it was just more patter from him, jocular gossip about the nearby Chicamacomico crew, conveyed as though he and I were yet friends.

I tuned him out two sentences along, keeping him going with a well-placed nod or a mutter meant to signify interest, knowing that soon he would stop and continue on his way. A studied peace better served me than outright disdain, as we were fellow station keepers and thus peers, and sometimes had to band our crews in order to effect rescues.

This studied peace—I had learned its usefulness early on. When newly returned from the Army—years before, in 1867—while I was still sleeping at my ma'am's cabin in the Freedman's Colony, Patrick came by one morning and hailed me outside. Though surprised and none too pleased, I ignored Ma'am's enjoinful glare and went and faced him.

It was the first I'd seen him since our encounter in the pocosin.

"Heard tell you was back," said he, and I offered, "Indeed I am."

"You look well," he said, and I, "It is a comfort to no longer have to cross Rebel fire."

I hadn't invited this reunion and felt no need to allay any awkwardness.

"I've been thinking, Dick. There's money to be made, fishing and ferrying and suchlike. The time is favorable. I figured you and me might have at it."

It sounded more a direction than a request, and I wasn't much patient of being ordered, by officers let alone by erstwhile masters. So I stood there, silent.

"I'm saying we should start up an enterprise together," he continued, adding, "You and me," as though this hadn't been clear.

He said, "Between your connections among yours and mine with mine, we could do well."

When I no more reacted to this than I had to the previous, he said, "Maybe, if you want to?" inflecting the last, an attempt to transform it into a query.

Finally.

"Maybe," said I, and I turned and went back indoors.

Right then was an ideal time for rupture, from the Etheridge House altogether and not only just from Patrick. But I thought on it long, and conferred with Fanny, and even with my ma'am, though I could aforehand divine her opinion on the matter. In the end, I agreed.

Patrick covered my portion of the investment at cost, and we bought the *Margery & Sarah* from John B. at below market price. We piloted the inlets and ferried folks to and from Elizabeth City. In the first years—before our venture got going good and Fanny and I could marry—John B. let us refit one of the slave cabins behind the Etheridge House, and Patrick and I moved into it together for lodgings.

Do not fret, the irony wasn't lost on me, not back then any more than now. For how do you forget the grievances that should not, by any right, ever be forgot?

You don't. But with time, you make do. In the Sand Banks, blood is blood, even if it is never fully family, and so you come, day in and day out, to cease to remember your justified resentments. By and by, they find their way into dark places you rarely allow yourself to visit.

It's true: I never did know for certain what had happened between Fanny and Patrick, if anything at all. She was ever Fanny, always, the manifest echo of my ma'am. If she did not need to relive it, whatever *it* might have been—and she never did—then neither did I.

And so why shouldn't I have availed myself of the chance to prosper by a fruitful enterprise? It was an opportunity that presented

itself and that I capitalized on. I made money, good money, and I
gained standing in the Banks. I was an American, by God—all of
us former Colored Troops were. Our exploits during the war had
been written on far and wide, and had earned us the right to make
whatever we might of this freedom. Why should I not have taken
the utmost advantage?

After our return to Fortress Freedom, the newspaperman Tewksbury published in the *New York Times* his account of the raid, and
though the man's presence had tried my last patience, I still to this
day find his words stirring to read. He lauded us as "sable braves"
and detailed our every accomplishment. "An army of 50,000 blacks
could march from one end of Rebeldom to the other almost without
opposition," Tewksbury concluded, "the terror they would inspire
making them invincible." I return to the yellowed newsprint often,
so much so that this last bit is committed to memory, word for word.

Southern newspapers reported our foray otherwise, as was to
be expected, harping on the "defenseless women and children" into
whose houses we forced entry and on the depredations committed
therein. I have kept this old newsprint, too. If what Tewksbury
described does not in every regard square with my own recall of
events, his gushing account cast a cleansing light upon the lies of
the Southern reports, for theirs were lies to the core.

On New Year's Day, 1864, a week after my battalion's night
march from Pungo Point, the African Brigade marched down the
main street of Fortress Freedom in full-dress military parade, wearing white gloves and with fixed bayonets. The Colored Ladies' Association of Norfolk had made for us a regimental flag, with CORPS
D'AFRIQUE stitched across it, and our new guidon whipped about for
all to see. All of Negro Portsmouth and Chesapeake and Norfolk
turned out to celebrate our victorious return, as did sizable segments

of the garrison entire—even many of the white soldiers who, before then, had always jeered us. Benjamin Butler, the commander of the Department of Virginia, watched from atop a raised dais, saluting our passage. He held an especially long salute to Colonel Draper as he passed by, atop his mount.

We were brave soldiers and, around Fortress Freedom, heroes all. Yet this did not in every regard serve us. To the Union brass, our December raid merely proved that General Wild would not be bent to its will, even less after the accolades. Before the end of the winter, he was removed from command.

In truth, I missed Wild's dash but never his derring-do. No, in the fighting we later undertook, under Draper—three forays along the Rappahannock, defending the canal at Dutch Gap, and charging the Confederate artillery at New Market Heights during the siege of Richmond—we benefited from Draper's steady, predictable direction and authority. I served in his staff through his rise to general, as his regimental commissary sergeant, the second-ranking non-comm after Henry Adkins, who was regimental sergeant major.

Wild's boldness and brash had marked us, all the same. When news arrived that Bobby Lee's army was pulling back from Richmond, the African Brigade raced up Old Osborne Turnpike and were the first troops to enter the Rebel capital—this, even though Draper had been commanded to give up the road to the white Twenty-Fourth Corps, to allow them to arrive first. Such a gesture was pure Wild, even as Draper had executed it.

After Dixie fell, the brass wanted all colored troops out of there quicker than quick. General Draper led the African Brigade to the southmost lick of Texas, to Brazos Santiago, nigh on in Mexico. It was a mean, dry land, piercingly bright and cut of gulches they called arroyos but that served as flues for the stinging, hot winds. On a leisurely ride from camp one day—just the general and me, and Simon Gaylord, who'd become a corporal and served as his orderly—Draper dropped from the saddle and just lay there on the ground. Gaylord and I scrambled to his side. Neither of us had heard a shot discharged nor seen a muzzle flash, nothing. Yet a ball had entered below his collarbone and blown a hole the size of a fist out his lower back.

I told him, "You're okay, Allie, you will be all right," though I knew this was not so.

He knew as much himself. Still, he managed a smile. "The irony of it! Now, after all the fighting is done. Isn't that how a literary man would put it?"

It was the last he said.

I've read that the Comanche tribe of Indians attacked in this way, stealthy-like, unseen and from afar. Perhaps them, or maybe some Rebby-boy with a sharp-eyed aim, of which there were still plenty about. All I knew was that I'd lost a friend true.

Patrick's is the Janus face of Alonzo Draper's, his uninvited appearance prompting nostalgia about the proving ground of my past. What I know of leading I owe to Alonzo Draper. His example lives on in my own captaincy at Pea Island, I make sure of it, and my life-saving service crew has earned a strong reputation along the coast. A few seasons ago, we rescued the ten mariners aboard the foundered three-master *E. S. Newman* during a hurricane so severe that other crews had sought shelter inland from the storm. It was noteworthy, all as much as Patrick's exploits in relief of the bark *Ephraim William*, and when now I sail to headquarters at Elizabeth City, for supplies or other matters, I'm always heartily greeted as a result. Even by the likes of R. B. Creecy!

The "Our Colored People" column of Creecy's newspaper, the *Economist*, just last week proclaimed:

The worthy Keeper of Pea Island Life-Saving Station, Captain Dick Etheridge (colored), our old friend, was in town on business today. He is a representative of the old-time colored man—polite, respectful, considerate and self-respecting.

Always I wonder, does he remember me from those three decades ago and our late-night walk through the occupied city, when he promised to see me dead?

The *Economist* is an important organ of the statewide Democratic Party, advancing the plank of White Supremacy, and Creecy was a key player in riling up the mob that rioted last year, down to Wilmington, and overthrew the duly elected government, killing numberless colored in the process. So maybe this is just what freedom looks like: colored with colored and white with white, and a courteous nod allowed to us ones who do not threaten to upset the new order of things—which, as I have aforehand said, is not so new and, for colored, not much orderly.

New and not so new, much my interrelation with Patrick—our studied peace. The doggedness of his silent gaze, as we stood together a-front of my station house, brought me back from my musings. He was leaning forward, not a step farther up onto my porch, but about as close to my face as he could be, given the distance.

Having succeeded at staring me out of my reverie, he started up again. "Sometimes I'd just as soon give it all up and return to my youth. Things seemed easier. A man could be a man, have an enthusiasm and pursue it. What seemed right was clear back then."

He stared, insistent, seeming to press for a response. I watched from above without offering one. His last comment did not warrant it.

It never surprised, a white man's capacity for convenient blindness.

"I got a boy," he said, abruptly, "a baby, not six months old. Did you know that, Dick?"

Neither did this surprise, for I already knew it.

"My boy, he's black like you."

By Catherine Pruden—one of the orphan slave children who had turned up at the Freedman's Colony during the war and stayed on after. Her husband, Micah, was lost off Hatteras in the 1896 storm season, and since, Patrick has been known to spend time at her house of an evening. Known among us, anyway, in the colored quarter. She named the baby George Edward.

John B. had died nigh on a score years before, and things had ended up much as he had wished. Patrick had become him, a grandee by Sand Banks standards. And now this, too.

With age, John B. had taken to asking after my ma'am's well-being, though she felt no improved warmth of feeling toward him and never reciprocated. She had likewise aged visibly, but not so much as to limit her. She lived in a cabin off the rear of Fanny's and my house, and her nearby presence was generally a blessing, and sometimes not. And when she passed also, it was so sudden and unexpected that it took me going on a year to daily remember that I need not go out back and look in on her. This was four years ago.

I stared down at Patrick, John B. anew. His face was unsettled, his eyes fixed upon me but seeming to seek a faraway horizon beyond, one he did not know how to attain. He looked incapable of even *beginning* to understand how to.

Me, I could have explained his disquiet to him, if he'd truly wanted the knowledge. For Patrick, a world where a nigger was a man—even this nigger—could only mean that being a man meant less. Now the nigger would be of his own loins, a darker hue of him.

This realization had surely been the spur that pricked his need to seek me out today and take an accounting of things.

But had he actually desired to know, I also would have told him that time would temper his feelings of confusion and dread, that it would whittle down his foreboding sense of responsibility to a stub of indifference. John B. had taught me this.

Patrick righted himself, flattening the front of his coat with the palms of his hands, and he smiled true. "My boy," he said, "when he grows up, I'd be proud to see him at your station, in your crew. That's all. I wanted to say this because I thought you should know it."

And this last piece did surprise. Surprised me entirely.

He turned and tossed up a hand. "Okay, Dick. So long."

I watched him walk up the dune's face, then over, myself feeling suddenly bewildered.

I'm an old man now, I am grown old—fifty-nine years on the sixteenth day of the new century. And it is with the utmost shame that I admit this: the memories unloosed by Patrick's visit—of who I was back then, and who I thought I have become since—have rousened a sentiment that I thought lost in me when it came to Etheridges, one I was sure that I had willed gone. The sentiment feels like heartache, a contemptible longing for something that never truly was.

And it is this feeling of shame that leads me to the last bit, to the story of how it ended with Revere. For it could not just end thusly with Revere, with him popping off shots and me more and more looking over my shoulder. No, our dispute had required conclusion.

On the evening after the New Year's Day parade at Fortress Freedom, in 1864, the African Brigade held a frolic on the regimental grounds with lively music and hearty dancing, a shindig to fête our having been commended. Many of the officers attended, including for a time Generals Wild and Butler. The officers stayed largely to the side, now and again clapping along to the beat. All but Allie Draper! He took several turns, even once with my Fanny.

Me, I remained vigilant, a-seat on a bench with my back to a wall, as I knew Revere to be about. I carried Private Lindsey Babley's pepper-box pistol in my pocket, borrowed earlier in the day. I did not offer a reason for requesting it; Babley did not inquire after my motives.

Along past midnight, I finally saw Revere, lurking on the edge of the onlookers opposite me, alone, without any of the swamp men. I supposed them to have returned to the Great Dismal, as our mission was done and their temporary enlistments correspondingly. I invented a pretext for our leave-taking—a sour stomach or some such thing—then accompanied Fanny back to the barracks for lady contrabands. I professed to be on my way to turn in, too.

I had told a similar lie to Fields before quitting the frolic with Fanny. He would have insisted on seconding me had he known my intentions, and I refused to put him in danger. No, it would be just me and Revere.

After leaving Fanny, I doubled back, aiming to settle it once and for all. The festivities had died down considerable by this time. The surrounding campfires, unattended, had faded to embers, and the lantern light was spare. Two musician boys still played fiddle, and a few troopers danced with women who yet lingered. Paps Prentiss threw bones for stakes against three others at a long table, a crowd amassed around, sometimes mocking, sometimes cheering.

It was then that I spotted him anew. Revere walked toward the sinks, at the far end of the ground. It didn't seem that he had seen me, so I followed, several paces to his rear. The surroundings grew darker as the frolic became more distant. This suited my purpose should I need to justify or defend my actions.

Separate lines had formed for the sinks—and long ones, even at that hour. I did not see Revere in nan one of them. I didn't know how I could have lost him.

It occurred to me that he had maybe opted for the trees, just beyond, to avoid the wait. It's what I would have done. I circled wide around the queues, keeping to the shadows. It was even darker out there at the camp's edge, and the brush and fallen leaves crackled under my slow steps.

I felt a strong arm, restraining me from behind, and the urgent line of a blade nicking longwise at my neck.

"Where you off to, Etheridge? Where is it you think you are going?"

It was him.

I saw the rest of them then, shadows separating from the shadowy trees, their feet shuffling over the dead foliage, loud as cicadas, and how had I not heard or noted their movements before this?

I was entirely surrounded. They were twenty or more, pushing in on me. I thought I perceived Golar, the silhouette of his wild head. If it wasn't to be by Revere's knife, there would still be no exit for me from there.

Revere had kept his free hand atop the pistol in my pocket but did not disarm me of it when he backed away.

"You think me a bogeyman, just like the whitey do."

I heard him more than I could see him, his shadow shifting toward the dark mass of the swamp men, who had stopped at a short distance of me.

"I'm but a man, yet a better one than you." I thought myself to see his smile, though the pitch of night was deep. "I better you, Etheridge. Had I wanted you dead, you would be. And you! You have a pistol and will not use it."

And he was right. I could not bring myself to loose the pepperbox and shoot him, though it was workable presently and this had been my aim. I had stood with a gun leveled on him once before, out there in the pocosin, and why had I not shot then either?

If conviction is the measure of the man, I was indeed lesser.

I heard his laugh, inmost and broad. Saw his shadow turn and move away, toward the woods into which the swamp men were likewise disappearing. There was a rustling over dry leaves, and before long, not even this.

Then was his voice: "You do not see, Etheridge, just like whitey does not see—that which is right and real, direct in front of your eyes. That we the labor and we the music, our women rear their children and birth their sons. Niggers are *everything*, Etheridge. Not what they think they see, but us in fact!"

The man spoke truly, the lesson my ma'am had tried to teach me from the start. Ma'am and Fanny, Fields and the rest—none had ever doubted this truth, not once. It inhered in the marrow of their bones. Me, I seemed capable only of seeking truth elsewhere.

Top to bottom, that nigger proved out right again.

ACKNOWLEDGMENTS

Thanks to Eric Simonoff, Morgan Entrekin, Sara Vitale, Alicia Burns, and Jessica Spitz, and to Cressida Leyshon and the staff of the *New Yorker*, for championing this work from the start. And to Antoinette Burton, Nancy Castro, and the Humanities Research Institute, and Bob Markley and the English Department of the University of Illinois, for support and community.

And to Beth Clary, Dina Guidubaldi, Steve Davenport, Monica Berlin, Audrey Petty, Jill Petty, Sylvie Moreau, Luc Bouchard, Scott Greenhaw, Caroline Morris, Jonathan Wei, Molly Martinez, Manuel Luis Martinez, David Zoby, Lorna Owen, Cathy Bryson, Robert Pyeatt, and Michael Larhman—great readers all, and even better friends.